D0251309

Remain true to yourself,
but move ever upward toward greater
consciousness and greater love!
At the summit you will find yourselves
united with all those who,
from every direction,
have made the same ascent.
For everything that rises must converge.

—PIERRE TEILHARD DE CHARDIN

The Hidden Gate

Savannah Secrets

The Hidden Gate

MARLENE CHASE

Guideposts

Danbury, Connecticut

Savannah Secrets is a trademark of Guideposts.

Published by Guideposts Books & Inspirational Media
100 Reserve Road, Suite E200
Danbury, CT 06810
Guideposts.org

Copyright © 2020 by Guideposts. All rights reserved.

This book, or parts thereof, may not be reproduced, stored in a retrieval system, or transmitted in any form or by any means, electronic, mechanical, photocopying, recording, or otherwise, without the written permission of the publisher.

This is a work of fiction. Savannah, Georgia, actually exists, and some places and characters may be based on actual places and people whose identities have been used with permission or fictionalized to protect their privacy. Apart from the actual people, events, and locales that figure into the fiction narrative, all other names, characters, businesses, and events are the creation of the author's imagination and any resemblance to actual persons or events is coincidental.

Every attempt has been made to credit the sources of copyrighted material used in this book. If any such acknowledgment has been inadvertently omitted or miscredited, receipt of such information would be appreciated.

Scripture references are from the following sources: *The Holy Bible, King James Version* (KJV). *The Holy Bible, New International Version.* Copyright ©1973, 1978, 1984, 2011 by Biblica, Inc. Used by permission of Zondervan. All rights reserved worldwide. www.zondervan.com

Cover and interior design by Müllerhaus
Cover illustration by Pierre Droal, represented by Deborah Wolfe, LTD.
Typeset by Aptara, Inc.

Printed and bound in the United States of America
10 9 8 7 6 5 4 3 2 1

The Hidden Gate

Chapter One

"DO YOU THINK FLANNERY O'CONNOR really taught a chicken to walk backward?"

Meredith Bellefontaine stopped in midbreath. Captivated as she had been with the fragrance of camellias drifting in through the open window of her car, Julia's question had the effect of a sudden blast of cold air. She gave her old friend a quick glance. "What?"

Julia Foley leaned forward and rolled her eyes at Meredith. A lock of silver hair fell over her forehead. "Well, do you think she did?"

"It's spring," Meredith said. "The camellias and dogwoods are blooming everywhere, and you're asking me about chickens!"

Julia sat back and folded her arms over her soft cotton blouse. She'd tossed her mauve Preston & York suit jacket into the back of Meredith's SUV. Meredith had picked her up this morning so Julia could leave her car at the shop for an oil change. "Well, we just drove past her childhood home and museum. Call me curious. What can I say?"

"Well, to answer your question, she did," Meredith said, feeling a bubble of laughter rise. "She wrote an essay about it back in 1961. She called it 'Living with a Peacock.'"

Any historian living in Savannah had to know about Flannery O'Connor, who wrote ironic, subtly allegorical fiction populated with eccentric Southern characters. These transformations were often accomplished through pain, violence, and ludicrous behavior in the pursuit of the holy. Meredith had often told visitors to Savannah about O'Connor's nineteenth-century Greek revival townhouse that was even now undergoing major renovations. The living room on the parlor-level floor was open to the public. The walled garden in the backyard, where the five-year-old O'Connor was said to have taught a chicken to walk backward, was added in 1993.

"Well, I guess you would know," Julia said.

Meredith could tell Julia was digesting her brief historical sketch, eyebrows raised in her high forehead. Analyzing it, no doubt, as someone with the legal mind and experience of a retired court judge would. Meredith waited, glad for the company of her friend and now business partner.

They'd roomed together their senior year in college and later kept in touch, over the miles, with Christmas cards and occasional notes. After University of Virginia Law School, Julia had practiced in Atlanta. However, when she returned to Savannah fifteen years ago to become a presiding judge in Chatham County's Juvenile Court, they had quickly renewed their close friendship. They had become a foursome—Julia and Beau, Meredith and her husband, Ron, sharing life and supporting each other. But four had become three when Ron died in September almost two years ago.

Meredith had been content with her work as head of Savannah's Historical Society. Well, *content* was a relative term. Some things weren't easy to dismiss. She had decided a complete change was in order—especially after her own scary heart attack on the first anniversary of Ron's death made her reexamine her priorities. Reopening her husband's detective agency and serving the community certainly qualified as a complete change. And Julia's critical thinking and experience made her the perfect choice for a partner.

"Still wearing your historian's hat," Julia said warmly, giving Meredith's arm an affectionate nudge. "Fits you well, but so does your new one. And I love being back in the day-to-day grind with you." She leaned forward again and said, "Let's take the long way. It's a drop-dead gorgeous day." She sighed. "No time to sit back and let life happen around us. Beau is happy as a clam with a nine-iron or a fishing pole in his hand. Goodness knows he's earned a rest after those years championing the new children's wing at the hospital. But retirement's not for me."

Beau, better known as Beauregard Eugene Foley, expressed no qualms about his wife joining Meredith to reopen the agency. But was her old college friend being set up to fail? Meredith felt a twinge of the old fear nudging at the back of her mind. She'd always been interested in what Ron was doing—she'd even gotten her PI license so she could assist him by gathering historical background for his cases, but what did she really know about the day-to-day ins and outs of running an investigations agency?

"You sure about this, Mom?" her older son, Carter, had asked when she told him her plans. He'd run a hand through thick chestnut hair that was so like his father's and jingled the keys in the pocket of his pleated chinos. A banker had to dress the part, and Carter's trim waist wore pleats well. He was skeptical about her decision, though he tried not to show it. But Meredith recognized the gesture—the jingling keys that always signaled some inner conflict. Ron had done the same.

Wise, compassionate Ron with his hardheaded determination and acute sense of justice. He'd joined the police force right out of college, but he hadn't been satisfied with his vocation. He'd wanted something more, some way to bring hope to those lost in the struggle of living with no one to fight for them.

A wave of sadness washed over her with such force that for a moment she thought she might drown. The surprise of it left her winded. She had worked through all that—moved ahead with her life—hadn't she?

"You all right?" Julia asked softly.

Meredith drew in a breath, embarrassed by her own reflections. And chastened too. She'd gotten through those difficult first days, her faith holding her up like virtual wings. And she had been sure—well, most of the time—that she was attuned to God's leading in reopening the agency. Still, she couldn't tamp the doubts all the way down, even with the help of Julia, who was clearly a stabilizing force.

Julia had needed her too. She'd had a successful career, but she'd needed something on which to focus her still bright energies, a cause that would give her a sense of renewed purpose. Meredith believed that joining her in reopening Ron's agency had been good for Julia—good for them both.

Meredith glanced at her watch. "Maybe we should head to the office instead of meandering through country roads smelling the oleander." But she took a long, slow breath as the road narrowed, and centuries-old trees arched overhead like a leafy cathedral. "Suppose there are clients waiting?" She grinned wryly. *Sure. Like they're beating down our doors clamoring for us to solve their dilemmas!*

Julia snatched her new iPhone from her lap. When she wasn't clutching it like a physical appendage, it was close at hand. Julia liked the latest gadgets and used them with ease. She put the phone on SPEAKER mode, and pressed the number that would undoubtedly summon Carmen Lopez.

They really couldn't afford a receptionist, but they had to at least *look* like they were successful. Meredith hadn't been left without means, but they'd sunk a lot of money into the agency. Julia was happily contributing to the renovation too. She had worked hard cleaning up the back garden where charred items had been thrown after a fire in Ron's office shortly after his death.

The fire had been attributed to faulty wiring and was quickly extinguished, but a credenza, a reading lamp, and several cardboard file boxes had been lost. Before it was all hauled away, they had painstakingly picked through everything.

While clearing away leaves and grass in the back garden, Julia had found a key—a small, outdated, unimpressive bit of metal, which despite numerous tries had fit nothing in the agency. Nor did it match the lock in the burned credenza. They had put the key away safely but not before making up mysterious stories about it, each one more outlandish than the last, over a pot of Earl Grey tea.

Inside, renovations were still in progress. They had decided to update the reception area and two of the offices, leaving Ron's old office, which required extensive drywall work, and the kitchen, for later.

"It's long past time that the place had a face-lift," Julia had said. "This floral wallpaper went out of style years ago. Besides, it's coming loose in places. I even saw some crumbling plaster on the rug last week."

Julia had also recommended the hiring of Carmen Lopez, citing her remarkable intuitive sense where people were concerned. Meredith heard Carmen answer the phone, and Julia said, "That you, Carmen?"

"Uh, just a minute. I'll check," came the mellow voice, tinged with her usual good-natured irony. Who else would be answering the phone?

Carmen, twentysomething and street-smart, had immigrated from Guatemala with her parents years ago. But when they were killed in an automobile accident and there were no siblings or relatives for her to go to, ten-year-old Carmen became a ward of the state and not with the best result. Tossed from one foster situation to another, she had pretty much raised herself.

Meredith pictured the attractive young woman with glossy black hair and dark eyes that revealed no secret. She was seldom at a loss for words, and tact had, so far, eluded her. She was most at home in jeans and a sweatshirt but showed a good sense of career-woman style.

"Cute," Julia said dryly into her phone. She rolled her gray eyes at Meredith as she continued her conversation with Carmen. "We'll be along pretty soon. Anything going on?"

"No, just the demolition derby giving me the *dolor de cabeza.*"

Carmen was bilingual, and she liked throwing in the occasional Spanish phrase. Meredith couldn't restrain a laugh picturing the wily receptionist with hand to brow feigning a headache.

Julia clicked off and dropped the phone in her lap. "She's a trip, but ya gotta love her, right? Actually, she's come a long way since showing up in my court a few years ago." Julia pursed her lips in thought. "Petty thefts, disorderly conduct—that sort of thing. It's a wonder she turned out so well considering the start she had in life."

That was vintage Julia. A heart attuned to others.

Julia's voice broke into Meredith's reverie. "Let's go by the old Besset plantation. Since the news about Geoffrey Besset, I haven't been able to get that place off my mind."

The wealthy plantation owner turned lawyer had practiced in Charleston, South Carolina, but the *Savannah Tribune* had carried the obituary three days ago. At the age of eighty-two, Geoffrey Philpott Besset was dead.

Under his great-grandfather's control, the plantation had been one of the richest in Savannah. Years later, Geoffrey's grandfather, and then father, had overseen sharecroppers. The property was nothing now but overgrown trees, a crumbling antebellum mansion, and a terrible secret. Geoffrey's twelve-year-old sister, Harriet, had disappeared almost sixty-five years ago. She was presumed to have been killed, but her body was never found.

They parked on the street in front of the mansion, and Julia climbed out of the car, that can't-wait look turning her cheeks pink. Meredith knew something about the place through her work with the historical society. She had learned that Geoffrey Besset left the plantation shortly after his father's death, posting a prominent notice of nonadmittance on the door of the mansion.

The city occasionally monitored the old place to be sure it didn't become the target of vandals or drug dealers. Beatrice Enterline, who replaced Meredith as head of the historical society, seemed bent on seeing the plantation restored. What a feather that would be in the Queen Bee's bonnet.

"Now that we're in the business of solving crimes, maybe we'll crack that old case," Julia said, grinning as they approached the pitted driveway. "I wish we could, because I don't like to see the old place turned into a haunt for ghosts. All for the sake of commerce, of course. Nothing like a good ghost story to lure folks to the historic homes tour."

Meredith sighed, wondering what cracking the six-and-a-half-decades-old case might mean. "Once we have some time on our hands, of course," she responded wryly, because they had nothing *but* time on their hands. "One thing is for sure. Geoffrey Besset won't be any help now."

They walked among arching cypress and live oak trees dripping with Spanish moss. Enormous swathes of it hung from twisting branches like old women's hair. The dangling moss was considered picturesque and charming in most settings. But here Meredith felt a chill, like being transported to an ancient cemetery with names no one knew anymore or wanted to know. She shivered.

In the distance loomed the remains of the mansion, forlorn in the May sunshine. It had once been magnificent with its huge pillars, a handsome balcony running along the outside edge of the house, large windows, and big center entrances at the front and rear. Grand gardens with geometrically cut hedges had likely complemented the symmetry at one time. Meredith paused, surveying the overgrown grounds. "Let's just walk a little and enjoy the beauty of this splendid day." She stepped into a narrow path, where a yellow pine warbler twittered on a tangle of low pine scrub.

Julia followed, pushing branches and weeds aside. "Good thing I wore my flats today," she said, laughing. She seldom wore anything else. She was tall, slender, straight, and even more imposing in her judge's robe.

They walked in silence for a while before Julia spoke again. "Imagine, these were once thriving fields of cotton with hundreds of slave families working the land, singing to keep their spirits up."

Meredith stopped walking. "They weren't just singing, they were praying," she said almost in a whisper. "And they were rising. 'Everything that rises must converge.'"

"Flannery O'Connor again," Julia said, dropping down to rest on a nearby boulder.

"She got the title from Pierre Teilhard de Chardin, the French philosopher and Jesuit priest. He wrote about moving upward toward greater consciousness and love." Meredith paused, surprised at her own recall of a quote that had often inspired her. "'At the summit you will find yourselves united with all those who, from every direction, have made the same ascent. For everything that rises must converge.'"

"Heavy thoughts on a brilliant morning," Julia said as she got up from the boulder on which they were resting.

Meredith started walking again. "Just a bit farther, and then let's take our weary selves back to civilization."

"I'm with you, girlfriend. Guess we're not going to learn anything about that old mystery this way." She tucked her arm through Meredith's, and the twinkle was back in her eye. "So, what do you suppose it was like for folks who worked here back in the 1950s?"

"I was just a child then," Meredith said. "Maybe *you* can tell me."

Julia laughed. "Yes, you're a whole eight-and-a-half months younger than I am." She sobered. "We know that things were far from restful."

"Even for a child of privilege like Harriet Besset those years could have been tumultuous," Meredith added. "Girls were expected to identify as wives and mothers with no encouragement beyond domestic bliss. When I was a girl—"

"Ouch!" Julia, who had dropped Meredith's arm when the path grew narrower and was now in the rear, tripped, knocking Meredith to her knees into a bed of pine needles along the path.

There in front of her, just beyond a cluster of loblolly pines, Meredith saw the broken-down remains of a gate, some of its iron bars still welded into the stone gateposts. Most of the overhead arch had fallen in, but the posts rose in a tangled mass of woody vines and black gum branches. Just beyond the crumbling gate was a partial stone structure with a low wall.

"It looks like it could be what's left of an old summerhouse." Meredith stood unsteadily, feeling her heart pound triple time. With a little gasp, she bent to creep under a rusted bar.

"I wonder why this wasn't demolished with the rest of the old shacks and outbuildings," Julia said in a whisper. "I can just imagine young Harriet stealing away from the heat and bustle of the house and coming here. Maybe meeting someone."

"Or maybe she just wanted the solitude of a place like this." Meredith sat down on the low wall, feeling a strange hush. "I remember a place like this at my grandmother's house. She had a gazebo painted white with wild roses twining through the slats. I'd take my Diet-Rite cola and curl up on the seat to read. I can still feel the prickles from the rosebushes that kept poking in. But *Heidi*, *Winnie the Pooh*, and *Anne of Green Gables* took me away."

"I used to love *Little Women*," Julia breathed.

Meredith tented her fingers at her lips. Why were they whispering? The silence was deep, yet it seemed to echo so loudly around them. Was it just the crackling of small creatures stirring in the brush or the warble of a bird launching itself into the brittle air? Or was someone there, peering through taut branches ready to snap? "It feels like someone is watching," she whispered. "Watching or waiting for something—or someone."

Julia shifted uncomfortably on the low wall. "I think it's time to go." Glancing around, she clutched her arms as though chilled. "I feel it too. Maybe it's the eyes and voices of the past, the long march of history that won't stop, still rising to converge."

Chapter Two

LOUVENIA BROWN KING TOOK A deep breath before entering the room where her dear friend Delyse lay in bed. Delyse's eyes were shut, but Louvenia knew she was awake. The veins in her temples pulsated beneath the disheveled halo of gray-white hair that always gave her a look of shock. Her lips settled in the ghostly smile Louvenia had come to recognize after weeks of visiting her in the nursing home. She touched Delyse's arm lightly, wondering what was passing through her old friend's mind.

The illegitimate daughter of a Jamaican planter, Delyse Watson found refuge with an Atlanta minister and rose to become a teacher and champion for literacy. She and Louvenia had met ten years ago after both of them retired from teaching and volunteered at the same library. Then Delyse was diagnosed with Alzheimer's, and three years ago, Louvenia moved in with her to take care of her.

Truth was, she had to go somewhere, and Delyse's cottage was far from the town proper and from her Le Grand Street house. Now that Delyse's condition had deteriorated to the point where she was unable to stay at home even with Louvenia's help, Louvenia was alone at Delyse's cottage except for her memories and Delyse's pet cat, Sydney.

Louvenia felt a cramp in her chest and leaned forward in her chair. For years, she'd lived just a few blocks from her daughter, and they'd been thicker than thieves. But when Charlene bought her condo and Louvenia moved into Delyse's house, she didn't tell Charlene where she was going. Charlene didn't know why her mother had to disappear, and Louvenia wasn't about to endanger Charlene's life or her grandchild's life by telling her. *Dear God, keep your eye on my little sparrow.*

"Magnolia?"

Delyse's eyes opened wide. Her quirky eyebrows lifted, and Louvenia knew she'd been aware of her presence even with her eyes closed.

Magnolia? The name startled Louvenia. No one had called her that in decades. When she'd had to run away as a twelve-year-old, she'd taken her mama's name and added Brown. Louvenia Brown. Then when she married Darwin, she became Louvenia King. She hadn't been Magnolia Clement for many years. She'd buried that sad girl long ago.

Her heart returned to its normal rhythm as she realized that Delyse was referring to the character in the diary Louvenia had been reading to her. A diary she'd unearthed days ago, one that she knew her unconscious mind had gone searching for. It was time to remember. Reading it to Delyse was a way to depersonalize the events and pretend it wasn't she herself who had written the words all those years ago.

"*Wah gwaan wid yuh todeh?*" Delyse asked in her native patois. She closed her eyes, her fragile energy spent already. Louvenia thought she was going to sleep, but then her eyes opened once more.

"I'm here for this afternoon," Louvenia answered.

"Yah, you here, but why you here?" Delyse asked. "You've been a good friend since my Willie's gone and since the sickness came."

She took a noisy breath. "But time for you to go home now." She patted her chest with a fragile hand. "They can take care of this old woman here."

Louvenia smiled at her. "You know what Thomas Wolfe said. 'You can't go home again.'"

"Read it to me," Delyse said, her eyelids fluttering and then closing. Her voice softened and fell away into a resigned whisper. "God knows I won't tell your secrets, even if I should remember them. But if you don't let the past die, it ain't gonna' let you live." She closed her eyes.

Louvenia froze. Delyse knew. Somehow, she knew. Somewhere in the fading recesses of her mind was the ability to discern this truth. Louvenia felt exposed, raw, but she kept telling herself, it's *her* life. Magnolia Clement's, not Louvenia Brown King's. She opened the old notebook and began to read.

May 7, 1955

The sun's been shining steady for hours, and I've been waiting here to see Bella. She's the prettiest mare in the world. It's Saturday, and Benny let me ride in his truck to the plantation where he works. He says if I mind my manners, he'll bring Bella out and I can give her the treat I hide in my pocket. She's a Morgan mare, brown as chestnuts shimmering in a red sunrise. Her mane and tail are golden. They look like wheat rippling in a field.

Benny says being here is no good for a girl like me. "Go on and wait out yonder till I come get you," he says when we get to Mister Besset's stable. "Stay out of sight and mind your manners." He glowers at me like an ugly troll. "Do like I tell you, Maggie Lu."

But my big brother never could keep the smile out of his voice when he talks to me, and he's not ugly. He's the strongest, handsomest man I know. Big and proud with muscles hard as rock. He's smart too and says someday the world will be different. It will be a world for everyone to live in and be safe. It will be a world where smart will not be a skin color. I tell him I don't know what that means, and he looks sad when he says that someday I will.

Benny knows more about horses than anybody. That's how he got the job taking care of Mister Besset's horses. Mister Besset is powerful proud of his Morgans and Arabians and sells some of them at a big auction in town. He has Benny do other stuff too, like clean the stables and keep the saddles and tack oiled and polished.

Benny knows horses, but that's not all he knows. His teacher says he was at the top of his class. Always got his nose in a book. He'd be going to college full time if he could. Even got it in his mind to be the first black student at the big white university. Clementine and me, we laugh at that, but Granny Luv gets all stormy-eyed and tells him to hush that kind of talk.

But he's gotta work now that Luke's here. That's Benny and Clementine's baby, Luke Benjamin, after his daddy, and he's almost a year old already.

"Luke baby, you get fatter every day," I tell him when I bounce him on my knee. I get to take care of him a lot, mornings and after school on account of Clementine being sick a lot. He's even more beautiful than Bella, who's about the prettiest thing there is. Bella belongs to Harriet, and I never ask can I ride her.

I'm sitting here in the old summerhouse behind the stables, trying to get the jitters out. I never did like waiting, so I always write down in this notebook stuff I think about. Nobody comes to the broken-down summerhouse anymore.

I reach up to touch the big magnolia tree that spreads over the summerhouse. The branches get all mixed up with vines that tangle around you like a thousand arms. Friendly arms, I think. Like they're trying to wrap around you and keep you safe.

I remember Benny telling me that safe is just a word, a word people like us don't know. He says lots of things that make Granny Luv's forehead scrunch up like a prune. "That big brother of yours gonna be the death of me." And I know it's because she's afraid. Afraid of his secret talks with friends in the old garage down from our street. Afraid of papers and magazines that talk about rights and advancement and freedom for people like him and me.

My name is Magnolia. Magnolia Louvenia Clement, but everybody calls me "Maggie Lu" which is okay I guess, because I'm nothing like those big white flowers that smell like candy. Well, sometimes they smell like candy. Other times, like now, they make me think of lemons. Lovely, luscious lemons. I like the sound of that: "Lovely, luscious lemons." My teacher read us a poem about lemons once, and I say "lovely, luscious lemons" over and over.

I make lemonade at home when Granny Luv can find lemons cheap enough for us to buy. "Not too much sugar, Maggie Lu," Clementine tells me. I think it's funny that now she's married to my big brother her name is Clementine Clement! I say that in my mind three times and can't help but grin.

Clementine and Benny and Luke live with Granny Luv and me. Granny Luv's the only mama I know. Sometimes I get to thinking about my real mama who died having me. I don't remember her. Funny how sometimes I miss her anyway. I think about her even when Granny Luv pulls me to her soft chest and hugs me hard like she's never gonna let go.

Her name is Louvenia Emmaline Clement, but I've called her Granny Luv for as long as I can remember. And most other folk I know call her that too. "Your granny is the prayin'est woman in all of Savannah," my Sunday school teacher says.

I'm ten, so I'm in Miss Williams's Bible class. Miss Williams tells Bible stories like she's been there living them, and she prays out loud. Real loud! Louder than Pastor Ray Bill Samuels. But I'm not sure my prayers climb any higher than the craggy old roof of this summerhouse.

Our house is down the road from here and is nothing like this big plantation, but it's got three good rooms. The house seems smaller now that Luke is here. Someday Benny will have a house just for him and Clementine and baby Luke, but I hope that day doesn't come too soon. That sweet baby stole *my heart the minute I saw his red face and big gummy smile. He's working on teeth now. Law, he gets cranky sometimes.*

Clementine came up from Alabama to marry Benny. She came up looking like an angel in her wedding dress and braided hair wound on top of her head like a halo. She has eyes like milk chocolate and skin the color of pecans in the shell all shining golden in the light. Benny says she's "delicious" like she's something to eat. Sometimes those two go on a-huggin' and kissin' like there's no tomorrow.

When I hear someone coming I peek out between the vines and see the shiny pickup truck Mister Besset drives. He's pulling up alongside the stable where Benny's working, and I can see that Mister Geoffrey's with him. I feel a hitch in my chest, hold my breath. Benny says he's mean as a snake in a wagon rut.

They get out of the truck, first Mister B, wearing that big gray hat with a glittery gold buckle in the band and walking like he owns the place—which he does and makes certain everybody knows it. He has brown hair with white frosting at his ears and a belly that sticks out over his pants.

Mister Geoffrey climbs down and nearly stumbles trying to keep up with his daddy, who's yelling about something with a fierce look on his face. I can't hear what they're saying, but I can tell it's nothin' good as they head into the stable.

Mister Geoffrey is eighteen, Benny says, and tall as his daddy. I don't remember my daddy, but Granny Luv says Benny was the light in his daddy's eye, and they could hoe up the best garden a man and his son ever planted. She says they loved nothing better than going off fishing together when their day's work was done. I don't think Mister B and Mister Geoffrey ever go fishing together. They don't hardly even look at each other.

Benny won't come and get me now, and I'm feeling cranky as Luke when he's working on sprouting a tooth. I push away my jitters and edge away from the summerhouse. I inch along like a caterpillar and scoot toward the stable. But when I see Benny coming out leading Bella, I hide behind a fat clump of bushes.

"You for darn sure should have been out here working those horses with Benjamin, getting them ready for the auction," Mister Besset says to his cowering son. His face goes all red and his eyebrows are fierce, like a tornado's coming. "Instead you're out raising Cain with that gang of hoodlums you run with."

This scares me because I know Mister Geoffrey got no love for Benny, and here his daddy is hitching their two names up like ponies in a yoke. Mister Geoffrey pulls on a long brown sideburn and looks toward Benny through eyes black as burned peas.

Benny's over by the fence currying Bella and keeps his back to the two men. Mister B shakes a finger in Mister Geoffrey's face. He jerks a thumb over his shoulder at Benny. "That boy there's got more guts and brawn than the pup I raised," the old man says and spins around to head for his truck.

I freeze behind the bracken and scrunch low till the truck roars away. I heard about those "hoodlums" Mister B was talking about. Some say as how they set fires and come jumping out of the woods on a dark night.

Mister Geoffrey strolls toward the corral, arms hanging at his side and not moving at all. He hoists his skinny self up on the fence and watches my big brother curry Bella. He says nothing, and his nothing bears down on my heart like a rock. And I remember what Granny Luv says to me with her eyes all round and sorrowful: "You just mind yourself and stay out of white folks' business."

When the door to Delyse's room opened, Louvenia dropped her hand over the page she was reading. A round-faced CNA with a straggly ponytail poked her head in. "Miss Watson all right?"

Louvenia looked at the bed. Delyse was asleep, snoring softly through her open mouth. Louvenia was pretty sure that when she woke up, she wouldn't remember what was just read to her. She sighed, wishing she could forget too.

Chapter Three

MEREDITH DREW IN HER BREATH as Beatrice Enterline whisked up the bus steps in her low-heeled lavender pumps. The historical society director was herding the group of eager guests forward, checking their tickets, smiling a broad welcome bright enough to carry to the back where Meredith and Julia were already seated.

"Tell me again why we're doing this," Meredith said, pulling back the latch on the bus window to let in the morning's fresh breeze before the overly controlled air-conditioning kicked on.

Julia inhaled deeply of the fresh air. "Because Beatrice practically got on her knees and begged us to."

Meredith took her own deep breath. "Yes, but we've taken this tour about a hundred times. What does she really want?"

Julia waved her hand. "I don't much care," she said. "She had me when she said she'd pay for lunch at the Downhome Diner." The diner had opened about three years before and had quickly become a popular spot in the historic district.

Meredith sighed as Beatrice swooped up the microphone from its holder at the front of the tour bus. "Well, good morning, y'all, and welcome to charming, scintillating, gorgeous Savannah!"

Over the top. That was Beatrice, from her shiny lavender shoes and matching linen suit to the piled-up adjectives that reminded Meredith of a preacher pounding the pulpit.

But Meredith had to acknowledge that the new director of the historical society, who occasionally conducted tours herself rather than leave it strictly to volunteers, was serious about her job. She'd graduated from the University of North Carolina at Chapel Hill before coming to Savannah but deemed herself as much a belle of the Georgia South as Scarlett O'Hara.

"At least she isn't dressed in an antebellum costume today," Julia said. "The last time I saw her, she looked like she'd made over the bedroom curtains." At Meredith's sidelong glance, she amended, "Well, they were pretty curtains, I suppose, but you could hide the family silver in all those ruffles."

Today, Beatrice's lavender suit lent an appropriate dignity and charm to the occasion. She flipped her sunglasses to the top of her head. Her hair was styled in a textured pixie the color of black walnuts. Unlike the classic pixie, her style featured longer hair at the top that strayed wherever it chose—a sort of windy look parading as carelessness.

"The woman knows how to make an entrance," Julia said with a roll of her eyes.

Meredith had been curious to meet her successor who took up her duties a few months earlier. Beatrice was somewhere around forty-five, nearly two decades younger than she was. Fresh enthusiasm and new ideas were to be applauded, to be sure, and Beatrice had them along with a liberal dose of ambition.

"Thousands of visitors come every year to Savannah," Beatrice drawled. "They're drawn to its elegant architecture, ornate iron-work, fabulous fountains, and luxurious green squares. But our city's beauty isn't the only feature. You'll find our reputation for hospitality has not been exaggerated. Now y'all sit back and enjoy. You're about to see sites finer than frogs' hair split four ways."

Julia's decided groan would likely have been heard were it not for the rise of laughter and chatter as visitors peered out of windows and exclaimed their appreciation. Beatrice always tried too hard in pursuit of Southern sayings.

As often as she'd viewed the city, Meredith couldn't help the swell of pride as they drove by the Olde Pink House Restaurant, site of Georgia's first bank, with sculpted trees in graceful symmetry; and the birthplace of Juliette Gordon Low, owned and operated now by the Girl Scouts of America as a memorial to its founder.

Internally, she echoed the hushed exclamations of guests as the beautiful Cathedral of St. John the Baptist came into view. Beatrice went on to point out Temple Mickve Israel, one of the oldest Jewish congregations in the country. A rare example of Gothic style architecture, it was placed on the Register of Historic Places in 1980.

They continued in a westerly direction, past the SCAD Museum of Art and the Georgia State Railroad Museum. Beatrice's excitable voice droned on as she described the famous places.

A few moments passed in silence as the bus wove through traffic, but before long they reached the Pulaski District. Beatrice picked up her microphone again. "Now look out your right-hand window and see one of the finest examples of Greek Revival and Regency architecture in Savannah. The Sorrel-Weed House was one of the first two homes in the State of Georgia to be made a State Landmark in 1954."

Meredith listened for the familiar description. "The house was built for Francis Sorrel, a wealthy shipping merchant in the early nineteenth century. Confederate General Lee visited there in 1870, shortly before his death. And in 1994, the movie *Forrest Gump* was shot from its rooftop—way up there!"

Now Beatrice lowered her voice. "But listen up, folks. This house has a reputation for being one of the most haunted buildings in Savannah. Don't go visiting alone, especially after dark!"

Listeners oohed and aahed appropriately as the bus slowed to give them a long look and then moved on. Julia nudged Meredith and gave another eye roll. "She's got them going. Sounds like a feature for *Southern Living*. The woman is indefatigable."

"She claims she's a Gemini," Meredith said. "You know—her sign. She says Geminis are talkers, outgoing, adaptable, and intelligent."

Did Beatrice really put any stock in astrological signs? Meredith felt the pull of sadness. Without a moral compass, life was a wilderness impossible to navigate. Beatrice was eager to make a name for herself. Perhaps most people were. Meredith told herself she shouldn't be too hard on the new historical director.

"We'll take a roundabout scenic route on our way back to camp," Beatrice intoned now, interrupting Meredith's reverie. "Take note of the lush green acreage out your left viewing window and don't miss those mighty oaks with Spanish moss dipping long fingers to the ground. And saints preserve us! Have y'all ever seen magnolia trees looking so gorgeous? I declare it would make a frog spit in a rabbit's eye."

"She didn't just say that," Julia groaned.

It was then Meredith recognized where they were, where they had been just the day before when Julia had encouraged her to take the long way to the office.

"Just ahead you'll get a glimpse of an antebellum mansion through those loblolly pines and black gum brush." Beatrice extended her microphone in a northerly direction. "It needs a little spit and polish, but that's the site of one of Savannah's most alluring mysteries."

Julia nudged Meredith as the bus slowed and idled along the road. She sat up straighter in the seat. "We're going by the Besset place," she said with a lift of her eyebrows. "That's not quite on the list of historic homes."

"I didn't expect we'd be here again so soon," Meredith said softly, feeling a chill. She peered into the distance to the tangle of vine-infested shrubs and trees where they had found the hidden gate and the crumbling summerhouse. Leaning forward, she shielded her eyes, the chill in her bones deepening. "Remember when we were sitting there on those old stones and we felt like someone was watching?"

"It was just a haunt of history," Julia replied. "That's all it was, don't you think?"

"Well, right now I'm not so sure," Meredith said slowly.

"What do you mean?"

"Look back toward that road to the left where the trees are thickest." Meredith whispered, sensing the same foreboding she'd experienced the day before. "I'm sure I saw someone jump back into the brush."

Julia turned so abruptly that her silver hair swiped across Meredith's cheek. When she turned back around, she said nothing for several seconds. "Probably some curious visitor to the area—or kids. We know the police monitor the place occasionally."

But Julia's pale gray eyes had darkened, and she was twining a strand of hair behind her ear like she always did when confronted with a knotty problem. "The Queen Bee has us spooked is all," she said.

"That house surrounded by all this land belonged to the Bessets, one of Savannah's oldest families dating back to the seventeenth century," Beatrice was saying. "Thousands of bales of cotton were raised on those acres, worked by slaves before the Civil War and later by sharecroppers raising soybeans and tobacco and corn. And, of course, peaches. There's nothing like Georgia peaches."

When the ensuing chatter died down, she went on. "But to get back to the mystery, the last Besset to oversee the plantation left the land after his daddy died. Folks say he had no heart to continue after his twelve-year-old sister disappeared. It's believed she might have been murdered, but her body was never found, and no one was ever arrested."

When the gasps died away, Beatrice added, "That was almost sixty-five years ago. Yes, the last Besset moved out, lock, stock, and barrel and left the place to molder and waste, but with any luck and the good assistance of the Historic Foundation, we hope to see this place restored. Some three hundred fifty buildings throughout Savannah's National Register districts have been saved thanks to some bold, driven women who started the foundation. We'd like to see this plantation restored too. But we'll get you back to town now so you can continue your sightseeing."

The engine revved, and the bus pulled away from the overgrown byroad onto the highway.

A short time later, Meredith and Julia stepped into the Downhome Diner, which was conveniently located close to the historical society and the place where trolleys and buses picked up and unloaded tourists. Beatrice was handing them off to an associate standing by.

The diner projected a sense of Old Southern charm with cheery yellow walls on which hung prints of Old Savannah. Long solar shades blocked the sun's glare but maximized the customer's view to the outdoors. A sparkling counter with red vinyl-covered stools spanned the length of the diner. There were also several booths and tables, each with a vase of seasonal flowers.

"Welcome back! Just the two of you?" Charlene Jackson greeted them, grabbing menus with a practiced hand. She had spied them easily upon entering and hurried over as soon as she finished helping a customer at the register.

In her midfifties, Charlene had an athletic build, iron-gray hair curled tight to her head and beautiful dark skin—the kind a fair-haired woman who freckled and burned in summer could envy. And Meredith did. "One more coming," she said, and then the door opened with a flourish. "Oh, here's Beatrice now."

Charlene treated her customers like old friends. Her friendliness and generosity were undoubtedly secrets of her success. Of course, her special shrimp and grits sautéed and served in tomato gravy speckled with smoky bacon went a long way toward her growing popularity. The menu also offered culinary surprises like the Pot Likker Noodle Bowl—ramen noodles, pulled pork, and veggies in a spicy collard green and ham broth.

Charlene led them to a table in a sunny corner and adjusted the shade. "Tara will be along to take your orders in a sec," she said, hoop earrings bobbing as she bent to place their menus on the table. She straightened but not before giving Meredith a look of such focused intensity that Meredith was taken off guard. Some terrible yearning seemed to vibrate in Charlene's brown eyes.

"Ah, at last," the historical society director said grandly as she opened her menu. "I could eat a horse. It's positively amazing how hungry one gets guiding a bunch of tourists around the city." She settled herself at the table, laying her purse in her lap. She looked from Meredith to Julia and back again. "So, how'd I do?"

"You did fine," Meredith said with a quick smile. Of course, the new historical director hadn't made a single request of her during the tour or acknowledged that her predecessor was on board. Meredith sighed. Not that she should have. But hadn't she made a great show of asking her to come along for moral support?

"Um—I think you hit the highlights," Julia said when Beatrice turned to her, obviously seeking yet further approval of her prowess. "The tourists seemed to enjoy it." She tapped her menu and turned to Meredith. "What are you going to have?"

"Some Brunswick stew, I think, with one of those special sesame rolls I had last—"

"Yes," Beatrice went on, apparently unwilling to end the discussion of the tour. "And weren't they shocked out of their socks when I told them about Isaiah Davenport keeping a wife, ten children, and nine slaves in that little house?"

Mercifully, a waitress arrived to take their orders, and the topic of the tour was tabled for the moment. Meredith was surprised to realize she was quite hungry after all. And the cuisine didn't disappoint. Her stew was loaded with potatoes, corn, and chicken in a rich, tangy gravy. It had a touch of heat, just enough to make her sweet tea taste even better.

When coffee was served, Beatrice sat back in her chair and gave Meredith a studied look. "So, I understand you've reopened your husband's detective agency. That's quite a change for you, isn't it?" Before Meredith could answer, Beatrice continued, cocking her head to one side to include Julia. "And the two of you are working together." She seemed delighted with her astute deduction.

"We are," Julia said, picking up a spoon to stir her coffee. "Now that Beau and I are retired, we can take up new pursuits. But Meredith and I are not detectives. We're private investigators. There's a difference, you know. Detectives work with the police."

Beatrice raised her penciled brows and took a long, slow sip of her coffee before placing her cup on the table with finality. "Well, I heard that Mr. Bellefontaine's agency was reopening, and I think it's wonderful. Actually, that's the reason I wanted to meet with you today."

Meredith felt her inner antennae rising. Beatrice was an acquaintance, hardly a friend—at least not yet. But she had gone to great lengths to encourage their presence today. Flattery. Free lunch. *Ah, here we go.* What was the new historical society director up to?

Beatrice pulled her clutch purse from her lap and set it down next to her water glass with a decisive gesture. "I want to hire you."

Meredith was stunned. "Excuse me?"

Julia coughed and touched her napkin to her lips.

"I have the approval of the society and the backing of some prominent city officials," Beatrice continued. "As you know, I sit on several boards here, and we're all eager—" She paused, her hazel eyes sparking with enthusiasm. "We want to see that old Besset place restored and added to the register of historic sites. It would be such a boon to our fair city, generating interest and adding to our economy."

When Meredith said nothing, Beatrice continued. "I'm sure you've heard that the owner has passed away. Though he paid taxes on the place, he gave no attention to the violations levied for the derelict condition of the property. We tried to contact him many times without success. He was a virtual hermit from all we can gather. That's where you come in. We need to learn everything we can about the Bessets." Beatrice pursed her lips. "We're prepared to pay seventy-five dollars per hour and a substantial retainer of one thousand dollars. Of course, we understand there may be additional costs, and we can discuss all that." She seemed to run out of breath as her eyes remained fixed on Meredith. "What do you say?"

Ron had seldom received so large a retainer, as far as she knew. A thousand dollars seemed like a fortune, especially with their client list resting pitifully at zero. "You know you have to wait for the standard period to a see if someone comes forward—"

"We want you to look into any possible remaining heirs. No relatives have climbed out of the woodwork yet. Could be no one wants to be part of the stigma about the old place. You know—some of the darker history of our beloved South. And they say the Bessets were among the cruelest taskmasters of the day. But if someone should lay claim to the estate, we'll want to be sure it's legitimate." Beatrice

cleared her throat, hastening on. "Your late husband had an excellent reputation here, and I believe you and Julia will keep up that
standard." She planted both hands on the table. "I have the check
right here." She opened her purse, withdrew an envelope, and
handed it to Meredith. "That should be enough to help you consider
our offer."

With lips that suddenly felt dry as cotton, Meredith stammered
that they would consider it.

"Good! I knew I could count on you."

With that, Beatrice rose, snapped up the bill, and left the table,
her posture ruler straight, lavender heels clicking double-time on
the tiled floor of the diner.

Chapter Four

MEREDITH ROSE SLOWLY, TOO BLEARY-EYED to read the lighted dial on the clock next to her bed. Sleep hadn't come easily as she mulled over Beatrice Enterline's offer and recovered from hours at the computer searching for anything connected to Geoffrey Philpott Besset.

After discussion about the historical director's surprising request, Julia had agreed. "Why not? We have the time right now, and we've both been intrigued by what happened there."

Meredith had phoned Beatrice to say they would accept the case. But not without trepidation. If the mystery hadn't been solved in sixty-five years, what made her think they could do it? Still, the fact that a child had never seen her sweet sixteenth birthday, never walked down the aisle on her father's arm, was heartbreaking. What had happened to Harriet? And what would happen to the plantation where she had gone missing so long ago?

Thus, the night of searching. Meredith had found references connecting Geoffrey Besset to the plantation originally owned by his great-great-grandfather, Henri. "Besset" was a variant of the French "Bessete" and the family likely migrated to America from Canada. But which branch of the Bessete family among the many did they come from, and how long would it take to trace them all and find the puzzle pieces that fit? Like the key Julia had found behind the agency, Geoffrey continued to be an enigma.

"What do you think, GK?"

The Russian Blue regarded her through vivid green eyes, characteristic of the breed. Yellow eyes in adulthood were considered flaws in show cats. On the edge of the bed, which was as far as she'd gotten this morning, Meredith returned the cat's stare and smiled.

She'd named him for the foremost Christian apologist, G.K. Chesterton, when she bought him three years ago from a friend of her younger son.

"He does look rather scholarly," Chase had said when she told him what she'd named him.

Chase William Bellefontaine, history professor at Emory University in Atlanta, could lay claim to scholarship himself, she mused. Her sandy-haired youngest had excelled in academics from the very beginning and never tired of learning. History was his passion, but he shared Meredith's love of words. He was still single, though vigorously pursued by many an adoring coed, like the one she'd gotten GK from.

"And what are your thoughts this morning?" she asked the cat, whose full name had been quickly shortened for ease in summoning him, though he seldom came when called anyway. He might be among the most sought-after breeds because of his beauty, intelligence, and kind disposition, but he was still a cat.

As for his thoughts, they were anyone's guess. GK merely looked at her, wide-apart eyes in his distinctive blue-gray face mild and unreadable. Though he treated her to his mellow "mrrow"—his peculiar variant of "meow"—from time to time, he was without a doubt the strong, silent type.

She bent to stroke his fur. Like all Russian Blues he had a "double coat" with the undercoat soft and downy and equal in length to the guard hairs which were an even blue with silver tips. Russian Blues were also treasured for their friendliness and sensitivity to human emotions, and the handsome cat had indeed been a surprising comfort to her in the two years since Ron's passing and even more so while recovering from her heart attack scare.

Her eyes fell on the gold-edged photo on her highboy dresser. Her father, a tall, silver-haired engineer in his signature three-piece suit and broad tie, stood beside the much shorter blond woman with an enigmatic smile and blue eyes that never seemed to fade, even when cancer began to wear her down. The family had celebrated her mother's sixtieth birthday around her bed singing her favorite hymn, "There Is a Balm in Gilead." Dad followed her to the Source of all comfort fifteen years later when he experienced a fatal heart attack.

"She died so young, GK," Meredith said softly. "I've already lived five years longer than Mom did." Her eyes misty, Meredith slipped past GK and made her way to the bathroom.

She regarded herself in the mirror, widening her eyes. They were blue like her mother's but not consistently blue. Rather, they reflected other colors close by. This morning they were more green than blue, thanks to her aqua robe.

She ran a hand through her short blond hair, its natural curl having its own way for the moment. She sighed. It was time for another trip to Mamie's Super Cuts. If only her hair grayed to a sleek, even silver like Julia's, she'd banish the box of Clairol Legally Blonde and go au naturel.

"Well, time's a'wastin'," Meredith said as she walked to the kitchen. She pulled out the box of GK's favorite kibble. "Here you go, cat." She'd just put the bowl on the floor when her cell phone went off.

She smiled with delight when she heard John Denver singing "Grandma's Feather Bed." Carter had loaded it onto her cell phone a couple of months ago, and she got tickled every time she heard it.

She picked up her phone and swiped the green phone icon. "Which one am I talking to?" she asked playfully.

"Hi, Grandma!" It was Kaden Micah, her older grandchild, who looked a lot like Opie Taylor. Complete with copper-colored hair and a spray of reddish-brown freckles across his nose, he might have been little Ron Howard's double. But personality-wise he was quieter, an almost too studious ten-year-old who excelled in science.

"Hello, sweetheart!" Meredith said. She knew she didn't have to ask why he called. Kaden was never reluctant to talk about his interests.

"Grandma, do you think someday we'll get to spend summer vacations on the moon? Or Mars? Kinsley says she'd rather go to Hawaii, but you'd rather go to Mars, wouldn't you?"

Meredith smiled. Nine-year-old Kinsley Faith, fair-haired and gorgeous, was a girly-girl, to be sure. The family lived in Charleston. It was only a couple of hours away, but life often got too busy for them all, and the kids were growing so fast.

"If I wanted a vacation for adventure and excitement, I think I'd choose Mars. But if I wanted to wear a lei and have flowers in my hair, you can't beat Hawaii." She'd become pretty adept at toeing a fine line between her two delightful grandchildren.

"Ah, Grandma," Kaden protested. "You always choose both."

Well, maybe not quite so adept.

She continued to chat with Kaden as she hurried through breakfast. When he'd finally exhausted his subject, she hung up determined to suggest another weekend at Grandma's—a real one—when she had her Snapchat visit with Carter and Sherri Lynn and the kids on Saturday.

Meredith dressed quickly, stroked GK lovingly, and left for the agency. As she steered her vehicle down the tree-lined street, she thanked God for the family she'd been given. And for her beautiful stucco Italianate home she'd inherited from her great-grandfather as a newlywed.

God had provided just the right house for her needs. Small enough for a working woman to handle and big enough for sleepovers with her favorite people.

She was counting on Him to guide her and Julia in the days ahead, however uncertain the future felt now. Victor Hugo's words seemed to descend like a blessing: "Have courage for the great sorrows of life and patience for the small ones; when you have laboriously accomplished your daily tasks, go to sleep in peace. God is awake."

When she arrived at the agency, Arnold's truck and Julia's car were parked in the agency lot, along with Carmen's Toyota distinguished by a bobblehead Chihuahua in the back window.

Arnold Mains and his crew had done wonders with the reception area and two of the offices, which she and Julia occupied. Now they would be taking on the renovation of Ron's former office.

They'd left his space the last of the four office areas, knowing it would require the most work, and they needed to get the agency up and running. But Meredith realized that she hadn't wanted to disturb that space that had been so distinctly his—she had wanted it to remain as Ron had left it. But that was crazy, she knew. The fire had desecrated it already. Not his wonderful old walnut desk, though, or the heavy, gilt-framed historical plat map of Savannah that hung over it.

Meredith was used to tender flashbacks that came at the strangest moments when you weren't expecting them. In her memory Ron sat at his desk beneath the map that had hung there since he opened the agency.

Her husband had loved that map. Renovating the office would require its removal. But she would restore it to its place, however fitting it might or might not be for a investigative agency run now by two well-heeled women in their seventh decade of life.

Meredith shook her mind free of its ghosts and pushed open one of the handsome double-glass doors recently installed and entered the empty reception area. Where was everyone? She glanced at her watch, chagrined to be the last one in. But soon she heard voices coming from the back where Ron's office was located.

Julia came around the corner, her face a mix of surprise and confusion. "Hey, we've been waiting for you!" She thrust back a lock of silver hair that had escaped her smooth coiffure.

"What? I'm not that late," Meredith protested, glancing at her activity tracker, poised at the time of day.

Julia tugged on Meredith's arm. "Come on. We have something to show you." She led her into Ron's office where Carmen, Arnold Mains, and a younger man in spackle-covered jeans hovered over

Ron's desk, their backs to her. She blinked at the blank space above them where the map had hung. It had been lowered to the floor and now leaned awkwardly against an adjacent wall.

Everyone turned as Meredith entered, and she stood transfixed at the sight of a metal box centered on the desk. Roughly eight inches by six, it was battered and scarred, its color undiscernible.

Arnold stepped back, giving Meredith access. "Found this behind the old plat map there when we went to check the lath work," he said, brushing a rough hand across his chin. "Must have been hidden there for some reason."

Meredith lifted her gaze from the box to a small recess in the wall, hardly larger than the box. Ron had bought a good safe, but it was empty and had been since she first considered reopening her husband's agency. Perhaps the recess behind the map had once served as his safe.

"We never thought to look behind that map," Julia said, color rising in her cheeks. "Who would have thought anything would be hidden there?"

"Took two of us to get it down," Arnold admitted, jerking a thumb toward his younger partner, who looked to have muscles hard enough to lift a horse.

It was no surprise that the map was heavy. It covered almost half the wall. Meredith moved closer to inspect the box. Julia crouched over it and began wiping the top surface with a tissue from a box Carmen held toward her. She glanced meaningfully at Meredith when her fingers swiped over the small silver lock.

Was it possible that the key Julia had found in the garden could fit this box? The lock looked about the right size. Meredith recovered from her quick excitement and said casually, "Thanks, Arnold. We'll take care of it. Oh, and thanks for keeping that desk covered while you work on the walls. And do advise us if anything else unusual shows up."

She picked up the lightweight box with a wad of tissues in each hand and carried it into her office.

"Look, there's scotch tape on the top of the lid—like something had been attached to it." Julia reached into Meredith's left-hand desk drawer with a look like a light bulb going off. "Like this key," she said, her eyes bright as she pulled it out and studied it in the palm of her hand. "Maybe it was taped to the box and got torn off, but how it ended up in the back garden is a puzzle."

Meredith wiped the lock area carefully and took the key from Julia's hand without a word. She touched the key to the lock and turned it.

"*Ay, caramba!*" Carmen gasped as the lock clicked open.

When they lifted the lid, they saw only dry pinecones and wing-like seeds, which appeared to fill the box. But touches of color appeared here and there. Meredith poked at the debris with a ball-point pen and separated some of the seeds and cones.

They could only stare at the meager contents. Meredith lifted out a narrow ribbon about twenty-four inches long. Faded and satiny, a lovely sky blue.

"A girl's hair ribbon," Julia said softly. "Not much of a treasure." She peered into the box as Meredith pulled out another object—a rattle shaped like a clown and made of five pink and blue plastic balls.

"This looks old," Meredith said, giving the rattle a gentle shake. "But it still works." A dull, thin clatter of tiny balls hit the inner plastic.

Carmen leaned in over Julia's shoulder. "I can find out how old that is on Vintage Toys Online. That site has some amazing old pieces." True to one trait of the millennial stereotype, Carmen favored the digital track to information. She shook back a lock of thick black hair and pressed in closer. "Is that a book?"

"*Little Women*," Meredith whispered, feeling a tender stirring. Like Julia, she had always loved the book. "What we have here is a cache of treasures—probably a girl's, but whose?" She picked up the book and riffled through the pages, checking the margins. She traced her finger over the worn but well-conditioned cover of the Alcott favorite. No inscription, no marginalia, nothing to hint at its owner.

Together, Meredith and Julia picked out the cones and seed pods and found in the bottom a folded piece of paper yellowed at the edges. Meredith's mind raced, eager to begin analysis. It wouldn't be hard to determine its age. Carefully she turned it over.

"A horse. A child's drawing of a horse," Julia said.

"Not bad," Carmen said.

It was a pencil sketch, blurred and smudged by lead. The horse had no harness or saddle; there was no background to provide a clue to its owner or place. The rendering was rough, the horse's legs a bit too long for its body, its ears too short beneath a scribbled mane. Yet there was a certain charm to it that touched Meredith's heart. Some doting grandmother would lovingly showcase it on her refrigerator.

Julia, who was parsing through the natural debris they had pulled out onto the desk, lifted a small scrap of paper no bigger than a wallet-size photo. "There's something written here," she said, holding the paper gingerly by one corner. Her voice rose excitedly. "Carmen, get the magnifying glass in my desk."

Meredith felt her breath catch in her throat as seconds later the powerful lens picked up the penciled words. After a few moments, she read them aloud.

Is that You God
in the rainbow
high in the sky
Is that Your whisper
in the summer breeze
waking up leaves
Is that Your touch
in the cuddle of kittens
like wooly mittens
Or do You hide from me still

No one spoke for a full ten seconds. The words on the scrap of paper, unpunctuated and simple in a juvenile half print, half cursive, read like a poem. Could anyone more beautifully express the angst of a soul seeking the divine?

"A child's box of treasures," Julia said, breaking the silence. "I wonder who she is—or was."

A thousand questions leaped to Meredith's mind as the three of them talked, but the most important was, how had this simple treasure come into Ron's possession? It could belong to any young girl, but was it possible that Ron had been investigating the mystery of Harriet Besset? Were these the missing girl's treasures?

"Besset," Carmen mused at one point in their discussion of the mystery. "Geoffrey Besset... Didn't he own that broken-down old place they talk about on Halloween?"

"Yep," Julia responded, folding her arms over her chest and giving Carmen a knowing glare. "As I recall, you and some of your friends got into trouble for horsing around and throwing rockets into the woods on that property."

"Ah, part of my evil past," Carmen said, in mock chagrin. "But I'm reformed, no?"

Banter continued for a while between Carmen and Julia, the judge who had helped the teenaged ward of the court embrace the straight and narrow. Then Carmen left the room, her fingers likely itching to search Vintage Toys Online.

Meredith tried to remember if Ron had ever discussed the decades-old disappearance of Harriet Besset, other than in casual conversation. Her mind yielded no clues. It was odd that just when the case had been handed to them, this box with its peculiar contents should turn up.

They carefully returned each of the items into the box. "This may have nothing at all to do with Harriet Besset, you know," Meredith said. "But we do have an obligation now to the historical society. Any thoughts on how we should begin investigating?"

"Well, there will be plenty of research and paperwork to do," Julia said, her words trailing off.

Carmen suddenly reappeared, a sheaf of papers in her hand and a look of puzzled excitement. She tapped the top sheet with a pink enameled fingernail.

"What's this?" Meredith asked.

"You know those handwritten logs of Mr. Bellefontaine's that you asked me to key into the computer?"

Meredith nodded hesitantly. Ron had always kept a list of anyone who called, and she had found ten years of names and numbers in a cardboard box. There might have been more logs, but only one box had been spared from the fire. She had asked Carmen to record the lists as time allowed.

"These go back a while," Carmen said. "But when we were talking about that old plantation, I remembered something." She tapped her temple with her index finger and pressed the paper toward Meredith. "Those initials next to the dates. There were several that year."

Meredith felt her pulse begin to race. She stared at the listings that Carmen had marked in yellow.

Twelve highlighted entries in Ron's hurried scrawl read "GB."

Chapter Five

MEREDITH PULLED UP TO THE Downhome Diner and took a seat at a booth near the back to wait for Julia. She smoothed her blond curls, which the early-morning humidity had already turned to frizz, and pondered the odd events of the previous day. The strange box of dubious treasures, the phone logs with the initials GB in Ron's handwriting.

She had found the address of the law office where Geoffrey Besset had worked until retiring twenty years ago. Maybe tomorrow she'd take a trip to Raleigh to see what information she might uncover about the man who had, for all intents and purposes, dropped off the radar.

But if he belonged to those scrawled initials, the recluse must have contacted Ron in recent years. It was strange that her husband could be involved with the case she and Julia had just taken on. Strange that first a half-buried key turned up, then Beatrice Enterline hired them to explore the Besset family for the historical society. Strange that a hidden box that might belong to the missing twelve-year-old Harriet had been found behind a picture in her husband's office. Strange that Ron had never mentioned any of this to her. Strange indeed.

"What can I get you, honey?"

A waitress with straight strawberry-blond hair wiped her hands on her apron and cocked her head to one side.

"Just coffee for now," Meredith said. "I'm waiting for a friend who should be here any minute." As the waitress bounced off to get the coffeepot, Meredith scanned the cheery diner for Charlene, remembering the wordless exchange she and the owner of the Downhome Diner had shared after the tour with Beatrice.

It had lasted only seconds, but it had been a look of such focused intensity that it had taken Meredith off guard. Charlene seemed to want to say something—something of considerable import by the look in her dark, expressive eyes. Meredith and Julia had patronized the diner several times since its opening, and Charlene had been courteous and friendly, always acknowledging them with a smile.

Not seeing Charlene, Meredith shifted her curiosity to a back burner in her mind. There were certainly more pressing concerns. Still, that look had unnerved her.

Julia was usually prompt. Maybe she'd gotten a late start this morning. Meredith glanced around at the antique prints of the city that covered the yellow walls. A vintage map of Savannah from 1734 in sepia tones, the imposing National Bank Building at the turn of the twentieth century, Fort Jackson, the oldest brick fort in Georgia standing on the banks of the Savannah River.

On an adjacent wall the old Cotton Exchange dominated. It was built in 1887 during the era when Savannah ranked first as a cotton seaport on the Atlantic and second in the world. In its heyday as a cotton port, over two million bales a year moved through the city. She had pointed out the building, which was now the headquarters of the Savannah Chamber of Commerce, on many a historic tour. Ah, she did love this city!

The glass doors opened, and Julia appeared, tall and regal in chic slacks and a cotton blazer imprinted with delicate leaves in black and white. Her low-heeled pumps made quick taps on the gleaming floor. Catching Meredith's eye, she hurried to join her in the booth.

"Hope you weren't waiting long," she said, pulling out a chair. "I had to help Beau with some drops to prepare for his second cataract surgery tomorrow. One of these days I suppose we'll have to clear our aging windshields too."

"Everything okay?" Meredith pushed a menu toward Julia.

"Oh, everything's fine," she said, laughing. "He just can't keep his eyes open long enough to get the drops in by himself. They just drip down his face."

"Men are so helpless sometimes," Meredith said, not really meaning it. Certainly not where the hunky outdoors enthusiast Beau Foley was concerned. "Have some coffee."

"Did I tell you I'll be away most of tomorrow? The surgery doesn't usually take long, but Beau is determined to go to Atlanta where his former optician moved. There are perfectly good doctors right here in Savannah, and he decides to drive three-and-a-half hours to Atlanta. Go figure!"

They each ordered one of the delectable breakfast scrambles pictured in the menu and concentrated on eating. For Meredith's part—and likely Julia's from the way she was frowning—there was a lot to think about.

They were on their third cup of the diner's special blend coffee when Julia put words to her pensive demeanor. "I keep thinking about that little poem—or was it a prayer?—that we found in the box."

"It is remarkable, isn't it?" Meredith asked, imagining the childish hand posing the question, "Is that you, God?" and then her poignant images of a breeze waking up leaves and a cuddle of kittens.

"Harriet must have been a remarkable girl—if it was Harriet," Julia said thoughtfully.

"Yes, well spoken but perhaps something of a skeptic too. That final line, 'Or do You hide from me still.' It's sad and at the same time disarming. Children feel and hear much more than we realize, I think."

"I remember when my Grampa died," Julia said, her eyes growing misty. "I told God how mean He was to let that good man fall into an elevator shaft. I was only six, but I told God I would never like Him again—ever!"

Meredith said nothing, her heart filling with sympathy.

After a moment, Julia's eyebrows arched, and a twinkle reappeared in the soft depths of her gray eyes. "He forgave my foolish little-girl rant—He's that kind of God."

"He is," Meredith said quietly. "I think we've all from time to time questioned why He allows some things. Maybe something happened in Harriet's life that broke her small heart. Childhood is a world apart from grown-up reality."

"I'd like to go back there," Julia said after a pause.

"To childhood?"

"No, I mean to the summerhouse. It's probably crazy to think we might find clues to the Besset mystery there after all these years.

Well, not without a bulldozer and, of course, permission to excavate. But it was odd being there. It was like you could almost hear the ground whispering or something."

Meredith smiled with a half shiver because she was remembering that odd feeling of being watched that they had put down to imagination or a sense of protracted history. "Our long-lost girl might well have penciled her bit of poetry in that very spot or sketched the horse as she sat on those crumbling stones."

They sipped their coffee quietly for a while as the chatter and laughter of patrons swirled in the background. A young couple was being seated at a table a few feet away. They held the hands of a little flaxen-haired girl, one on each side. The child, probably three or four, looked up into her parents' faces expectantly.

Meredith smiled. "I think Harriet might have had hair like that—and blue eyes. A mother might well buy a blue ribbon like the one in that old box for such a child."

"I was a blond once," Julia said, giving her smooth gray coif a little toss. "But my mother said red and pink were my best colors." She shrugged, acknowledging the lightness of her reverie. She picked up the check and said with sudden resolve, "So, it's early yet. We should take the long way to the office again. You game?"

"Why not? I could do with a drive in the country."

Soon they found themselves walking among arching cypress trees along the border of the old Besset plantation. The crumbling house, hardly grand enough now to be called a mansion, stood in the distance, an example of Greek architecture with Doric columns and a Byzantine dome.

"It must have been quite a handsome structure at one time. I wonder why it was abandoned by the last Besset to live there." Julia drew an audible breath. "It's been empty for something like thirty years, hasn't it?"

"Yes," Meredith replied, recalling what she knew about the place from her historical society days. "Geoffrey didn't exactly abandon it, though, because from the records we know he continued to pay taxes on the place."

"Strange," Julia murmured, "but he was a cryptic character from all we can surmise."

They walked on along the edge of the property's forested section that grew denser as they went. Massive oaks dripped with Spanish moss, long fingers pointing to the secretive ground.

"If these grounds could speak," Meredith said, "I wonder if we would want to hear the tales. The ones history repeats are horrifying enough. When Harriet Besset went missing—or was murdered, as many think—Martin Luther King Jr. hadn't yet arrived on the scene of the Civil Rights Movement, but things were building up."

Julia was quiet for several paces as they walked on toward the site they had discovered on their first visit. When a familiar cluster of loblolly pines came into view, she edged deeper into the bracken. Meredith followed, and shortly the broken-down remains of the hidden gate with its iron bars still welded into the stone gateposts came into view.

They pushed through the woody vines and tangled branches to reach the low stone wall, the remains of the summerhouse. They sat together in silence for several moments. Meredith listened for birdsong, but it was strangely absent. And this far from the road, no traffic noises penetrated either.

"What was that phrase from Flannery O'Connor you mentioned last time we were here?" Julia asked, tucking her hands into the pockets of her linen jacket, as though she were feeling the cold. "Something about rising—"

"'Everything that rises must converge,'" Meredith said. "It was de Chardin's line, but O'Connor quoted it in the title of her book about uniting with all those making the same ascent."

"Well, I hope things come together in this case that's been thrust into our laps," Julia said softly. "Not so much for the sake of the historical society, though I suppose that's important. But to find out what really happened to that young girl and others in her circle of family and friends."

"Yes. She deserves so much more than a few lines in a sixty-five-year-old newspaper." Meredith recalled the brief stark lines: *The case of twelve-year-old Harriet Besset, daughter of Charles P. Besset, reported missing July 13, 1956, from Chatham County, Georgia, remains unsolved. The body has not been recovered.*

As though in protest, something stirred in the quiet enclave. A rustling and a light snap of branches. Perhaps a chipmunk or squirrel was foraging among the dried leaves. Or a breeze had suddenly risen to portend a coming storm.

"Did you hear that?" Julia asked, straightening and drawing her hands from her pockets.

Meredith nodded, feeling again the shiver she'd experienced before when they sat on that crumbling stone wall. They'd laid it to the bleakness of the surrounding, to imagination. Certainly not to ghosts, though many a tale of the unsettled dead circulated in the Old South. Ghost tours were probably the most popular among tourists and even the locals.

Real or not, God's Word warned of the futility and the danger of putting credence in "familiar spirits," urging rather that trust be placed in God. Meredith felt a surge of confidence as she leaned once again on the God she had come to trust. "If it's His will, the truth about Harriet Besset will be uncovered," she said.

Julia nodded. "We'll do what we can and leave the rest to—"

A loud thrashing and a burst of wind broke the silence. Whipping around, Meredith stared at the largest man she'd ever seen. Wide eyes in a deeply lined and dark face framed by wild hair leered at them through the bushes. His great arms in a faded work shirt gripped a limb of the ancient magnolia tree behind the wall where she and Julia had been sitting. Now they were both on their feet staring at the fierce-looking man whose girth rivaled the trunk of the tree. His feet in heavy work boots came down with a thud on the ground, scattering tangled wood vines and forest debris.

"Y'all get out!" he shouted in a craggy bullhorn voice that could easily wake the dead if such were possible. "You don't belong here!" He raised one meaty fist and brought it down on another thick magnolia branch in a threatening gesture.

Julia struggled to press a button on the cell phone in her hand and dropped it. Meredith saw her stoop to retrieve it, saw at the same time the angry expression on the big man's face change into a questioning one. His huge eyes flashed from one woman to the other.

The seconds dragged like minutes in which a series of thoughts raced through her mind, sorted themselves, and left her inexplicably calm. "We mean no harm here," Meredith said. "We've been hired by the historical society to explore the Besset family and holdings. I'm Meredith Bellefontaine, and this is Julia Foley." She took a step toward the man, whose fingers clutched the limb of the magnolia tree. Whoever this bull of a man was, what right did he have to be there? "We've told you who we are. Now, who are you?" she demanded.

The man dropped his hands to his sides and shook his huge head with its mop of scruffy hair. Meredith was surprised to see his massive shoulders droop and his mouth go slack as he surveyed them through eyes not quite clear. Meredith blinked. He was an old man, his leathery face etched with the years—at least six decades plus—as far as she could surmise. "And why are you jumping out at us like this and scaring us half to death?"

"They call me Lucky," came the voice that had lost more than half its volume. "I was just doin' what the lady from the society told me—keeping busybodies and folk up to no good from comin' round, messin' up the place."

Julia, once again clutching the phone tightly, took another step closer to the magnolia tree. Obviously struck by curiosity, she made no move to call for help and stared at the massive man. The city occasionally monitored the old plantation to be sure it didn't become the target of vandals or drug dealers. Was this ancient mountain of a man here for that purpose?

Meredith studied the now wary face. She'd never seen him before that she could recall, but could he have been the figure that leaped into the bushes when the tour bus paused outside the plantation grounds a few days earlier? When Julia had turned around to see what she was talking about, the figure had vanished. Meredith had shrugged it away until now.

"What society lady?" Julia asked.

"Ms. Enterline," he said, lifting his chin. The lined brow furrowed deeper. "And I'm just doing what I'm supposed to." He stepped into the bushes as though to take his leave. Branches snapped back in place, and he stumbled off into the woods.

As he hobbled away, something fell from the pocket of his denim overalls. A bottle that looked suspiciously like a whiskey bottle but was clearly empty, the sun shining through it. He stooped to retrieve it before stuffing it back into his pocket. Meredith turned to a frowning Julia. "What do you make of that? Did Beatrice really hire that man to guard the Besset estate?"

Julia pressed her lips together in thought. Her silver brows rose as she pressed a button on her phone. She nodded to indicate that she was about to find out exactly what Beatrice Enterline had done. "I saw the bottle," she said as she waited for someone to pick up. "But he didn't appear in the slightest inebriated."

"You know him?"

"No, but believe me, I know a drunk when I see one. And when I don't." She put up a finger to halt further discussion. "Julia Foley here, Beatrice. We're at the Besset place and ran into someone who says you hired him—"

Obviously, Beatrice had interrupted and was explaining, though Meredith couldn't hear what was said. She sat down on the wall to wait and pondered the man whose footfalls were swallowed by the unforgiving land as he shuffled away from the old summerhouse.

"You might have warned us," Julia said into the phone. "He scared us half to death." She clicked off and joined Meredith on the wall. "Yep, apparently, Lucky lives in an old house at the end of the lane that adjoins the Besset property. He came from someplace north a couple of years ago. Harmless, Beatrice says. Just an old retired man who passes this place a lot when he goes to fish in Sutter's Creek. So, they decided he might want to earn a few dollars to watch the place."

"The bottle?" Meredith asked.

She shrugged, raising her eyebrows again. "Police say he's sober—doesn't drink, at least not anymore. They agreed to let him keep an eye on the property to scare away kids and such."

"Well, he certainly had my heart pumping," Meredith said. "And I bet he's the one I saw from the bus when we went with Beatrice on that drive-around tour." She snugged her jacket tighter around herself, surprised at how much cooler it was in the woods. She stopped at the magnolia tree where the old man had stood.

Many magnolias ushered in spring with their February and March bloom times, but others like the beautiful specimen near the hidden gate didn't flower until much later. "Isn't it unusual that this tree is flourishing without benefit of the sun that magnolias crave?"

"The blooms are gorgeous," Julia agreed. She examined a slender branch bursting with pure white flowers. "Almost like someone has been taking care of it." She pursed her lips and added quietly, "Besides the bountiful Creator."

"Hardly likely," Meredith said, turning away. "But we'd better get to the office before Carmen sends out the National Guard." A shiver passed through her again. Though his presence had been explained, the old man called "Lucky" had unnerved her. She bent her head toward the welcome shaft of sunlight.

Chapter Six

THE MORNING HAD COME SLOWLY, the sun hidden in a thin blanket of cloud. Intent on her plan for the day, Meredith had hurried through her morning routine and bid a fond but hasty farewell to GK, who had been morose over the lack of warmth on his favorite windowsill. Her cat hardly blinked when she left the house, umbrella in hand. "Be a good boy today, Mr. Chesterton," she had warned in parting, but no answering "mrrow" had come from the handsome Russian Blue.

She would miss the company of Julia today. Beau needed her to go with him to Atlanta for his eye surgery. The two were well fitted to each other. Beau, a recently retired anesthesiologist, was a few years older than Julia but an excellent foil for his wife's analytical mind and fun-loving ways.

They had never had children. Julia had cited polycystic ovary syndrome, the most common cause of infertility in women, as the reason. It was a hormonal imbalance that resulted in a series of small cysts on the ovaries. Acceptance of the condition had come, and both Beau and Julia had successful careers that absorbed their time and energy. Julia had poured her heart into many of the children she'd come across in her years as a children's court judge and was thankful for the freedom she had to do so.

Meredith slipped into her SUV with a prayer of gratitude for her sons and grandchildren. Carter and Chase were precious when Ron was alive, and they were even dearer now that she was alone. And adding to her joy were her two grandchildren, Kaden and Kinsley. *Lord, how excellent and beautiful are Your gifts!*

As she drove she found herself thinking of another young girl. Harriet Besset had been a child robbed of years in which she might have known the joy of a late spring morning like this one—rain and all.

In the four hours it would take to get to Raleigh, she had plenty of time to contemplate the lives of Harriet Besset and her older brother, Geoffrey. It was a long shot to imagine she could learn anything about Geoffrey Philpott Besset by visiting his former law office. He had retired two decades ago. Still, perhaps the man had had a partner whose son could have succeeded him. Someone might know something. She was taking a chance that one of the partners would be there and make time for her, but she had the day. And a long drive often worked to sort out her thoughts.

She drove past green lawns and well-proportioned homes, greening farms with long white fences that spanned the highway, and hoped for the best. She turned on the windshield wipers against an insistent shower. April had been a chartreuse ballerina swept on gossamer wings, cherished as she danced lightly across the stage of spring. But she was changed now, a seasoned matron surrounded by May's grand panoply of color and richness.

Meredith swallowed against a sense of melancholy that rose unbidden. She too was no spring ballerina but well-seasoned, and at times lonely, despite her loving family and circle of trusted friends. Funny how such a feeling could present itself at the oddest times.

Even people who knew the comforting presence of God were not immune to loneliness. But perhaps it had its purpose. She'd read somewhere that, like the Grand Canyon, loneliness is a deep incision in the surface of our existence that becomes an inexhaustible source of beauty and self-understanding.

She sighed and listened to the rhythmic tempo of the windshield wipers. Long drives by oneself could lead to such introspective moments, she realized. It was her son Carter who now and then brought up the subject of his mother's future, hinting that she had his permission if she should find someone with whom to share her life.

Ever the pragmatist, Carter would say, "It wouldn't hurt to go out now and then. Lots of women your age find male companionship a fulfilling experience. Besides, you work much too hard. You know what they say about all work and no play."

She always derailed the subject. Ron had been enough—more than enough, and when you'd experienced the very best in a life partner, it was hard to imagine giving your heart to anyone else. She'd had to fend off the attentions of Bob Nestor, a contractor who had updated her current house. He was kind, thoughtful, and well placed in life, but she wasn't interested or ready. She didn't need the complication of such a relationship, especially now that she and Julia had taken on their first case.

As the miles passed, she rehearsed the events that began with a small key turning up in the yard behind the agency. She prayed for guidance in knowing what to do about the old mystery that had become more than a case. It had become personal somehow.

What did those childish objects in an old metal box mean? Who was the girl who sketched a horse with a golden mane, who saved a bit of blue ribbon and looked for God?

And what, dear husband, did you know about it?

As she neared the section of Raleigh where Geoffrey Besset had once practiced law, she had to turn the wipers on high against the downpour. Rumbles of thunder accompanied the urgent drops. She turned up the mechanical voice giving her directions and peered anxiously through a blurred windshield for street signs and numbers.

She took New Bern Road to Battery Heights and relaxed slightly when she found Storm Road. *How appropriate! Storm Road on a stormy day.* Now if she could just find a parking place in the busy section of the city near number 2016. And if the wipers would cooperate. She needed new blades and wished she'd taken care of that before heading out of Savannah.

She didn't see the number on the building described by the GPS as her destination in time and made a pass around the block. A crash of thunder and a renewed weeping from the skies made for even poorer visibility, but there it was now. Just ahead.

Happily, there was a good spot along the curb, and she headed for it—at the same time another car signaled for a right turn and veered into the spot ahead of her. Oh well, there was room for two. She braked to let the car in and followed. She could easily park behind it.

Whomp!

She gasped as her bumper connected with a red Land Rover Sport. *This didn't just happen!* Its driver hadn't pulled up far enough and stopped too quickly. And she hadn't had time to brake fast enough. *Great!*

She eased back from the bumper and jumped out, heedless of the pouring rain. "What are you doing?" she demanded as a silver-haired man stepped out of his car and walked with agonizing slowness to view the damage. He'd even taken time to grab an umbrella, which he extended toward her, affording ample coverage for them both.

"Why in the world didn't you pull all the way up?" Meredith spouted. "Didn't you see my signal? Didn't you see me behind you?" She stared into the unperturbed face of a trim sixtyish man in a sleek gray suit. Its color mimicked the silver of his hair in which threads of visible copper intertwined. He'd been a redhead! *Figures.*

"Are you all right?" he asked in a frustratingly calm baritone voice.

"No, I'm not all right. I mean, I'm not hurt or anything, but I'm soaking wet now and I have an important meeting. Why couldn't you—" She broke off, aware she was close to frantic tears.

He had been inspecting the two bumpers, which appeared to Meredith to have sustained no damage, and looked at her more closely. Utterly disconcerting, that face. What was it? And why was he so all-fired calm?

"I'm sorry," he said, unruffled. "But let me remind you that you are the one who bumped into me."

"Only because I thought...because this rain..." How could he be so smug? She really hated smug. And yet she knew he was right. She supposed he'd now whip out a cell phone and report the accident with that superior air of his.

"The important thing is that you're okay. And I don't think our cars suffered much either." He paused and stroked his cheek. "Unless you have a different opinion, I don't think we need to call this in."

He gave her a searching look, and it was then she realized that the man had one very blue eye and one very brown eye. He had heterochromia. She knew only one other person with that condition, a young woman in a Bible class, who most of the time wore contacts to make each eye an even blue.

She drew in her breath, willing herself to calm down. "No," she said, looking away to the bumpers. "I appreciate—that is, I'm fine so long as you are." She paused, ashamed at her outburst, but it was just so unnerving to feel the impact and hear the scrape of metal on metal.

"Why don't we step into the building over there and get out of the rain," he suggested with a wave of his hand to 2016 Storm Street. "We can exchange phone numbers and insurance companies if needed."

"Yes, of course," she said, feeling only slightly mollified. "I'll just get my purse." She leaned in to retrieve her umbrella and purse. "As it happens, that's where I was going anyway," she said stiffly.

They walked into the brick building, still under cover of the gentleman's huge black umbrella. When they were inside the vestibule, Meredith smoothed her damp hair and brushed the front of her cotton A-line dress. It was at least five years old but a business favorite in a soft shade of blue. She probably looked like a semi-drowned rat. He, on the other hand, looked impeccable from his crimson and silver striped tie to his Derby dress shoes.

He waited as she dug in her purse for her card holder. "So, your meeting is here?" he asked as he pulled a business card from his wallet. "My appointment is here as well."

She looked around then for the first time. The vestibule of the building was small and led into what seemed to be a single office. A plaque above the glass door read "HOLDER AND SONS, ATTORNEYS AT LAW." Adjoining the office was a small coffee shop.

She took the card held out to her, drawing her attention back to her accidental companion. ARTHUR "QUIN" CROWLEY, ATTORNEY AT LAW. She might have known! She'd rear-ended a lawyer!

"'Bellefontaine Investigations,'" he read with a lift of silver brows. A decided twinkle appeared in his heterochromatic eyes. "Ms. Bellefontaine? Or is it Ms. Foley?"

She swallowed "Ms. Bellefontaine. That is, Mrs. Bellefontaine. Please, call me Meredith. My friend and I have recently reopened my late husband's agency."

He angled his head to one side, still staring at the card. "Your partner wouldn't be *Judge* Julia Foley, would it?"

She nodded, too surprised to respond verbally.

"I never had the pleasure of appearing in her court, but she has a reputation for intelligence and fair-mindedness."

At that second, she realized that the address on Arthur Crowley's card read "Savannah, Georgia." She scanned it, noting the holder's specialties: CORPORATE LAW INCLUDING PATENT, CONTRACT, BANK-RUPTCY, TAX, ZONING REGULATIONS, AND LAND USE. "You're from Savannah, Mr. Crowley," she said, looking up in surprise.

"Quin, please. And yes, it appears that we both made the same trip this morning." He looked around, making a quick survey of their surroundings. "I'm here to see Jerrod Holder," he said, expressive brows rising once more. "And since there is no other office in this building, I must surmise that you're here to see him as well. What time is your appointment?"

"Well, I don't actually have an appointment," she said, doing her best to sound self-assured. "I was hoping to have a chance to talk to one of the partners. I—" She broke off, realizing how unbusinesslike this must sound. "The—um—drive appealed to me as well. At least it did until the rain turned into a deluge and—" She paused and allowed a light bubble of laughter to rise up. "Until I bumped into you. Literally!"

He smiled then, a gracious smile that wreathed his eyes with light. "How very strange," he mused.

Was he enjoying her discomfiture?

He glanced at a watch on his wrist. "Actually, I have thirty minutes until my appointment. What do you say to continuing our conversation over there?" He gestured to the coffee shop.

She wasn't altogether sure it was a good idea, but she was damp and chilled in the highly air-conditioned vestibule. A hot drink might settle her nerves. And she was curious to know his reason for driving to Raleigh to see the same lawyer or lawyers she needed to see. "Sure," she said, feeling quite unsure.

"I wish someone would open a coffee shop in my office building," he said as he held the door for her. He wasn't tall—probably would stand eye to eye with Julia, who was three inches taller than Meredith was.

They sat at one of only two tables in the small shop. A middle-aged waitress with a thick, decorative hairnet came from behind the counter. "Will it be coffee?" she inquired. "And perhaps a cruller or donut to go with it? We have some excellent peach pie. Also, coconut cream."

Meredith requested only coffee, as did Arthur "Quin" Crowley. What was that "Quin" all about, anyway?

Though she hadn't asked, he said, "I'm rather a latecomer to Savannah. My practice was in Columbus, near the Alabama border. My daughter still lives there with her family."

She waited for more. Like why he had moved to Savannah. When he picked up his cup, she said, "I see. How do you like the oldest city in the state of Georgia?"

"I've always admired it. Still do," he said.

"I was director of the historical society there for a number of years. I never tire of its enterprise and beauty."

"And now you're a private investigator. Unusual switch. Ah, but then you said your husband was in the business." He set his cup down and looked at her with unabashed interest.

"Yes, he passed away a little over a year and a half ago." She was surprised to feel somewhat easier. "I didn't plan to take up his line of work, but then I had a little episode with my heart and realized I wanted to do something different. Not that focusing on history isn't important. It's just—" She gave a little shrug.

He didn't say anything right away, but after a lingering pause said simply, "I'm sorry for your loss."

"We had a lot of good years together—two sons and now a couple of grandchildren. Don't worry, I won't whip out the photographs, though the truth is my grands are quite perfect."

"I just have one, a granddaughter. Also perfect," he offered with a laugh that had music in it. After another pause, he added, "I lost my wife five years ago. I guess my change of venue had something to do with that. In any case, I'm now a citizen of the oldest city in Georgia."

Meredith grinned. He even talked like a lawyer.

A twinkle glittered in his eyes. "Now that we've run into each other, may I ask why you've come all the way to Raleigh to see a lawyer?" He passed a hand over his jaw again, which might imply thought, or perhaps it was a nervous gesture. "You don't have to answer if you don't want to, of course."

She leaned back and folded her hands on the table. "Actually, it has something to do with a case Julia and I have taken on behalf of Savannah's Historical Society."

He waited, his gaze growing more intense.

"You may have heard about the old Besset plantation even though you're new to the area. Well, the society has been interested in it for a long time, and now that the last owner is dead and no will has been found, they're eager to acquire the land and probably rebuild the mansion."

"That would be Mr. Geoffrey Philpott Besset?" His eyes narrowed briefly.

"I see you know about him. Well, he is rather infamous, I suppose, even though he'd dropped out of sight and managed to remain hidden for a couple of decades. The society hired us to find out all we can about him and any possible heirs that might turn up."

"I see." A cryptic expression crossed his face, and a vein in his temple quivered. "Interesting. This whole day has been...very interesting."

She looked at him expectantly. "Why is that? I mean, aside from the fact that I put a dent in your Land Rover and made something of a fool of myself."

"You did nothing of the kind," he said quickly. "I'm only referring to the strange coincidence that we should meet here. You see, I too need to gather information that might shed light on a case of mine. I've been hired by a potential heir to the Besset Plantation. He claims his mother was married to Charles Besset."

Meredith caught her breath and stared hard into Quin's unusual eyes. "Did you say your client's mother was married to Charles Besset?"

"His name is Langston Butler. And yes, he tells me that Charles Besset married his mother after Charles's first wife, Sarah Jean Templeton, died. Langston has asked me to represent his claim to inherit."

"And there's proof of this relationship?" she asked, feeling quick distaste. If this was the same Langston Butler she knew of, his reputation preceded him.

Quin paused, considered her. "He says his mother took back her maiden name after the split from Besset. But I probably shouldn't talk about this yet. I'm still exploring the matter on behalf of my client."

"You did say the man's name is Langston Butler—the same Langston Butler whose real estate dealings have incurred some rather intense scrutiny by the authorities?"

Quin raised expressive silver brows and stroked his chin thoughtfully. After a few seconds, he glanced at his watch and smiled a strange half smile. "I'm afraid I have to go. I'll be late for my appointment."

So he was that kind of lawyer. Someone who could work a deal, find a convenient loophole to wriggle his client through if it was worth his while. Langston Butler, of all people! The man had been around the Savannah area for only a few years, but he'd had business deals throughout the South—and beyond, for all she knew. The thought of Quin Crowley representing Butler hurt because she liked the enigmatic lawyer, found his manner calming and forthright. But maybe he was only putting on the charm—part of his modus operandi.

So, he didn't want to discuss the Besset plantation, wanted to end their conversation and get to his scheduled appointment. Fine with her. "Well, don't let me keep you—" she began but was quickly interrupted. He seemed at a loss, which gratified her to some extent.

"Look, I'm sorry." He shifted his feet, cocked his head in a boyish way. "I—uh—really enjoyed running into you." An irritating twinkle lit his bicolored eyes. "Or...being run into by you."

The twinkle faded in the face of her silence, and his voice softened. "Meredith, I could wait until after your visit with Holder if you care to—"

"Oh no. Please don't disrupt your schedule on my account. I have to get back to Savannah right away in any case."

It was the last she saw of him, for when she came away from her fruitless quest in Holder's office, Arthur "Quin" Crowley was gone. She'd told him not to bother waiting, but she was puzzled and irritated by her disappointment at his acquiescence.

Chapter Seven

THE NEXT DAY LOUVENIA AGAIN made her way to Delyse's bedside. Once again, as she did every day, she told Delyse that Sydney, her little tabby, ate all his kibble and that everything at her cottage was fine. The cottage that had become Louvenia's refuge from a world that held danger. Danger for her and her little family. The close-knit family that had come unraveled.

Benny was gone. Long gone—like Clementine and Granny Luv. Safe in the arms of Jesus. Where Luke was, she didn't know. He'd lost his way, but she prayed every day he'd find it again. Right now, for her, keeping Charlene and Clarissa safe from the man who still looked for her after all these years was her highest priority.

She drew closer to the bed and saw that Delyse had had her bath for the day and was dressed in a pale blue nightgown. Her old friend looked almost girlish. Louvenia patted the wrinkled hand resting on the coverlet.

Sometimes, when Louvenia visited, Delyse was in her own world, maybe back at the library, wanting to run an inventory on all the self-help books. But this morning she seemed much more alert, which gladdened Louvenia's heart. At the same time, she wondered if Delyse remembered what she read to her yesterday.

"Are you all right, Louvenia?" Delyse asked suddenly.

"Of course I'm all right," Louvenia said with a defiant lift of her chin.

"You are a sassy girl, aren't you?" Delyse teased.

Louvenia remembered that's what Granny Luv used to tell her with a cloud of worry in her eyes.

"I see you're fine today too," Louvenia said. And then something froze inside her. The care home staff had tied a blue ribbon around Delyse's thick gray hair. Louvenia swallowed, catapulted in time to another blue ribbon.

Delyse closed her eyes for a full thirty seconds. She opened them, black and wide with the world in them. "You bring your journal today, sassy girl?" she asked.

Louvenia patted the large fabric bag draped over her shoulder and took out the notebook.

"Then read to me," Delyse said, folding her hands over the covers and closing her eyes.

Louvenia sat down and turned the pages, looking for the girl she once was. She forced her eyes away from the blue ribbon around Delyse's hair and read how it was when she met Harriet for the first time.

May 21, 1955

Granny Luv took me with her to Mister and Missus Besset's place because they're having a big party for Miss Harriet's birthday. She's gonna be 11 today, Granny Luv says.

I know that's Mister Besset's daughter, and I say that if she's anything like her daddy, I don't want to help with her old party. Granny Luv rolls her eyes at me and tells me to mind my manners.

Granny Luv told me to come with her today because she needs help for the party. She's been cooking and cleaning for Missus Sarah Jean Besset for as long as I can remember. Benny says Granny Luv's too old to work so hard. Her legs are about wore out, he says, and tells her she should stop working here, 'specially when they don't pay her a smidgen what she's worth.

"Missus Besset needs me," Granny Luv tells him.

I know Missus Besset takes to her bed a lot, and I try to feel sorry. Maybe she really is sick, and maybe her stepsister got to do a lot to keep the plantation in order, since Missus Besset can't. But it seems to me that it's Granny Luv doing all the work in that house.

When it's time for the party, I find Miss Harriet at a fancy table in the garden. The big mansion is so pretty it makes my heart ache. They got roses of every color you can imagine blooming all around. And there are tables covered in white linen so bright it makes stars swim in my eyes. Umbrellas and chairs are set up on green grass so thick it swallows you up when you walk. Pink and purple balloons bloom everywhere, and a whole flock of girls are bouncing around Miss Harriet, chattering and laughing. They're dressed up real fancy—like they're going to church.

Miss Harriet's wearing a blue dress with ruffles at the hem and around her neck. "It can't be much fun to play all gussied up like that," I say to Granny Luv when I take the trays of sandwiches and cake from her hand.

"They have their ways," she says when I roll my eyes. "Besides, Miss Harriet can't do much jumping around what with that bad leg of hers."

That's when I see that she doesn't move right. She gives a little hop on her left foot when she walks, like it might not be strong enough to hold her up.

Next time I bring out a tray, I sneak behind a pillar to see her face better. The first thing I notice are her eyes. They're blue as a summer sky, the same color as her dress. She has light gold hair shinier than Bella's mane, and it goes all the way past her shoulders. A sky-blue ribbon is tied on top of her head. She smiles, and I like the way her eyes sparkle. But she seems embarrassed, like she doesn't know what to say.

"Let's all sing 'Happy Birthday'!" A shrill voice soars over the giggles and gab of the guests. Most of them are kids, but there are two adults. I recognize Missus Besset's voice right off because I hear her calling Granny Luv when she wants something. "Louveenie! Do bring that pitcher of ice and see that it doesn't sweat all over this linen tablecloth." Or "Louveenie, put up the umbrella on that table over yonder." Now she puts her hand on Miss Harriet's shoulder. "After we sing, Harriet can open all the wonderful presents ya'll brought," she says and starts the tune in her high voice that peters out almost to a whisper.

I remember Granny Luv saying how Missus Besset be fragile as a newborn kitten. The others join in, including

Miss Amelia Percyman, who is Missus Besset's stepsister and always hanging around like she doesn't have a house of her own. Granny Luv says Miss Percyman got her nose stuck up so high in the air, she's like to drown in a rainstorm.

I laugh thinking about that and decide right then and there to call that lady "Miss Persimmon." 'Cause she's sour as a persimmon. The sound of it makes me giggle and in my mind I say it again and again while I watch Miss Harriet open her presents.

I don't want to like Miss Harriet, but she smiles over every gift, and her voice sounds happy when she thanks everyone who gathers around her. Paper doll books, paints and crayons, a little box with a dancer on it, ribbons and bows and even a fancy dressed-up doll with a pink parasol. I never saw so many pretty things at one time, and I try not to be jealous.

"Don't be wishing for what others got," Granny Luv has told me a hundred times. "Envy don't get you nothing but trouble."

So I keep bringing out more lemonade and watch the girls playing with Miss Harriet's new things. I watch as the party goes on, and I wonder what it must be like to have anything you want. If I could have anything I wanted, I'd have all the picture books ever written and a golden horse like Bella.

Benny says Bella is Miss Harriet's horse, the one she always rides. Maybe I'd ask for one even more beautiful that could fly like the wind. Yes, if I could have anything... But then I think how Mister and Missus Besset have anything they want, and they always look like someone just died.

Miss Harriet takes the paper off yet another present—a huge round red thing. "It's a Hula-Hoop, the latest thing," someone says. Miss Harriet looks confused and runs her small hand around its wide circle.

"Show us how you do it," a girl a little older than Miss Harriet says. She has a long, freckled face and red hair in two braids by the side of her head. "Here, I'll show you!" and she whips the thing over her head and starts wigglin' her hips in circles like her upper half and bottom half aren't connected anymore.

Some other girls take a turn too, and then Miss Redbraids looks at Miss Harriet with a glitter in her eyes that spells meanness to me. She flings out her spindly arms like she's talking for all the girls. "Let's watch Harriet do it!" she says.

I look around for the grown-ups, feeling uneasy. Missus Besset has gone inside, pressing her hands to her head and looking miserable. Miss Persimmon is stretched out on a blanket across the yard, fanning herself with her eyes closed. I think she is about the laziest person I ever saw except when Mister Besset is nearby. Then she flits around him asking does he need something or can she do anything for him.

Sometimes Missus Besset notices her stepsister batting her eyelashes at Mister Besset, and I think she looks sadder than a hound in a cage.

The kids ooh and aah at the presents piled up on the table, saying how much they like this or that. One holds up some purple beads and drapes them around her neck. They look up at Miss Redbraids and gather around Miss Harriet looking curious as a cat by a mousehole.

Miss Harriet's face goes whiter than I thought a white girl could get. She looks around, as though she'd like to run away, and I wish Missus Besset hadn't gone inside.

"Come on. You have to take a turn," the red-haired girl says, sticking out her lips in a pout. She puts the hoop over Miss Harriet's head. "Just start wiggling your hips. You got to keep it going around all the time! You can't let it fall to the ground."

"Yeah," says a girl with long brown hair in two ponytails. "Don't be a sissy girl. Do it like this!" When she swings her skinny hips around, her ponytails bob like two brown toads hopping on a rock.

All the girls pretend to whirl the hoop around, and Miss Harriet tries to copy them. But her left foot doesn't seem strong enough to hold her. She stumbles and tries hard not to let the hoop fall. Two red spots appear on her cheeks. Her eyes go all wild and scary.

The party girls are laughing. "Go! Go! Go!" they shout and point their fingers at Miss Harriet, who whirls even harder. But her feet give way, and she falls with the hoop trapping her inside. She falls into some bushes that snag her dress and her beautiful blue ribbon. I hear her cry out in pain, but the girls are still laughing.

She moans and tries to get up. There's a nasty scrape on her left arm, and I can see the blood fall on her blue dress. Blood just as red as my blood when I fall playing dodgeball on the playground.

Pastor Ray Bill Samuels's words flash through my mind. His voice thunders, and he holds out his big beefy arms like he expects someone to run into them. "God made of one blood all nations of the earth."

I drop the pitcher of lemonade and run to her. I don't think about it—somebody's gotta help her. "You okay, miss?" I ask, reaching for Miss Harriet's hand.

"I—I think so," she says, scrambling to get up, putting her weight on her good foot. It takes a few seconds to realize that none of the other girls have made a move to help. They just stand there and gawk. Miss Redbraids's face is scrunched up like she thinks it's a funny sight to see Miss Harriet sprawled out on the grass.

I remember a sick hen Granny Luv had once and how all the other chickens kept pecking on it till all its feathers were gone. Now I see people can be just as mean, picking on a girl whose feet are different.

Suddenly two men come running across the lawn. Wasn't supposed to be any men here today. My heart goes crazy when I see that one of them is Mister Geoffrey. His boots pound the thick grass, and there's fury in his steps. With him is a big man with haystack hair named Waylon Jute. Benny says Jute is as mean as Mister Geoffrey and twice as dumb. They both make my insides turn to jelly.

"What in blazes is going on here?" Mister Geoffrey yells. He looks around for his mother, who hasn't come back out of the house yet.

Miss Harriet is on both her feet now. I'm holding her Hula-Hoop in one hand, her satiny blue ribbon in the other. We both stand there, stunned into silence. The other girls look like they see a ghost.

I hear a high-pitched voice, see Miss Redbraids push her way toward them and point at me. "She done it! She pushed Harriet!" And she uses that word that makes Benny's face grow hard and cold when someone says it.

Miss Persimmon comes over, waving her fan and looking like a boiled crawdad from sunning herself. "Harriet, darlin'! What in the world?" She says it like it's two words—"wo-ruld"— and opens her green marble eyes wide.

Next thing I know, Granny Luv is running toward us, her apron flapping like a white flag in the wind.

Mister Geoffrey pulls Miss Harriet toward him, gripping her by the shoulder. I know he has a powerful liking for his little sister and looks like he'd put a dagger in me if he had one.

Jute looks down at Miss Harriet with eyes that look sort of sleepy or hungry. He rings his tongue around his thin lips and says something I can't hear. Benny always tells me stay away from Jute, that he ain't safe. He touches Miss Harriet's head, strokes it lightly, and drops his gangly arm to his side.

Granny Luv has hold of my hand and pulls me hard toward her. She clasps me to her chest, and I feel the fear in her when Mister Geoffrey demands to know what I'm doing there.

"She just helpin' me serve, sir," Granny Luv says. "She don't mean no harm."

"She pushed Harriet in the bushes," Miss Redbraids says. She has her nose stuck in the air like Miss Persimmon.

I feel shaky, and I want to scream that I didn't do anything. I see the blood still oozing from Harriet's arm, and I look at the trickle on my hand from the spiny bushes.

Miss Harriet pulls away from her brother's hand. "No!" she shouts, and her cheeks suddenly get red as flame. She shakes a finger at the girl with the red braids. "Pamela Sue Rayburn, you take that back." I can't believe how bold she looks. "You know it's not true. I was trying to do the Hula-Hoop, and I fell in the bushes." She points to me. "She helped me!" I hear the proud Southern lady she'll be one day when she's the mistress of her own place. "Maggie Lu didn't push me," she says. "She helped me, do you hear?" She stamps her good foot.

The girl named Pamela shrugs her shoulders and turns away like the whole thing doesn't matter a lick. The other girls look down at their shoes and take little embarrassed steps back.

"I'll take Harriet to her mama," says Miss Persimmon. "And you—" She waves her fan toward me. "You best go with your grandma. I declare, this lovely birthday party is in tatters." She sticks her nose up in the air like she's the one been put upon.

Granny Luv whisks me away and into the back door of the house, but I can still feel Mister Geoffrey's cold eyes on my back.

Granny Luv and I don't say anything for a long time while we clean up from the ruined party. I wipe the china carefully and put the silver into the drawers like Granny Luv taught me. There's something glad rising inside of me. She stood up for me! Miss Harriet stood up for me.

That was the start of things for us. "You don't need to call me 'Miss Harriet,'" she said when she tiptoed into the kitchen later. "I want to thank you—for being kind to me today," she says. She lowered her pale eyelashes, and a lock of her yellow hair fell over her forehead.

When she looked up again, she stared right into my eyes. And very slowly she took the blue ribbon from her hair, looped it over me, and tied it up in a bow on top of my curly head.

When I got back to the summerhouse the next day, I tucked the ribbon away in the metal box Benny hammered for me in the stable. I bury the box under the magnolia tree and think about how sweet it is to know somebody likes me just for me.

When Louvenia looked up from the journal, Delyse's eyes were closed and she was snoring softly, her hands still clasped over her frail chest. Louvenia felt hot tears well up in her eyes and begin to spill down her face. "Oh, Harriet. Gentle Harriet. I'm so sorry," she whispered.

Chapter Eight

"WHAT? CHARLES BESSET HAD ANOTHER son?" Julia stared at Meredith through incredulous eyes. "I've been through every twig on the Besset family tree, and there's no record that Charles had a son other than Geoffrey—living or dead! There were just the two children, Geoffrey born in 1938 and Harriet in 1944."

Meredith leaned back with a resigned sigh. Julia had come into the office late, having presided over an early meeting of her local professional women's club that morning—the morning after Meredith's late return from Raleigh.

Her meeting with one of the two lawyers in the office where Geoffrey Besset once worked had yielded nothing about the former plantation owner. Nor had any documents been left behind when he had vacated the premises twenty years before.

A wasted trip. With the possible exception that she had met Arthur "Quin" Crowley, Attorney at Law, and legal counsel for Langston Butler, alleged son of Charles Besset.

Now, after a night of fitful sleep, Meredith sat at her desk, her computer not yet booted up. She met Julia's eyes. Her partner was leaning in, waiting for a response to the surprising discovery.

"Yes. Apparently he has a claim to the Besset plantation."

Julia splayed both hands on Meredith's desk. "Charles Besset married Sarah Jean Templeton in 1935. June, I believe."

"Apparently, Besset remarried after Sarah Jean died, to a Kendra Ellen Butler in 1965. She took back her maiden name of Butler after the marriage failed."

Julia's puzzlement spread across her features, and she was quiet for a moment. Then narrowing her eyes, she said, "I never saw any record of that. How'd you find that out anyway?"

"I ran into Butler's lawyer in Raleigh."

"His lawyer? But nothing's come out about a claim."

Meredith shrugged. Perhaps Quin hadn't gotten around to that yet. Maybe he had been in Raleigh to collaborate with Holder and Sons. She suppressed a sigh.

Julia jumped up and zipped into the outer office, calling for Carmen. "Did we get the morning paper?"

"*Sí*," came the quick reply. "But there's nothing in there about the Besset plantation. *Nada*."

She'd been listening. Carmen had eyes in the back of her head and ears attuned to whispers. Maybe that was how she always knew what was going on around town.

"Already read it," Carmen said. She lifted the *Savannah Morning News* from the bottom drawer of her desk and handed it to Julia, who began leafing through, scanning the section where claims might be printed.

Coming back into Meredith's office, Julia said, "So you ran into this Butler guy's lawyer when you were in Raleigh. What lawyer is that?"

"He's new to Savannah," Meredith said in as offhand a manner as she could muster. "Actually, we ran into each other. Uh—that is, I ran into him. But it was his fault. It was raining, and he pulled into the parking spot I was aiming for, and, well, I sort of rear-ended him."

Julia sat down again across from Meredith and looked at her quizzically. "Everyone okay?"

"Oh, it was really nothing. We didn't even call it in. We just agreed to forget it over a cup of coffee." Meredith fiddled with the business card she hadn't even realized she was holding.

"Well, that's good. But who is this understanding fellow?"

Meredith flipped the card toward Julia. "A very self-assured lawyer named Arthur Crowley," she said. "Out of Savannah, as it happens."

"Quin Crowley?" Julia's lips pursed in surprise.

"You know him?"

"Well, yes, that is, not personally, but I've heard through colleagues I used to work with that he's quite good—and reliable. Rather attractive too." She gave Meredith a sidelong look, her hair falling over her left eye. "He's a widower, I'm told." She shrugged. "The legal community is to some extent a close-knit one, you know."

"Well," Meredith said, recalling Quin's words, "it seems he thinks rather highly of you too."

Julia's expressive gray eyes widened. "Really?"

"When he saw your name on the business card, he asked if you were Judge Julia Foley. Says he was never in your court but that you had a reputation for intelligence and fair-mindedness."

"So, he's not only understanding, he's remarkably insightful," Julia said with a grin.

"Or condescending," Meredith said quickly.

Julia regarded her closely. "You like him," she said with the certainty of considered judgment.

"I don't even know him," Meredith began and stopped when she heard the hot denial in her own voice. The truth was, she had liked him. Not since Ron's passing had she given another man more than two minutes' thought. She was sixty plus, had a promising career, a great family, magnificent memories. The last thing she needed was a man. She released an exasperated breath. "Well, when you hear who he's representing, you may question your opinion."

Julia looked from the business card to Meredith's face. "Butler, you said."

"Yes, Langston Butler."

Julia's eyes widened. "You mean the real estate mogul—the one who's got his fingers in a lot of mud pies? The one who came to Savannah wanting to build a casino here?"

"That'd be the one," Meredith said, picking at a ragged nail she'd just identified.

"Well, well," Julia said, her features inscrutable. "So, one can only wonder about the man's sudden appearance on the scene and his lack of interest in the Besset property until now." She began drumming her fingernails on Meredith's desk and looked intently into some analytical space in her head.

"An opportunist, I'd say," Meredith said. "And the first order of business is to investigate his claim, find out if he really is related to Charles. I'd hate to see the historical society lose out to a money-grubber like Butler. To a guy who might turn that beautiful old plantation into who knows what."

"Yes. There are some sites that dig more deeply into genealogical backgrounds—for a price, of course. If there was a marriage to this Kendra person—however brief—there's got to be a record. But, recluse or not, it sure is odd that Geoffrey didn't leave a will on file somewhere. After all, he went into the legal business after he left the plantation."

Meredith sighed. "Unless it was destroyed or stolen." She placed Quin's business card back in her desk drawer, feeling at odds with herself. She had taken an uncharitable attitude toward Langston Butler. Maybe Arthur Crowley too—even before all the facts were in. Lack of sleep, perhaps. She'd been at sixes and sevens all morning. "I guess we should notify Beatrice about a possible heir," she said resignedly.

"I suppose," Julia said. "But I'd really like to see Langston Butler on his own turf. He's got an office in Tybee Island." Julia's eyes lit suddenly. "No reason why we shouldn't check out a little real estate."

The small city and barrier island known for its wide, sandy beaches, light station, and museum, boasted homes and properties that drew wealthy beach lovers to its shores. Meredith leaned forward, warming to the prospect. "It's just a half hour jaunt down Truman Parkway to US 80." She shrugged. "Why not?"

"We'll be out this afternoon," Julia told Carmen as they passed her desk in the reception area.

"Yes," Meredith added. "While we're gone, check—"

"Check out info on Kendra or Langston Butler," she finished, giving a toss of her glossy black hair and winking one cocoa-brown eye. "I'm on it. *¡No hay problema!*"

The offices were small, and they had made no effort to keep their conversation private. Still, it was uncanny how Carmen could intuit their thoughts and instructions before they were even stated.

"Before you go, here's a list of calls," Carmen said, handing Meredith a few pink "while you were out" slips. "By the way, there are two from Miss Jackson. And she called again just a little while ago. I said you were busy but that you'd call." She tugged at a dangly red earring. "She says it's important she speak with you."

"Jackson? Charlene Jackson?"

"Yes, you know, from the diner."

Meredith caught the inside of her cheek with her teeth and once again remembered the diner owner's cryptic look. Her call had come in yesterday while Julia was gone with Beau for his eye appointment and while she was running after a dead end in Raleigh. Why was Charlene Jackson calling at the agency? She tucked the slip into the pocket of her linen slacks. "I'll take care of it."

It was another gorgeous May day as they approached Tybee Island via US Highway 80. Following their GPS instructions, they drove over Bull River Bridge and through the Fort Pulaski National Monument. Once they passed over the Lazaretto Creek Bridge they were on the island. They found Butler Real Estate at the west end of a shopping mall.

"I hear he owns a restaurant on the island and part interest in a start-up development company," Meredith said. "I researched it when I got back from Raleigh."

"Ambitious guy," Julia said. Butler Real Estate didn't look like much. Just a small shop squeezed in between a day spa and a dental office promising "affordable care." But it was possible to make anything look good through buildups on social media and glossy, pumped-up flyers. As they pushed open the glass door, Meredith gave a hopeful shrug and exchanged a glance with Julia.

A willowy blond with gleaming white teeth and heavy mascara looked up from her desk. She wore a pale green dress with a gold belt at her narrow waist. Damp, crimped hair hung like a cloud around her shoulders. "May I help you, ladies?" she asked in diction that didn't deny her Southern roots. "We have some absolutely to-die-for properties available today."

Meredith smiled, genuinely liking the young woman who seemed like she'd be happier walking on the beach in flip-flops. "We'd like to see Mr. Butler."

But there was no need to phone or check his availability. From the one inner door in the cramped office, a man likely well into his fifties emerged in a white shirt with no tie and sleeves rolled up to the elbows. He had carefully groomed dark hair flecked with silver and a much-too-handsome Roman face. A mature Marlon Brando *On the Waterfront* look.

"Ladies, welcome to Tybee Island." His teeth vied for gleam with his secretary's.

He probably pegged them for tourists on the spot. Tourists with possible buying interests. But Meredith and Julia had agreed to be straightforward—the quickest way to getting the information they needed. Perhaps.

Meredith pressed a business card toward him and introduced herself and Julia. "The Savannah Historical Society has asked us to look into the disposition of the Besset Plantation, and we understand that you have a claim pending on the property."

His dark brows rose toward his receding hairline. A muscle in his temple quivered as his smile widened. "Crowley works fast. I didn't know he'd filed yet. Good man. I like a fast worker. 'Time and tide wait for no man.'"

But Crowley hadn't publicized the claim yet. Meredith had checked. She cleared her throat as they were ushered into Butler's office with its cluttered desk and dark walnut furnishings. "You may know perhaps that the historical society is interested in restoring the Besset mansion should it become available," she began.

He motioned for them to take the two chairs across from his untidy desk. "You caught me working," he said, hastily stuffing papers into a drawer. The vein in his temple trembled again, and his left eye closed and reopened in rapid-fire movement.

A nervous tic, Meredith realized with surprise and watched it happen once more as he folded his hands on his desk to signal that they had his full attention. A showy diamond ring glittered on his pinky finger.

As though he had not heard Meredith's explanation, he asked with an indulgent smile, "So, ladies from the historical society. How may I be of assistance?"

"We're not *from* the society," Julia answered. "We are looking into the Besset plantation on their behalf."

"Ah, yes, of course. Bellefontaine Investigations. Impressive." He rubbed his hands together briefly and settled them on the desk once again, then took his time responding. "Well, you see, I haven't decided yet what I will do with the old place, and you must admit this conversation is a bit premature. Technically, I haven't taken up ownership."

"But I assume you are in possession of your brother's will," Meredith said.

"Well, not exactly, though I'm sure a thorough search will uncover it. But, as you may know, a will isn't necessary. If none is found, family members stand to inherit." He paused with his full lips slightly open and glanced from her to Julia and back again. "I—uh—assume *you* haven't seen a will either." His voice lifted in question as the tic resurfaced, revealing his anxiety.

Meredith chose not to respond to the question of a will. "Mr. Butler, we've been told that Geoffrey Besset lived in seclusion and was not available to discuss any potential plans for the property with the historical society. May I ask if you had contact with your alleged half brother in recent years?"

He considered this for a moment, his brown eyes sparking at the word *alleged*. He cleared his throat and directed his gaze to a point over the heads of his visitors. "I have not, though it's not germane to the issue here," he said with icy coldness. "The high and mighty Charles Besset sent my mother packing. Without a cent, I might add. She had to work as a waitress in a two-bit dive to support herself and me. She's gone, God rest her soul. She took back her maiden name, which I too have adopted—as you know. She despised Besset. And I wanted nothing to do with my so-called father."

"Until now," Julia said meaningfully, eliciting a glare from Langston Butler that Meredith thought could easily be described as malevolent.

"We're sorry," Meredith put in quickly, "about your mother and those difficult years." Was it possible she was actually talking to

Geoffrey's half brother? She took a quick breath, attempting a look of sympathy. "How long since your mother passed?"

"She died when I was twenty-two. An auto accident," he said, cracking his knuckles as he spoke. "Too bad she didn't live long enough to get something out of the old skinflint."

"So, the marriage is a matter of record?" Julia asked, softening her intrusive question with a smile.

"I don't carry a birth certificate around, but I'll prove my connection in court." He narrowed his eyes at Julia, perhaps aware of her former judicial position.

He got up quickly, placed his hands on his slim hips, and took a step to one side of his desk. Below his rigid jaw, the muscles in his neck pulsated. He appeared to steel himself, and abruptly his manner changed. He flashed a smile that didn't reach his eyes. "I don't need to prove anything to you. Besides, I'm a businessman. The Besset name would do nothing to advance my position." His lips turned down at the corners, and his voice became caustic. "For all I know one of them murdered my poor half sister Harriet way back in 1956—nearly a decade before I was born."

Something hard and dark seemed to permeate the small office with his unfounded accusation. Meredith and Julia stood as one and stepped toward the door.

"Thank you for dropping by, ladies," came the arrogant dismissal. "I'm a busy man. If you have further questions concerning my claim, you may contact my lawyer, Arthur Crowley. I'm sure you'll have no trouble reaching him."

Chapter Nine

It was early to call, but it had occurred to Meredith that her banker son might have had occasion to deal with the man claiming to be related to Geoffrey Besset. Or at least have some knowledge of his financial standing. Besides, she wanted to hear Carter's voice this morning—that steady voice that said, *Everything will be all right.*

"Mom? Everything okay?" Carter's deep baritone held a note of anxiety.

"Everything's fine, Carter. I'm just getting an early start today. I wonder if you might have any information about a Mr. Langston Butler," she said, forging ahead.

He didn't respond right away, and Meredith imagined him running a hand through his hair and frowning into the receiver. He had been unenthusiastic about her decision to reopen Ron's detective agency. He would have preferred that she relax into a well-earned retirement, write her memoirs, perhaps take up knitting. She waited, tapping her fingers on her desk.

"You're not working some case for Butler, are you?"

"No, but it appears he's become involved in the case we're working on. You know, for the historical society." She had told him and Sherri Lynn about Beatrice Enterline's request during their recent family Snapchat. "Turns out Butler thinks he's in line to inherit the Besset plantation, though we have yet to determine that for a fact."

Records confirmed that his mother had indeed married Charles in 1965, but the marriage was annulled less than a month later. Julia was even now going through some public information at Chatham County's offices looking for a reference to Kendra Butler's son. Now Meredith awaited a response from Carter.

"Langston Butler is connected to the Besset plantation?" Carter seemed momentarily stunned. "How is it this is just coming up now?"

Meredith sighed. "Well, apparently, there hasn't been any communication. And there's no love lost between Butler and his erstwhile relatives."

"You've spoken with Butler?" Carter's voice climbed another step on the enharmonic scale.

"Julia and I visited him at his real estate office on Tybee Island," she explained patiently. "Seems he's in earnest about putting in a claim. Feels he's deserving of it since Besset apparently sent his mother away without the means to support herself back in the 1960s. He says his mother realized later that she was pregnant and took back her maiden name. Kendra has passed away, leaving Langston the sole heir, or so he says. A will hasn't been found yet."

Carter said nothing immediately but released an audible breath. "Butler has no accounts or holdings in this bank, and of course I couldn't disclose his business in any case. But you must know that there have been some questions. He doesn't enjoy the best of business reputations. I've heard talk of shady dealings in Atlanta and some possible insider trading in Louisiana. Mom, you should keep your distance from him."

When does the child become the parent? Meredith imagined her strong-minded son jingling keys in his pockets.

As the older son, Carter had always taken his job as protector seriously, often getting in the middle of Chase's playground battles. Now with Ron gone, he'd taken on a special mantle where she was concerned. She supposed he might always be Don Quixote tilting at windmills.

"I don't suppose I could convince you to let someone else handle the investigation of Geoffrey Besset and the characters connected with him," he said with gentle urgency.

"Well, no. We've taken this on, Carter, and we believe it's important. Someone needs to get to the bottom of this old mystery, to which, by the way, your father may have had some connection. We found some old phone records implying that there was communication going on between him and Geoffrey Besset."

Meredith hadn't intended to mention those phone logs and was glad she'd said nothing about the key and the hidden metal box, all of which would only worry him more. She hurried on. "Well, look, I just wanted to let you know about the Butler connection in case you hear anything among your financial colleagues that you can share. And please don't worry. Love to Sherri Lynn, and kiss Kaden and Kinsley for me."

She smiled, thinking how that would go over with Kaden, who struggled with physical contact. His mom and dad would need all the patience and understanding they could get to help him negotiate the labyrinthine nuances of social interaction. *Bless him,* she prayed. *Bless all my dear hearts, Lord!*

Carter clicked off after another plea for her to be careful.

Meredith settled into her chair, ready to tackle her inbox when Carmen called from the outer office. They had a perfectly good phone system with light-up buttons for intercom discourse, but Carmen often simply announced a caller.

"The Queen Bee calling," Carmen said in her lilting contralto.

Had they openly referred to the new historical society director by that moniker? *We've really got to be more respectful and careful with our words*, she thought.

"*Lo siento*," Carmen apologized. "It's Beatrice Enterline for you."

Meredith pushed the blinking red light and picked up the receiver. "Meredith Bellefontaine."

"Meredith, darling, how are you this morning?"

"Fine, Beatrice." Meredith pictured the flamboyant director with one hand poised debutante style on the phone, the other removing one earring for comfort.

"There was something of a disturbance at the Besset plantation last night that I thought you should know about."

Oh dear.

"It may have been precipitated by your meeting with Mr. Langston Butler, which I can well understand," Beatrice continued. "But I thought you should know about it."

"I see," Meredith answered. Which she didn't.

"Apparently, Butler went to the Besset mansion, wanting to have a look, and Lucky dissuaded him—rather vehemently, I'm afraid. Bless him!"

Lucky had given Meredith and Julia a proper fright when they'd encountered him near the hidden gate. She could easily imagine

Langston Butler's alarm upon coming face to face with the huge man.

"I don't know what made Butler think it was all right just to walk in and defy the 'no-admittance' order when his claim to ownership hasn't been recorded. Thank goodness we had the foresight to hire Lucky. He did the right thing to scare him off. But I got an earful from Mr. Butler this morning, I can tell you."

Meredith could almost see Beatrice's feathers ruffling. "We're working on this," she said with an assurance she didn't quite feel. She had advised Beatrice about her visit with Butler but didn't expect the man to push ahead like a bulldozer. Still, she probably should have anticipated such a reaction after observing his earlier behavior. "I'm really sorry about this."

"Mr. Butler might be even sorrier. He was quite incensed when Lucky advised the police about the invasion." Beatrice gave a little harrumph. "And invasion it is, until there's anything official. Well, do keep us informed as you forge ahead, dear. And have a lovely day!"

Nothing daunted Beatrice Enterline, at least not for long. Meredith couldn't help but smile as she hung up the phone. But her humor faded quickly. Langston Butler wasn't going to lie low and let things progress in due course; he was a mover and a shaker, which could be a good thing in a person, but in Butler's case, it wasn't very welcome right now.

She leaned back in her chair with a sigh and wondered if Butler's lawyer had also been subjected to a loud harangue. No doubt, Quin Crowley would be unflappable, allowing the man's rant to play out. She recalled his slow walk, umbrella in hand, to view possible damage to his Land Rover after her car bumped into his.

It surprised her that Arthur "Quin" Crowley had lingered on her mind since their abrupt meeting. He was polite but infuriatingly self-assured. Still, he exuded a surprising warmth that made one feel safe. *Quixotic* came to mind, perhaps because of his amazing eyes, each so different from the other, yet wholly engaging. How would he proceed with his difficult client? Did he regret taking him on?

The sound of the agency door opening interrupted her reverie. She heard Carmen's chair scrape against the tile, and a moment later, Charlene Jackson was ushered into her office.

Meredith stepped around the desk to stretch her hands toward Charlene. "It's good to see you." Remembering that the woman had phoned at least twice and hadn't received a return call, she said, "I'm sorry I didn't get back to you. Things have been a bit hectic around here. I do apologize."

"I—I hope you don't mind my just dropping in," Charlene began, fumbling with her car keys. "I had a few minutes and thought I'd see if you were available. But if this is a bad time—"

The tall woman was clearly upset, the cocoa-brown eyes in her handsome face serious. Midsized silver hoops hung from her ears. Only small lines around her mouth troubled the surface of her flawless skin. She was in her midfifties but could easily pass for forty.

"This is a perfect time, Charlene. Please, sit down." Meredith indicated one of the olive-green designer chairs in one corner of her office. When Charlene sat, Meredith took the adjacent chair. Talking across a desk was so impersonal, so cold. She sensed Charlene's need of warmth. "Our coffee isn't as good as the diner's, but it's hot. I could use some. How about you?"

"I don't want to trouble you," Charlene began.

"It's no trouble. It will just take a second."

The stand with the coffeemaker was conveniently placed between her office and Julia's. She poured two cups and was back in a couple of minutes. A little delay could give her guest time to settle, if composure was necessary.

"Here we are." Meredith placed their cups on the small table near their chairs. Charlene had pocketed her car keys and arranged her long, athletic legs carefully. But the concern etched in her dark eyes remained.

"I suppose you know how much Julia and I enjoy the food at the Downhome Diner," Meredith began, hoping to put Charlene at ease. "Because we come so often!"

"I'm glad," Charlene said. The hoops in her ears bobbed awkwardly as she nodded her enthusiastic approval. "It's been an upward battle getting started, but then nothing worthwhile is easy." A little frown perched on her forehead. She took a sip of coffee and said nothing for what seemed a long moment. Presently, she set the cup down and studied it.

"Charlene," Meredith began calmly, "I can see something is troubling you. How can I help?"

Charlene's eyes widened. "I want to hire you—that is, you and Julia." She released a breath as though she could hold it in no longer.

Meredith waited. *Hire us?*

"I have thought about this for quite a while, and I just can't let this situation go on any longer." She lowered her head briefly, and when she lifted her eyes they were shiny with unshed tears.

"Oh, Charlene." Meredith leaned in toward her. "What is it?"

Charlene gave her head a small toss, as though to ward off panic. "I want you to find my mother." Her lips trembled on the word *mother*.

"I see," Meredith said, though she didn't see at all. *Find her mother? The woman would have to be in her seventies, wouldn't she?* Perhaps she was ill or had wandered away from home in mental confusion. Why didn't Charlene call the police? Meredith cleared her throat. "How long has she been missing?"

"Three years."

"Three years!" Meredith couldn't hide her surprise.

"It's not like she just disappeared or anything. Well, in a way, she did, but she left on purpose. I mean—" She shook her head. "Let me back up." She paused as though trying to sort out her thoughts. "After my father died in 1966, my mother raised me and my brother. I grew up, got married, and moved out of the house. Then five years ago my husband passed away, and I hoped she might move in with me." A vein in her temple quivered.

"I'm sorry," Meredith said softly. "I'm a widow too. I know how hard it is to pick up and go on."

Charlene nodded. She took a breath, then swallowed hard. "We always were a strong family. My brother and I were taught to work hard—like she did. She worked her way through college and became a teacher. Even after losing my father, she pressed on, making sure we had what we needed."

Not a small feat, Meredith realized, for an African American woman to accomplish during the tumultuous years of the Civil Rights movement.

Charlene made a tent of her fingers and continued. "She worked hard in our community, staying among her own people. But she knew how to make life fun for us too. When we were little, she would sometimes rent a cabin near the water. We'd take a canoe out on the river or fish with our homemade poles. Though we had very little money to spend on luxuries, we always had ice cream cones on the wharf." Charlene's eyes glistened. "Those were very special days."

"Does your brother live in Savannah too?" Meredith asked.

"Jacob died in 1991 during Operation Desert Storm," Charlene said softly. "It was an awful blow for Mother. She not only lost her husband but her son as well. My daddy was gone before I was born."

She paused so long that Meredith almost prodded her to continue.

"After graduation, I worked in the community I grew up in—in north Savannah, managing an advertising office, but I always wanted to do something on my own—something that would expand my view of the world.

"When the chance came to open a diner here in the historic district, it was a dream come true. It was like the good Lord just opened a door wide for me. My loan came through at an unbelievably low rate. I had plans—when business picked up—to get a condo for Mother and me close to the diner, with room for friends and relatives to visit. It would be big enough for my daughter Clarissa and then later for any babies she might have to roam around in."

"How wonderful," Meredith said.

But Charlene's face was etched with gloom. She shook her head slowly from side to side, fixing her gaze on a spot across the room. "I thought she would be eager to join me, but she wouldn't come. She told me she didn't want to move away from the community that had been her home for so long, from her friends who had become her family. She insisted that I didn't need an old woman to worry about. I was completely blindsided."

Meredith watched Charlene's eyes dart back and forth, not settling anywhere. Then her gaze dropped to her lap.

"I couldn't believe what was happening. I wanted to make her happy. I planned to make room for her and all the things that were important to her. Precious little they were. She didn't cling to possessions. 'Put your resources into things that last,' she would always say. I argued and pleaded. She's in her seventies and shouldn't be alone."

Meredith waited, feeling the tension Charlene clearly was experiencing. "What did she do then?" she asked.

"She said she had a friend who was ill and that she was going away to take care of her. But I needed her. Clarissa needed her. I couldn't believe my own mother would choose to nurse an old friend rather than stay with us."

Charlene's jaw tightened, and her fingers wove in and out in her lap. After a few seconds of silence, she went on. "She said I was not to contact her, but she wouldn't say why or when she would come back." She lowered her head. "I was angry, and the disagreement got so sharp between us that I just left. Of course, I was fully absorbed with getting the restaurant going, and before I knew it, months had passed with no words between us."

"Did you try to contact her?"

"Yes, but I didn't know where she'd gone, and I couldn't get any information from anyone. Not even from the library where she volunteered her time. She just closed up her little house and had her mail forwarded to wherever she's staying."

"She didn't contact you?" Meredith asked incredulously.

Charlene swallowed and lowered her head. "I got a letter. There was no return address, no stamp. It just appeared under my door. She said she was well but that I was not under any circumstances to try to reach her." She shook her head slowly. "She and I had our disagreements in the past but nothing really serious. And she always doted on Clarissa. But she simply broke away from us with no explanation! It's like she just dropped off the planet or something."

"Can you think of any reason why she would do that?"

Charlene sighed deeply. "My mother has always been secretive about her life—especially her past. I think, well, I think she may have been running from something."

Meredith's sadness grew as she listened to Charlene's story. A family estranged, an elderly woman who should be enjoying golden years with her family separated from them. Apparently by choice. She sighed. Even if she and Julia had the time to give, it seemed that looking for this woman would be a wasted endeavor.

"Charlene, it sounds like your mother simply wants to be left alone. She doesn't want to be found." She paused, sensing Charlene's frustration. "To be honest with you, Julia and I are in the middle of a case that demands a great deal of time. I don't think we could take on another right now."

Quick tears filled Charlene's eyes and streamed down her cheeks. "She will be seventy-six years old in July. I need to know she's all right. I want to see my mother."

"I'm really sorry," Meredith said, trying to remain objective. A rift had occurred between mother and daughter. It was a personal family matter, not a missing persons case.

"I don't know how to find her on my own," Charlene said through a flood of tears.

Meredith could feel Charlene's pain as though it were a living thing that had invaded her private space. She heard herself say, "We couldn't promise anything, but—"

The misty eyes lit with sudden hope. "I can pay you—not a lot right away, but I will—I promise." Her cheeks seemed to suddenly glow as she opened her handbag. She drew out a picture frame and thrust it toward Meredith.

"This was taken when Clarissa graduated from college. That's my mother with her."

The elderly woman in the photo was tall like Charlene with the same lithe body, though her shoulders were rounded, bowed down by the strain of living. Her complexion was darker than Charlene's but clear, remarkably unlined except around the very dark, pensive eyes. Intelligence shone through them. Intelligence and something else. Wariness perhaps.

"You favor her," Meredith said quietly, absorbing the image and wondering what lay behind it. "She looks well. Was she in good health?"

"Yes, I think so," Charlene said. "She's always been a very strong woman. Says she's like her grandmother. Her Granny Luv, as she was known. She was gone before I was born, so I never met her." She paused before adding wistfully, "I wish I had asked my mother about her—about a lot of things, but I was just too busy trying to get ahead, you know, making a better life for myself."

That resonated much too deeply. Meredith's own mother had died far too young. How she wished she had known her more intimately in the sixty years she'd been alive.

"Here's the address of the school where she taught until she retired ten years ago. Oh, and the library where she volunteered. Although like I said, they wouldn't tell me anything. Maybe you'll have better luck than I did." Charlene's words ran on rapidly, as though she feared Meredith would change her mind and decide not to help her.

"Someone there might know something," she continued. "I remember she had a close friend—" She paused. "A woman she met at the library." Charlene released a long breath, like her speech had winded her. "I wish I could remember her name, because I think she might be the one my mother went to take care of."

"We'll see what we can do," Meredith said. "I'd like to keep the photo. Would you take it from the frame?"

Charlene scrambled to comply, standing as she did so. "I'll write you a check today. Is two hundred dollars enough? It's all I can do right now, but I can pay more at the end of the week—"

Meredith touched Charlene's trembling arm. "It's fine. We'll take the two hundred dollars now as a retainer. You don't need to think about paying more until or if we find your mother. Of course, there may be some expenses we incur in the process."

Charlene's lips quivered, but her eyes shone with hope. She mumbled repeated thanks as she hurried to the door, perhaps fearing her good fortune might vanish.

"I'll walk out with you," Meredith said, taking Charlene's elbow with a light hand. "I want you to think about something that might have happened to bring about the change in your mother. What could make her so adamant about not contacting her?"

Charlene said nothing until they reached her Ford Fusion with its slightly faded exterior. It wasn't surprising that the owner of a struggling new business couldn't afford a more up-to-date model. She opened the driver's door but paused with her arm resting on it. "I told you I thought my mother might be afraid of something— something in her past that she never talked about."

"Yes," Meredith said, silently urging her to continue.

But Charlene was looking off into some space only she could see. She pressed her lips together and paused before continuing. "It's partly why I came to you," she said thoughtfully. "When I went to my mother's house looking for something that might explain where she'd gone, I found something under the hall table by her front door." She drew a small white card from the pocket of her tailored skirt and handed it to Meredith.

Meredith looked down, then up sharply into Charlene's searching eyes. A crow soared suddenly overhead, its raucous cry unnerving in the bright May morning. The name on the card read BELLEFONTAINE DETECTIVE AGENCY.

Chapter Ten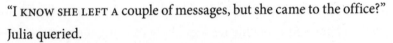

"I KNOW SHE LEFT A couple of messages, but she came to the office?" Julia queried.

Meredith gave a slow nod. "She wants to hire us."

Julia dropped down in the chair across from Meredith. "Whatever for?"

Meredith lined the stapler up with the pencil holder on her desk and studied them before looking up. "She wants us to find her mother. Seems there was a falling out between the two of them and now Charlene wants to set things right."

"Sounds like a family dispute to me—not our kind of job," Julia said. "Not to mention that we're up to our ears with the Besset case. Speaking of which—" She pulled a piece of paper from the pocket of her jacket. "I discovered that the former owner of the nearest property to the Besset plantation is still alive. Most likely he knew Geoffrey back in the day. He's in a nursing home, but it might be worth a visit to see what he knows."

Meredith looked down at the name. CORD ARMSTRONG, LINDSTROM NURSING CENTER, HINESVILLE, GA. But the unfamiliar name and address blurred as the words on the card Charlene had given her loomed in her mind. *Bellefontaine Detective Agency.*

How strange that Ron had been involved in a case with Charlene's mother while also involved in Geoffrey Besset's affairs—the same two cases that had landed in her lap. But then, there weren't that many detective agencies in Savannah. Perhaps it wasn't so odd that her husband, who had a good track record, had been contacted in each instance.

"Well, what do you think?" Julia pressed. "Do you want to run over to Hinesville, or should I?"

Meredith returned her distracted thoughts to Julia. "What did you learn about Langston Butler's birth?" she asked.

Julia raised her brows, perhaps surprised by Meredith's disorientation. "I couldn't find a thing," she said.

"So we still don't have any proof that Langston is Charles's son." Meredith shook her head. "Surely he has *something* to corroborate his connection. It's hard to believe that Langston Butler would try to get away with a fraudulent claim to a fortune."

"He said he could prove it in court," Julia commented, referencing their visit to Tybee Island.

"Guess he isn't going to give us any up-front information, let alone do our work for us." Meredith sighed. What was the man up to?

"I did find out that Langston Butler has been at City Hall talking about commercial permits and revisiting his old casino agenda." Julia always kept an ear open to her former colleagues in jurisprudence.

"Butler is clever, cunning, and careful," Meredith said, thinking out loud. "Carter tells me there has been some speculation of shady dealings in Atlanta and some possible insider trading in Louisiana.

Who knows what Butler would do with that beautiful plantation if he got his hands on it?"

Julia remained silent as the incessant tick of the wall clock filled the office. Meredith had never noticed how much noise it made. It had been a troubling morning. She'd hardly made a dent in her paperwork, and then there was Charlene's visit with its attendant guilt and regret. Now it seemed likely that the Besset plantation would fall into the hands of a marketeer or shyster—or worse.

"Well, he doesn't have it yet," Julia said, breaking the silence with her steely determination.

Meredith smiled. What a blessing that Julia, with her forthright good sense and bright outlook, was in her life.

Julia straightened and leaned back in her chair. "Now, tell me more about Charlene's trouble."

"Well, apparently she was urging her mother to move in with her when the diner deal was settled. She bought a condo, fully intending to make room for her mom. Not only wouldn't her mother come, but she said she was going away to care for a sick friend. Got really strange about it, said Charlene was not to look for her under any circumstances. She just packed up and left her home with no clue to her whereabouts."

"She sounds pretty feisty."

Meredith pulled the photo from her center desk drawer. She handed it across to Julia. "Louvenia Brown King, seventy-six on her next birthday. Guess things got pretty heated between them, and Charlene gave up trying to change her mother's mind."

"Sad, but she hardly needs a private investigator to iron out a family squabble. How long has it gone on?"

"Three years," Meredith said, shocked anew by the long period of estrangement. "Charlene said their little family was very close at one time and that Clarissa, Charlene's daughter, was the joy of her mother's life."

Julia only shook her head. "That's really sad, but—"

"I told her we'd do what we could," Meredith said, interrupting and handing Charlene's two-hundred-dollar retainer across the desk.

Julia's mouth formed an astonished O. "You didn't!"

"She was so distraught. She's tried to find her mother, gone looking for her, but no one knew where she went or else they weren't willing to say. So, Mom has disappeared without a trace." Meredith bit her lip. "I know we're busy with the Besset case, but I couldn't turn Charlene down."

"You're such a softie," Julia said, but admiration shone in her eyes.

"We need much more information before we start any kind of search," Meredith said, giving Julia a beseeching look. "I told her we'd be in touch, and I'd like you to hear her story firsthand. But we've also got so much work to do for Beatrice...."

"So, it's divide and conquer," Julia said.

"Well, divide and discover anyway." Meredith wrinkled her nose. She tapped the piece of paper with Cord Armstrong's name and address. "How about I go look up Mr. Armstrong, and you gather some helpful data from Charlene. That way, we can compare our thoughts and determine a course of action."

Julia shrugged. "Looks like our caseload is growing."

"Like weeds in a garden."

"Flowers," Julia amended.

"Flowers," Meredith agreed, thankful once again for her part-ner's enduring optimism.

***

The sun's scorching rays beamed through the driver's-side window as Meredith headed toward Hinesville, a forty-seven-minute drive south down State Road 196. She had stopped for a Subway sandwich and lemonade before getting back into the car, grateful for air-conditioning in May's summery Georgia climate.

Yet she loved to feel the wind in her hair, to revel in the freedom of speeding along the fragrant countryside. She tested it, but only for a few seconds before rolling up the window with immense grat-itude for modern engineering.

She wondered about the man Julia had identified as a one-time neighbor of Charles or Geoffrey Besset. Would he, in his great age, remember anything from those years? And would he be able to express it? Had he perhaps known Harriet?

It was a long shot, but there had been no short ones where this case was concerned. What had happened to that young girl who had never had a chance to grow up, to walk down the aisle to a hand-some waiting groom? To hold a child in her arms, to know the sweet abandon of driving freely in God's wide, abundant world with the wind in her hair?

Lindstrom Nursing Center was a long, low brick building with sloping walkways edged with soft touch holly and hibiscus shrubs. The windows stretched in uniform squares, and the property looked cared for and solid. She'd seen many such institutions that were far less appealing but that still demanded exorbitant sums for the amenities they offered.

She felt an unwelcome return of melancholy. She would rather be talking to Charlene about her missing mother over a cup of coffee. But it was only right that Julia get the longer straw after having a new case thrust on her without consultation. Ah, well, who said investigative work was easy and pleasant?

After parking in the visitors' area, she checked her appearance in the car mirror. She repaired the damage to her hair from her brief open-window test and dabbed at her lips with pale coral gloss. She brushed a wrinkle from the white blouse she'd paired with a tangerine A-line skirt. She'd do, she supposed, for the aging Cord Armstrong—whoever he was.

Suddenly, her breath caught, and her stomach fluttered. A red Land Rover was pulling into the spot next to her. Not just any red Land Rover. There was no mistaking the profile of Arthur "Quin" Crowley, who hadn't yet turned to see who occupied the adjacent parking place.

He descended from the Land Rover in an open-collar white shirt and dark slacks, his silver hair slightly ruffled. Perhaps he too preferred fresh air when driving. He opened the rear door of the Rover and reached in to retrieve a gray suit coat. His gaze caught hers, and a smile lit his face.

She got out, hastily adjusting the straps of her low-heeled sandals. What on earth was he doing here? Had he followed her? Her thoughts leapfrogged over each other as she tried to steady herself. She had been completely flustered, hardly the soul of decorum the last time they "ran into" each other.

She put up a hand traffic-cop style. "Don't worry, I'm parked. Your bumper's safe."

"Ms. Bellefontaine!" he said, reaching to shake her hand.

"It's Meredith, remember?" she said, feeling her smile rise unbidden. "We meet again."

"Hey," he said, giving an informal greeting and scrutinizing her with his unusual bicolored eyes. "It's really good to see you again. I've been wanting to get in touch, and here you are." The smile faded slightly. "I'm sorry we had to part so abruptly last time...." The sentence trailed off. "I enjoyed our talk over coffee. How are you?"

The self-confidence she had found infuriating at their first meeting had altered, but she took no pleasure in his discomfiture. He seemed to genuinely want to make amends. "I'm fine," she said with a little lift of her chin. "I guess we've both been busy. I trust your visit to Raleigh was more productive than mine."

He didn't respond right away, and when he did it was not in reference to her comment. He pushed his arms through the sleeves of his suit coat. "I think we are both here to pay a visit to the same man. Mr. Cord Armstrong?" The final syllable implied a question. "I too have heard that Armstrong may have insight into the Besset family."

There was no use denying it. Obviously, Quin had uncovered the same information Julia had found. And if Langston Butler had a legitimate claim to the Besset plantation, it was his right to take ownership. The historical society would have to appeal to him in their pursuit to save the property for the enjoyment and benefit of the city of Savannah. Beatrice Enterline would be unhappy, and it would grieve them both that Butler's plans for the property most likely had little to do with redemption.

Meredith resettled her purse strap on her shoulder. "I assume, then, that Butler's claim hasn't been validated yet?" If it had, of course, it would have been made known, and, she reasoned, there would be no need for further corroboration. Also, no need for Bellefontaine Investigations to continue its exploration.

"Look," Quin said earnestly, "we're both trying to do our best for our clients." A small frown appeared above his eyes. "I don't think we have to be at cross-purposes here, do we?" The sun glinted on the copper hairs in his silvery head and ignited a spark on his gold watch.

Meredith hesitated. Everything she had heard about Quin Crowley had been positive. She had checked his record. She really had no reason to distrust him.

"I suggest we visit Mr. Armstrong together. We want the same thing—the truth." Quin paused and rubbed a hand over his jaw. "I've been reading up on that old mystery. A twelve-year-old child doesn't just disappear. Whatever happened there should be brought out in the open."

She felt suddenly lighter than she had since the day began. At least she wouldn't have to go into that gloomy place alone. Ever since her mother's lingering illness with its accompanying clinic and hospital visits, Meredith had found it difficult to enter establishments that dealt with sickness and incapacity. It was a failure on her part, and she often asked the Lord to help her look beyond misery to healing.

They walked together into the building and signed in with the receptionist. A pleasant-faced woman in her early forties directed them to the courtyard where a balding man with a bulbous nose sat in a wheelchair, a knitted shawl over his knees. He seemed to be mumbling, his chin nearly down on his chest. Meredith felt quick sympathy, but her hopes plummeted. Not much hope of useful information here.

"That's Mr. Armstrong over there," an aide said. She pointed to a surprisingly tall figure standing several yards away staring off into the distance beyond the courtyard. He was slightly stoop-shouldered and white-haired but looked a good deal more vigorous than the man in the wheelchair. He turned slowly, unsmiling when addressed.

Meredith was glad for Quin to take the lead. Extending his hand, he said, "I'm Arthur Crowley and this is Meredith Bellefontaine. I wonder if we could have a word."

Armstrong peered down to meet Quin's gaze. "Do I know you, sir?" he asked in a clear voice. He had a sharp, reddened nose and a narrow face that might once have been described as handsome. A white mustache and bushy sideburns in the style of nineteenth-century statesmen stood out on his ruddy cheeks.

"No, but we are looking into the disposition of the Besset plantation and need some information. We thought you might be able to help." Quin looked at Armstrong with directness and an encouraging smile.

"The historical society here in Savannah is very interested in the estate and hopes to see it rebuilt," Meredith put in quickly, avoiding Quin's eyes.

"Besset." Armstrong looked off into space again, and Meredith wondered if he had forgotten their question. "Charles Besset," he said, touching the left side of his abundant mustache. "He was very fond of his horses. They were Arabians, I believe. Some Morgans too, and even a golden palomino." He fingered his mustache again and stared off toward the horizon.

"Sounds like you know a lot about horses," Quin said.

"Bred quite a few," he said, thoughtfully. "In the old days." He broke off for a moment, as though picturing those "old days." He coughed and went on. "Charles put great stock by those horses. Raised them for auction—well, at least until his daughter disappeared."

"You were there when that happened?" Meredith's pulse quickened.

"I was a kid," he said. "The same age as Besset's son." He abruptly sat down on a bench nearby, as though he had grown suddenly tired.

"Geoffrey?" Meredith asked, feeling her breath catch.

"Geoffrey," he repeated and folded his large, gnarled hands over his lap. "Yes, that was the name. A wild kid." He raised his messy white eyebrows in recall. "My brother and I were warned to stay clear because of the shenanigans he got up to. He was cocky and even mean—had no liking for the African American men who worked for his father." He paused and pressed his lips together beneath the white mustache. "I heard that when his father became ill and Geoffrey took over the place he got rid of them all as well as every one of those magnificent horses."

"Do you remember Charles Besset's wife?" Meredith asked, fully aware that she was taking over the conversation. But Quin was listening with avid interest.

"She was a sickly sort and died shortly after the little girl went missing."

"Do you know what happened to her—to Harriet?"

"Nobody knows, though the police questioned everyone in the county. It was a terrible thing! Terrible!" The elderly man who looked like a statesman bowed his head.

"Mr. Armstrong," Quin said after a brief moment, "do you recall Mr. Besset taking another wife after his first passed on?"

"I heard somewhere that he had remarried, but by the early sixties I was in graduate studies at Georgia Tech and living in Atlanta. My folks went through some tough times and lost their home. I stayed in Atlanta after earning my degree."

"How long have you been here?" Meredith asked quietly.

"Only a few weeks." He patted his chest. "When my heart began to betray me, I came back to Savannah to live with my sister and her family. But I became a burden, and I didn't want that." He pulled a handkerchief from the pocket of his vest and blew his nose. "So, this is home now."

Quin waited until the handkerchief went back into the man's pocket, then asked, "Are you aware of any children resulting from Charles Besset's second marriage?"

Armstrong twirled his mustache idly. "Sorry. Guess I can't help you much." He lifted his gaze beyond them and heaved a sigh. "I was always sorry about losing our place—mostly for my father's sake. He was a good man—I never appreciated how good." He rose unsteadily.

Meredith jumped up to grasp his arm. "Are you all right?"

"I'm afraid we've taken up too much of your time," Quin said, getting up to take the man's other arm. "Can we walk inside with you?"

Cord Armstrong straightened his shoulders and gently pulled away from assisting hands. "No need. I'm quite all right, but I think I'd like to stay here in the sunshine a while." He turned away from his guests to resume staring off into the distance beyond the courtyard.

They thanked him and retreated into the care home foyer and then out into the May sunshine. Quin was quiet as they walked toward the parking lot, no doubt disappointed. He had left his business card, asking Armstrong to contact him should he remember anything helpful.

For her part, Meredith pondered what she had heard about Geoffrey. Armstrong had painted a picture of an angry man who had rid the plantation of black workers as well as the horses his father had been so proud of. It wasn't a good picture.

When they reached their cars parked side by side in the lot, Quin said, "Well, guess we didn't learn anything about Langston Butler that will help either of our clients." He paused, letting his gaze rest on Meredith's face.

"No, but it was interesting to hear about Geoffrey as a young man. Coincides with his reputation as we've heard it so far. But I suppose it was something of a wasted trip for you."

"Not at all," Quin said quickly. "I liked Cord Armstrong. I hope he has some good memories to think about in that place."

Meredith nodded, touched by Quin's sensitivity to the aging Armstrong. "Me too." She opened her purse to retrieve her car keys, wondering why she was so unwilling to end their conversation. "You know," she said thoughtfully, "another visit might be in order. Who knows what he might remember another day?"

"Good point." Quin made no move to open the Land Rover's door but stood looking at her. "Maybe we could come back together?"

His smile was tentative, his amazing eyes puppy-like, making Meredith smile back. "I mean, since we're really not at cross-purposes or anything." He dropped a hand into the pocket of his slacks. "Can I call you?"

She shrugged, not wanting to admit that the invitation pleased her. Though he represented a man she believed to be dishonest, the lawyer himself intrigued her. She struggled to give a businesslike response. "I suppose it would be good to share any significant findings." But she couldn't deny the smile that rose straight from her heart.

Chapter Eleven

RAIN DANCED DULLY ON THE roof of the little summer cottage where Louvenia sat with a half-knitted sweater in her lap. Usually she would be up and gone to sit with Delyse by this time, but she couldn't make herself leave the cottage. Not today.

Delyse's little tabby minced around her feet, arching his striped back. It almost seemed to her that he sensed what she was feeling. "Go on, Sydney!" Louvenia said, glaring in his whiskery face. "Don't mind this foolish old woman!" She gave him a little push with the toe of her shoe. She was ashamed of her fear—the same fear that had brought her to this place too many months ago.

But she'd lived with the fear so long, it had grown nearly comfortable. *Law, I'm a sorry sort! Hiding myself away—pretending I'm doing something good by watching Delyse's place and feeding her cat.*

She'd learned the news by accident when she was in the Super Dollar getting her groceries. She only went once a month. It was better that way, so folks didn't pay much mind. The words swirled in her mind. "Geoffrey Besset is dead." He couldn't be looking for her anymore or her little family. Was there any reason now to stay away? Yearning for her dear ones was like a tourniquet twisting tighter and tighter around her heart. It had been so long.

Geoffrey Besset is dead. All those years he'd tried to find her, all the hiding and running, were over. But it didn't seem real. She still felt danger like a real presence. Last night she saw a dark car circling around the cottage, slithering slowly like a snake ready to strike. She had waited, but no one had come. Yet fear was still her companion.

She picked up her knitting and thought about her granddaughter. One day last month she couldn't stand the not knowing and the yearning any longer. She'd ridden the bus and camped out on the bench at the bus stop across the street from the diner until she'd caught a glimpse of both Charlene and Clarissa leaving at closing time.

And she saw—with her own eyes—when it felt to her like time was a dead thing and her heart was drowning in the past—that her life was reaching into the future. A great-grandbaby on the way! She wished...

But she didn't let her heart wish. She knitted faster and faster until her fingers felt like they were going to jump up and run off all by themselves. And then, all of a sudden, she remembered when her fingers first felt yarn all soft and snuggly in her hands. She'd written it all down in the book hidden in her tapestry bag. The book Delyse made Louvenia read to her. The book that burned with a thousand memories.

Louvenia reached for the notebook, opened it, and felt her fingers tremble on the pages. Soundlessly, she read the labored little-girl scrawl....

It's Saturday, and Benny has taken me with him again to Mister Besset's where he works.

"You two keep your eyes open, ya hear?" Benny tells me with that slow, severe wink of his before he heads to the stables. He knows Harriet and I are friends, that we sneak away to this broken-down old summerhouse every chance we get to be together. He levels his gaze at me. "Mister B will be gone all day—maybe two days," he tells me. "Little Bee's gone with him," he says with a knowing wink. "But you never know when those two will come buzzing back to the hive."

Big Bee and Little Bee: It's kind of a joke Benny and I share. A sad one, really, because Mister Geoffrey is always trying to get close to his daddy, like a bee trying to suck nectar from the same flower as his daddy, only to be shooed angrily away. I just hope both Bees stay far from the hive today.

There are lots of things Harriet and I like to do. I show her how to fish and catch crawdads and how to skip stones in the creek. And she tells me things she learns in school. Harriet learns all kind of things at the white school. They even have classes in music and art and how to be "a lady."

We learn reading and writing at my school, but there are few extras, and there are never enough books to go around. We share pencils and paper because there's not enough for us all.

One day Harriet brought a pot holder she made at her school. "I had some yarn left over," she told me. "It's for you. Want to make one too?" Then she pulled out two long needles and a ball of bright yellow yarn.

I wasn't interested in learning how to be a lady, but I thought the yellow yarn was prettier than a daffodil in spring. I watched her push one needle into the other and wrap the yarn around and around. Over and over she showed me and then put the needles in my hands.

I was clumsy at the start, but I loved sitting under the boughs of the big friendly tree with Harriet. Before long I could make the stitches right. I couldn't wait to show Granny Luv. That day we sat for a long time while I practiced, and Harriet read out loud from Little Women.

I think I'm a lot like Jo, the girl with a sassy tongue who loves to write stories. I think I'm the happiest girl in the world sometimes when I sit with my big notebook and write, and when Harriet creeps through the heavy branches of the magnolia tree like she does now.

She has her fancy yellow dress on—the one almost the same color as her hair, which is tied back with a green ribbon. Miss Persimmon, her auntie, always dresses her like she's a princess on account of that's what Mister Besset calls her. "My little princess!" Harriet hides play clothes in the stable so she can change. Her mama knows, and they keep it a secret from Miss Amelia Percyman, who wouldn't approve. She doesn't approve of Harriet going anywhere with the colored help and their kin. We got more secrets than toads got warts!

"*Law, I thought you'd never get here,*" I say.

Harriet sets a sack down on the old wooden bench and grins a wide, happy grin that makes her eyes shine like two bright river stones. "*I wanted to get here sooner, but Mama's feeling poorly today.*" Her smile fades, and I know she is worried about her mama, who spends more and more time in her bed.

"*I'm sorry,*" I say to her.

Harriet shrugs and makes a little circle with the toe of her shoe. "*Granny Luv says not to worry, that God will take care of her.*"

"*Everyone says Granny Luv's the prayin'est woman in the county,*" I say, wanting to make Harriet's eyes shine again. I try not to think about Clementine, who, just like Harriet's mama, isn't getting any better, prayers or no prayers. I look at the sack Harriet brought and wonder what's in it.

Harriet does a little hop on her good leg and sits herself down on the bench under the big magnolia tree. She reaches into the sack. "*I brought this for you,*" she says. "*It's for your nephew.*" She pulls a funny plastic clown made of balls strung together on rubbery string. "*You said it's his birthday, didn't you?*" She shakes the clown, and its legs and arms wiggle and sound like peas bouncing in Granny Luv's metal bowl.

I jerk on the string, watch the clown bob up and down, and think it's the best toy I ever saw. "*You got this for Luke?*" I ask, and I feel my heart swell up like a balloon.

Harriet nods proudly. "*I even wrote his name on the back. You can see it if you look real close.*" Her eyes sparkle. "*I can't wait to show it to him. Can we go to your house now while my daddy—"

She means while her daddy and Geoffrey are gone and won't catch us. A couple of times we've walked the mile to my house. I don't think it's so easy for her, what with her limp and all. Riding is what we like best, and Benny taught us where some back trails are. But we can't ride horses to my house.

"You sure you want to?" I ask. I feel a little jumpy inside, thinking of sneaking away.

"We won't stay too long. C'mon, no one will miss us."

I may be the one with the sassy tongue, but Harriet isn't afraid of much. I don't know any other white girls, except for the ones I read about. Most don't want anything to do with me. Even Granny Luv says I should stay with my own kind. Harriet's a lot like Benny, and I hope she doesn't get in trouble with her strange ideas.

"I declare, it plain makes no sense to me what color our skin is," Harriet has said more than once. "You just been in the sun longer than me!"

She screws up her forehead and wiggles her nose. "Let's go," she says and grabs my hand.

"But you need to change out of your dress," I say.

"We don't have time," she says. "It'll be fine." She tucks the clown rattle into the paper sack, and we set off, careful to stay back from the road and follow the line of trees. When we get to my house, we scoot in the back door. I can still smell the jambalaya Granny Luv made for supper last night.

The first time she ever saw my house, Harriet said it felt friendly. I was worried about showing it to her, on account of her house is so grand. Like a mansion compared to ours. But Harriet doesn't seem to notice things like peeling paint or a tattered sofa.

We hear Luke fussing, and I look around for Clementine. There are dishes in the sink, sitting in water cold and gray as a stormy sky. "Clementine!" I call and hear her voice coming from the bedroom, and I know right away this is one of her bad days. I hurry in, see her curled on her side.

"Can you see to Luke Benjamin?" she asks weakly. Her eyes rove to Harriet and back to me, and there's a touch of a smile on her lips. "Hello," she says to her. "Sorry I can't get you some lemonade...."

"Never mind," Harriet says, her eyes turning soft. She covers her mouth and whispers in my ear, "She gonna be all right?"

I shrug because even though Granny Luv, the prayin'est woman in the county, says God be taking care of her, I don't see Benny's wife getting any better. I tell Clementine we'll see to the baby. I turn away from the pain in her cocoa-colored eyes and tuck a quilt over her thin body. I smile as big as I can. "We come to see Luke anyhow," I say. "You go back to sleep."

We change Luke's diaper and feed him his bottle, which Harriet asks can she please, please do! And then we show him the clown rattle. He coos and grins with delight, showing the two little teeth bursting through his bottom gum. Granny Luv will have a little cake for him when she comes home, and she'll cuddle him and sing to him when her day's work is done. We leave when he falls asleep, and I think he looks like an angel curled up on a cloud.

Later I will wish we had stayed looking into the face of that sweet angel and never set foot out the door.

The afternoon is dwindling away as we hurry back. With only a few rays pushing through the leafy trees, the woods seem darker, but we stay under cover, away from the open road. Harriet's daddy or Mister Geoffrey could be inside one of those passing cars.

I hear myself humming under my breath, like I do when I feel jumpy inside. Harriet limps along. I can tell she's getting tired, but she keeps talking in that lilting voice of hers that's light as a lily stem.

"Luke loved the clown rattle," she said. "I told Auntie Amelia that Mama said I could buy it for Missus Starkweather's new baby. For when they have the big midsummer dance next week." She giggled. "I guess that was a lie, but Auntie Amelia was busy trying on hats, so she didn't care."

Granny Luv would have said, "A lie displeases the Almighty whether it's a little one or not." But I don't say this. I just look at her and wonder if all my untruths are big ones and all Harriet's are little ones.

"Benny's wife is real sick, isn't she?" Harriet asks a little breathlessly.

"Uh-huh," I mutter, thinking Granny Luv better be praying harder than she ever did before.

"My mama too." She bites her lip hard, then looks up. "If I tell God I'm sorry for the lie, will He hear me if I pray for her

and Clementine too?" And I think maybe Harriet isn't as brave as she lets on.

"Granny Luv says He always hears," I say and let my thoughts run willy-nilly through my head without saying more.

"Well, I think—"

But suddenly Harriet stops talking. She stops walking too. And then we both hear it—low voices coming from deep in the woods just beyond us. Men's voices.

"Somebody's in there," I whisper. I don't like to admit it, but I'm afraid of ghosts. I don't even like it when Pastor Ray Bill calls down the Holy Ghost.

"Hush!" Harriet says. "It's probably nothing."

Even though I'm not grown up, I know that men gathering in the dark can be a powerful bad thing. I overheard Benny once say Tommy Roy Johnson got caught in these woods and was beat so bad he couldn't work for six weeks.

My heart jumps two feet into the sky when I hear a sound behind us. Harriet jerks around, nearly losing her footing. A man pushes through some brush and plants two big feet on our path. We recognize him right away, even though he's wearing something like a nightshirt, white and floppy on his skinny frame. In one hand he holds what looks like a pointy hat with ragged holes cut in it.

"Waylon Jute!" Harriet exclaims. "What are you doing out here?" She points her finger at him like an exasperated teacher. "Is my brother with you?" She looks around anxiously and then back to stare at Jute.

I couldn't see the others. Jute must have walked away on his own. I hold my breath. Mean as a snake and twice as dumb. Isn't that what Benny said about Jute?

"Why, if it isn't Miss Besset. And what are you up to?" He says "you" real strong and smiles crookedly as he takes a step toward Harriet.

"What my friend and I are doing is none of your business, Waylon Jute," Harriet says, placing both hands on her hips. "And I'll thank you to get out of our way."

He hasn't looked at me until now, and his eyes go so narrow they're like slits in his face. They bore into me. "You better be more careful what company you keep," he says to Harriet, not taking those steely eyes off me.

Harriet grabs my hand. Her voice doesn't waver. "I keep any company I want to, Waylon Jute, and now we're leaving."

"You wouldn't be so high and mighty if your father were here," Jute muttered. "Maybe I'll just tell him who I met in the woods today."

"You better not!" Harriet shouts. "My brother will beat you six ways to Sunday."

But her face has gone pale, just like at her birthday party when the girls teased her. Her eyes blaze like blue flames, and her lips shake.

"You think he will?" Jute says. "Let's just go ask him right now." And he lunges forward, hands outstretched.

Harriet scrambles back, nearly falling on the stony edge of the woods where tree roots stick up from the ground and ragged branches can snag a person something awful.

I hear myself gasp and squeal, and then without thinking I stick out my foot hard into Jute's shin, doubling him over into an awkward heap. He struggles against the long nightshirt that tangles around his feet. I grab Harriet's hand. "Run," I yell, still restraining myself, lest the others who I was sure weren't far would hear and maybe join in Jute's cause. I drag her, half carry her, running for all I'm worth toward the summerhouse.

The summerhouse is well hidden from view, but I know exactly where it is and how to get through the old gate. We'll be safe there.

I don't dare look back. I hear no footfalls, only the bleating of the clumsy man who no doubt is pulling himself up from the ground and staring after us with confusion and rage.

"Are you okay?" I gasp, peering into Harriet's stricken face.

She is half crying and breathing hard as she holds on to her bad leg. But I can see she's angry too. "That Waylon Jute!" she sputters. "He's ruined my dress—and yours too."

I begin to brush away the debris clinging to her dress, feel my hands trembling. I'm wishing I could run to Benny or Granny Luv, tell them what's happened. "Don't care about my dress," I say. But what would Harriet tell her mama or Miss Persimmon? "We got to clean you up before you go home." I go get my box from under the magnolia tree and the jug of water and rag I always keep there.

I wash her scraped knee, and she scrubs at her face.

"You gonna tell Mister Geoffrey?" I ask, but my heart is stuck in my throat, because if she tells her brother what

happened, he'll say it was my fault. And I can't think what he'd do to me. For sure he won't let me see Harriet anymore.

"I don't know why Geoffrey has anything to do with that moron," Harriet says angrily. She sits down on the bench carved from a pine log. She hunches forward and supports her chin on her hands. "Jute ruined our whole day," she says, pouting.

I gape at her. She should be much more afraid of the Jutes of this world. She should know that people like him could do a lot more than ruin a day. We should never have gone off to see Luke. What if something bad had really happened? It would be my fault.

I wait a long time in the summerhouse after Harriet leaves before I walk to the stable. Benny will be getting off work and going home to Luke's birthday party. He'll be tired but he will be his steady self. He'll smile and tell me what Harriet's golden horse got up to today.

Could I tell him that we'd seen men in the woods, standing in a circle? Tell him that Waylon Jute was there? That he looked at me with fire in his steely eyes?

No. I can't say any of these things. I can only shiver and pray to the scary Holy Ghost and hope He will hear me.

Chapter Twelve

SATURDAY DAWNED WITH MAY'S FINE gifts in her basket—a high platinum sun, azure skies with billowy clouds, and a plethora of flowers strewn across a green landscape.

Meredith carried deviled ham sandwiches and potato salad to the back deck, where the table was set up for the picnic she would share with Carter and Sherri Lynn and her grandchildren. She put Kaden's favorite Star Wars mug at his place and the pink and blue Cinderella cup at Kinsley's. She had made the special sausages in puff pastry that the kids always asked for and which they usually spoiled by dipping in ketchup.

She'd hummed through the morning's preparations, eager for her family's arrival. Charleston was only a couple of hours away, but the miles often stretched, making their visits fewer than she liked. She'd hoped Chase might have a free Saturday to join them, but he had sent regrets. He was attending a historical symposium in Atlanta.

Meredith sighed and paused at the ledge where GK was sunning himself in a long, languid sprawl. He looked up at her briefly through slanted green eyes and closed them again in sheer indolence. "Better take your ease now," she told the handsome Russian Blue. "The kids are about to descend." GK enjoyed her grandchildren, but he had his limits.

It had been a long, eventful week, and Meredith was ready to set aside for a while the business of the Besset Plantation and their newest case, Charlene Jackson's missing mother. She felt a pang of conscience. She'd had little time to devote to finding Louvenia Brown King.

And then there was Arthur "Quin" Crowley cluttering her thoughts. She hadn't expected to see the enigmatic lawyer at the retirement home where they'd interviewed Geoffrey Besset's former neighbor. She hadn't expected to be pleased about running into him again or even now to sense him intruding on her mind amid the whirl of domestic activity.

She shook off the interruption and set a big bowl of potato chips and a veggie tray on the laden table. She'd bought new cushions for the chairs, and she admired how nice they looked. There was something altogether soothing about being home. Today she would be Mom and Grandma, chief cook and bottle washer, and leave investigative worries behind.

At the sound of a car, she went to the front door, prepared to wave her family in. But it wasn't Carter's Nissan approaching. Nor did the vehicle park but idled for a few seconds before moving on. It wasn't a car she recognized. Just a run-of-the-mill dark sedan. She was surprised to feel slightly disturbed. No reason for it. She shrugged. Still, the sense of unease lingered.

When a few minutes later Carter's vehicle parked in one of the spaces in back of the house, Meredith stepped out onto the deck, eager to greet her family. True to his nature, Carter was on time. He was seldom early and never late. She waved joyfully as the rear passenger doors opened and two small bodies emerged.

Nine-year-old Kinsley Faith ran to her in pink capri pants and a ruffled white blouse with a large pink bow at the neckline. A purse shaped like a berry with green ribbons flared from her shoulder as she ran. She flung her arms around Meredith.

"We're here, Grandma!" she said breathlessly. She tossed her blond curls and showed off her purse. "It's a strawberry. I got it for my birthday. Are we having peach pie?"

Meredith's peach pie was legendary in her family and Ron's. Up until a few years ago she'd made it strictly by her mother's recipe, which called for nutmeg and sour cream as surprise ingredients. But then one day, on a whim, she pulled it out of the oven early, swirled some melted apple jelly over the top, and stuck it back in the oven. Now the moment the first ripe Georgia peach appeared at the farmer's market, her children and grandchildren asked her to make it at every get-together.

A more reserved Kaden came behind, red hair fringing his forehead, eyes blue-lit in his freckled face. As usual, he avoided direct eye contact and held up a small geometric shape made of plastic interlocking pieces. His latest polyhedron.

"That looks complicated," she said, lightly ruffling his coppery hair. He stepped back a little, uncomfortable as always with physical contact. She peered at the many-sided plastic bauble in his hand. He had given her a complete tutorial on the polyhedron in a recent Snapchat session. If memory served, it was a geometric solid in three dimensions with flat surfaces and sharp corners. The kind of brain teaser that would enthrall her curious grandson.

When the children ran to greet a semi-patient GK, Carter put his arm across Meredith's shoulders and leaned in to kiss her cheek.

He smelled like Irish Spring soap and old leather. But even in chinos and a striped golf shirt he still looked like a banker. His thick chestnut hair had been recently cut, leaving a light rim at his temples where the sun hadn't invaded.

Sherri Lynn climbed out in a white sundress with navy piping, her slim feet wrapped in delicate sandals. Honey-colored hair flowed straight and fine to her narrow shoulders.

"These are for you," she said, pressing a bouquet of red damask roses toward her mother-in-law. "I hope you didn't go to too much trouble." She gave Meredith a sidelong look through soft brown eyes. "But of course, you did!" She kissed Meredith's cheek, leaving the distinct fragrance of lavender that vied for essence with the roses.

The perfect homemaker, Sherri Lynn seemed always to know just how to dress, what to say, and what to do. The fifth of seven children from a hardworking farm family, she had learned everything about being the perfect hostess and homemaker from her mother and older sister.

Lunch on the deck progressed over the next hour or so—a warm, noisy affair covering a wide spectrum of childish and adult commentary. Presently, Kaden and Kinsley went off to play yard bowling with a curious GK frolicking after them. Sherri Lynn insisted on replenishing the pitcher of sweet tea, leaving Carter to survey his mother with a "let's-get-down-to-business" look.

"So, how are things going at the agency?" he asked, lifting dark brows and crossing his arms over his chest.

"Going well," Meredith said, studiously swirling her tea in the tall glass. If Carter had his way, she would be doing almost anything

but working as an investigator. He viewed her occupation as messy and dangerous, better left to the fictional Miss Marple or Hercule Poirot. She knew much of that mindset had to do with his concern for her, his sense of being responsible for her.

"We haven't solved the Besset mystery yet," she said carefully, "but we're making progress."

Carter's brows rose a bit higher in the smooth plane of his forehead as he waited for her to elaborate.

"We did have an interesting conversation with a former neighbor who knew Charles and Geoffrey to some degree. He didn't have much to add about what happened to Harriet, but he said something surprising." She paused, letting her shoulders relax. "He said Geoffrey sold off all the horses on the plantation after his father became ill."

"For the money, no doubt," Carter observed. "I understand Charles Besset had some pretty valuable animals."

"Maybe, but Mr. Armstrong—that's the neighbor—said Geoffrey never shared his father's fascination for horses. Or much of anything else his father prized, except keeping the traditions of the Old South."

Carter nodded knowingly. "Traditions that maintained the power of plantation owners. Even the sharecropping system that replaced slavery left black and white farmers alike in debt at the end of every harvest. It was equivalent to bondage."

They sat in silence for a moment before Carter spoke again. "I guess there will always be people who hold on to power at the expense of others." He paused. "Which brings me to the subject of Langston Butler. Anything new on his claim to inherit?" He leaned back in his chair and dropped his hands to his pockets, considering her.

Meredith drew in her breath. "Apparently, he's the sole heir, since no will has been found. His lawyer hasn't been able to confirm his claim. We know his mother married Charles, but Butler's birth record may have been lost."

"Probate may take a long time, but the man has a way of getting around and getting what he wants," Carter said, frowning. He fidgeted with the keys in the pocket of his chinos and went on. "A customer relocating from New Orleans applied for a loan last week. Seems he lost big-time on land he purchased from a company that promised the world but left him with property with no water access. He's still in litigation over it, so his loan will likely be denied." He looked meaningfully into Meredith's eyes. "One of the partners in the development he bought into was Langston Butler."

Meredith absorbed this information silently and wondered what, if anything, Quin Crowley knew about it. She exhaled a long breath. "The more I hear about Langston Butler, the more concerned I am about the future of the Besset Plantation."

Carter leaned forward as Sherri Lynn came out onto the deck. His gaze remained fixed on Meredith. "And the more I hear about Butler, the more concerned I am that he's involved in your investigation."

"Grandma, I almost won." A breathless Kinsley came running back up to the deck and practically launched herself at Meredith. "I would have too, if Kaden hadn't whistled just when I was about to throw my last ball!" She stuck out her bow-shaped lips in a pout.

"Did not!" Kaden said, rushing inside and stopping short of the table. He brushed unruly red hair out of his eyes. "She's just a sore loser."

"Am not!" Kinsley declared, but not nearly so vehemently. She and her brother seldom had any real conflicts, and small spats were usually quickly forgotten. Already, Kinsley was losing interest in her complaint and in yard bowling. "Can I have another cookie?" she implored, looking up into her grandma's face.

Meredith drew an arm around Kinsley, pulling her even closer against her knees. She felt quick gratitude for the kids' argumentative interruption. It had derailed the subject of Langston Butler and Carter's warning. She laughed and patted Kinsley's cheek. "You may if Mom says it's okay. You too, Kaden."

"One more," Sherri Lynn said. "One for the road, actually, because your father and I have to get going. We're on the committee for the church missionary society meeting tonight."

"Already?" Kinsley complained, reaching for a chocolate chip cookie.

"Yes. It's a long drive back to Charleston." She laid a warm hand on Meredith's shoulder. "It's been so good being here, and lunch was delicious." Ever the dutiful daughter-in-law, Sherri Lynn had already cleared the luncheon plates and rinsed all the dishes. Turning to the children, she said, "Now, what do you say to your grandma for making such a nice picnic?"

The two obediently responded with their thanks. Kaden clutched his polyhedron while Kinsley picked up GK to give his soft blue-gray fur a final stroke.

"I'll just help carry the rest of this into the kitchen," Sherri Lynn said, stooping to retrieve the glasses.

"No need," Meredith said. "I'll get the rest. Besides, Julia's coming by this afternoon. She had a heavy golf date with Beau today. She'll be ready for a glass of something cold and any leftovers she can beg." She laughed as she stood to help her family gather their belongings. "I was hoping she'd be here in time to see you."

"Give her our love," Sherri Lynn said.

Carter kissed Meredith's cheek and gave her a cautionary glance. "And remember what I said. You and Julia."

Hardly had five minutes passed after Carter and family left and then Julia arrived.

"I missed them, didn't I?" she asked, taking the chair next to Meredith on the deck and leaning down to unhook the straps of her sandals.

"Not by much. They just left. But they send their love."

Julia swept back a lock of soft gray hair. "What a cool family you have! You, my friend, are a lucky girl."

"And don't I know it." Meredith set her glass on the tray next to her chair. Sometimes she felt an irrational guilt that she should be so favored when Julia and Beau had never been able to have children. But she also knew that Julia would be the first to scold her for such feelings and inform her that she and Beau led very happy, fulfilled lives, thank you very much.

"Let me get you a glass of iced tea," Meredith said, getting up. "How about a sandwich? Deviled ham or sausage puffs? Kaden left one or two."

"Just tea," Julia said, drawing her feet up onto the wicker lounge with its thick striped cushion. "And one of those cookies there on the plate." She sighed with contentment as she stretched out on the chair. "Ah, this is the life."

Meredith returned with the plate of cookies, a glass, and a fresh pitcher of tea. She and Julia chatted about golf, about Kaden and Kinsley, and generally enjoyed the peaceful afternoon. But what Carter had told her about Langston Butler lingered in her mind.

"My son thinks we both should mind our p's and q's with Langston Butler," she said with a rueful smile.

"Hmm," Julia said after swallowing a generous sip of tea and placing the glass on a coaster. "I've read a lot of fanciful theories about what p's and q's might stand for. 'Children should save money by minding their pennies and quarters.' And then the more ridiculous—like sailors in the eighteenth century paying attention to their peas—pea coats—and queues—ponytails." She sighed. "I guess we'll have to keep minding our p's and q's without knowing why."

Meredith laughed at Julia's witty response, but she was grateful for Carter's attentiveness to family responsibility. "Did you know that Butler was involved in a real estate scam in New Orleans? Some development promising prime property, but it turns out there was no access to water."

"Ah," Julia said. "I think I recall reading about that. A place called Sunshine Springs. Pumping in water wound up costing so much that buyers couldn't afford to maintain their new homes." She sat up straighter. "Butler was involved in that?"

"Carter says he was one of the partners in the development. Guess my son was doing some investigating of his own after his customer applied for a loan. I'm going to pass this information on to Beatrice to give the town council a heads-up."

"That could come back to bite us. Butler's already got his shirt in a twist about our nosing into his business."

Meredith felt an inward shudder, recalling their visit to Tybee Island and the coldness of Butler's manner when they began to inquire about his family background and connection to Geoffrey Besset. There had been something in those cunning eyes that had chilled her to the bone. Momentarily she thought of the dark sedan idling near her house.

"You suppose his lawyer knows about this?" Julia asked.

"I think I'm going to find out," Meredith responded firmly, and in a flash recalled the warmth in Quin's eyes and his invitation to visit Cord Armstrong together. She wondered if Julia could see the blush she felt creeping into her cheeks.

Julia regarded her briefly and cleared her throat. "I learned something interesting too. The police and the coroner's office have been pretty closemouthed in releasing information about Geoffrey Besset, but I now know where he was living at the time of his death."

"Really?" Meredith exclaimed.

"He was in Walterboro," Julia said. "It's a popular day trip, something of an antiquing destination."

Meredith had driven past the small town in South Carolina, which used to be a summer retreat for local planters looking to escape their malaria-ridden Low-Country plantations. It was located midway between Savannah and Charleston. "Yes, I did some research a few years ago for the historical society. The downtown has kept many of its historic buildings dating back to the 1800s."

"There was a Slave Relic Museum too, as I recall," Julia said. "It's closed now. I'm not sure who owns it." She paused. "Imagine Geoffrey Besset secluding himself in that little town. Can't be more than five thousand population."

Meredith recalled Carter's impassioned comments about slavery and sharecroppers who perpetuated the oppressive system. It was interesting to think of the aging Besset living in the shadow of a museum dedicated to the thousands who had suffered bondage. Perhaps Julia's sober silence reflected the same thoughts. For a while, they sipped their sweet tea, saying nothing.

"I talked to Charlene," Julia said, breaking the stillness. "She really wants to find her mother, to end their separation." She paused. "She says her mother didn't talk about her childhood, but she was fiercely proud of her grandmother, whose ancestors came from slavery and who worked hard to advance herself. She had none of the opportunities African American women have today. She was constantly held up to Charlene as an example—a reason to make something of herself.

"I know I said it wasn't something we should get involved in," Julia went on. "But I'm glad you took the case. I told Charlene we'd come to her place tomorrow night to review some family photographs and gather the information we need to help find her mom. I hope that was all right."

Tomorrow night! Meredith swallowed, mildly surprised at her good friend and partner. Tit for tat, she supposed. Meredith had taken on Charlene's case without consulting Julia, and now Julia had made an appointment for an evening's work without consulting her.

"She's expecting us around seven," Julia said. "That should give us plenty of time tomorrow morning after church to run over to Walterboro." She pulled herself out of the chair with a satisfied grin. "I still haven't found that turn-of-the-century armoire I've been looking for."

Meredith drew a deep breath and held Julia's mock innocent gaze. "I won't tell Carter if you won't."

᪤ Chapter Thirteen ᪤

JULIA WAS READY PROMPTLY AT ten thirty when Meredith pulled up to her rambling house with its spacious green lawn fronted by ancient elms. The day was already hot, and Meredith was glad she'd worn her cotton ivory shift and sandals for the short trip to Walterboro. She waved to Beau, who circled around from the back of the property on his riding mower.

"I've tried to convince him to hire someone to cut this beast of a yard," Julia said as she jumped into the passenger side of Meredith's SUV. "But he's convinced no one can do the job right. Or the way he wants it done." She tossed her sweater into the back seat. "He's getting too old for all this toil and sweating, but that's a man for you!"

"But what a man," Meredith shot back with a smile. Julia had met the now retired anesthesiologist when she'd been taken to the ER with an infected insect bite sustained at a camp where she was a summer counselor. Beau was a young intern at the time, and according to Julia, it had been love at first sight. They had married in '77 and been sipping sweet tea from one straw ever since. "How did his cataract surgery go?"

"He says he can see like a hawk, but I can't quite get used to him without glasses. I look up sometimes and wonder who that strange guy across the table is." She waved goodbye to her husband out the window and promptly shut it against the morning's heat. "Hot day for antiquing," she said.

"Hot day for anything," Meredith added. Once onto the main road and past the usual flow of traffic, she asked, "Do you think we'll see anything but the outside of the house where Geoffrey supposedly lived?"

"We can only hope." Julia lifted one well-shaped silver brow. "But we're resourceful, right? According to Google Earth, the house is on the outskirts of the town—rather remote but quite a handsome structure."

"I guess the man could afford it," Meredith said, wondering about the much storied but little-known Geoffrey Besset who'd inherited the wealthy plantation. She imagined it as it had once been—magnificent with a robust economy owing first to cotton and later to peanuts, blueberries, and various vegetables indigenous to Georgia. There would have been pecan trees and acres of pasture for the horses Charles Besset had bred and sold.

They passed a large horse farm with miles of white fencing, and Meredith thought about what Cord Armstrong had said. *Imagine Geoffrey selling off all his father's prized horses!* She knew that current listings placed the average price for a champion Arabian at ten thousand dollars. Even a few would bring quite a purse. And that didn't include the Morgans and quarter horses supposedly owned by the Bessets.

As Meredith drove, Julia chatted about the charming antique shops, boutiques, and bistros of Walterboro. "Let's hope they don't sell all the good stuff off before we have a chance to look," she said.

But Meredith wasn't willing to delay the real reason for the day's excursion. The shopping would wait.

Unlike his former payments through anonymous third-party affiliates, Geoffrey had paid his last property tax bill through a bonding company in Walterboro. Julia had been able to pull in a favor from a colleague in the assessor's office to zero in on the address. They veered off the main road going east to take Highway 15 that continued the northerly route from Savannah to Walterboro. Vast farmlands and picturesque countryside stretched through that section of Colleton County. As they followed the series of turns indicated by the GPS, the area grew more suburban, the distances between homes wider but more prosperous. Most houses appeared less than twenty years old, some with circular drives popular of country homes of the '90s.

"Not too shabby," Julia said.

"Hmm, that one's huge—and look at all that land around it." Meredith slowed as the GPS gave yet another directive. Instructed to turn in five hundred feet, she was greeted by a long entrance road shrouded by thick foliage and propelled toward a rambling two-story house with tall columns and wide shuttered windows. Outbuildings in similar style and color spanned the acreage, including a fenced-in area obscured now by the expansive home.

Meredith pulled up the long driveway and parked so they could traverse the cobblestone walkway to the house. She was surprised to hear music wafting from somewhere. The house, the garage? Perhaps from behind. "Well, I guess someone is home," Meredith said, taking a startled breath. "I wonder who Geoffrey left behind—if indeed this is the place where he was found at the time of his death."

"Someone who likes Ravel. Bolero, to be exact," Julia said. "Sounds like the middle of the long march to a final crescendo."

"Give me country Gospel anytime," Meredith said, though she did love the piano concertos of Debussy and the intricate stylings of Bach when she was in a classical mood. She pressed the button on the left side of a wide panel. "Do you think anyone will hear us over this noise?"

Julia rapped on the door and continued doing so for several seconds. But there was no response as the music grew more and more intense. "Let's go around back."

They passed a large double garage and, rounding the house, were astonished to hear yet another sound—a piercing, raucous cry that put one in mind of a jungle rather than a tame suburban domicile. "What on earth?" Julia cried.

From a long, low shed, a large bird came sweeping into a fenced-in area, a scream emanating from its wide, open beak. And suddenly its white feathers began to spread and fan out in a dazzling display.

"Well slap my head and call me silly!" Julia said. "It's a peacock—an albino peacock. I've never seen one in all my born days!"

Meredith watched in stunned silence as the feathers expanded to their full width. A perfect fan. Long tail feathers dragged like a bridal train in the dirt as the bird strutted grandly to the fence. A crown-like crest bobbled atop its head as it advanced, continuing to screech its warning call. "Better than any watchdog I ever saw," she breathed between screeches.

From the patio behind them a voice nearly as raucous as the peacock's broke on the air. "Hush, John Henri! Hush, you silly bird. You're ruining Ravel and scaring these nice ladies."

The apparition in a flaring multicolored smock waved both arms to shoo the bird off. A woman—fortyish perhaps—held what looked like a wide housepainter's brush in one hand. She wore white capri pants, and her brown feet were bare. The scowl on her round face quickly gave way to a smile as she shooed the bird back toward its enclave.

"Come on up to the patio, ladies!" she called, making an invitational swoop of her arms. Messy dark hair spilled around a green and purple turban, and enormous gold earrings danced as she moved. "Don't worry about John Henri. He gets het up around visitors, but he's really a darling."

Meredith tried not to stare, especially when, drawing closer, she saw that the woman had a tattoo of a pink hibiscus covering her entire left cheek. The flower's green stem extended down the side of her face to the base of her neck. Meredith had seen lots of tattoos. Never one like this.

Julia was first to recover. "Sorry to disturb him," she called, her eyes round as a ring-tailed coon's. "We've never seen an albino peacock."

"Oh, he's not an albino. He has a condition called 'leucism.' His pigment cells didn't develop down to the feathers. So, he has no color and looks white. He's got the prettiest blue-gray eyes you ever saw."

Meredith and Julia approached the broad back patio. The wide doors to the inside of the house were flung open, revealing a vast room cluttered with what appeared to be numerous canvases as flamboyant as the woman herself.

"Come on in. John Henri will calm down. Come! Come!" the woman urged, pink lips bright in her coffee-with-cream complexion.

She waved them forward but stepped into the room first. She made another sweep of the arm that held the paintbrush, indicating an enormous canvas of swirls, jagged lines, and scallops. "What do you think?" she asked, her dark eyes lit with anticipation.

Meredith struggled to respond. "Well, it's really—really—" She pulled her eyes from the canvas to the animated face of her host. *Google Earth must have made a mistake.*

"I'm sorry," Julia began, "we were just looking—"

"This color here—" The woman extended the wide paintbrush and made another swirl of bright color on the canvas. "It's called Manic Magenta. Isn't it divine?" She paused, as though suddenly aware of her visitors' confusion. "You did come for a preview of my exhibition, didn't you? It's not till next week, but word gets around. I don't really mind."

Meredith spotted a small stack of business cards among the pots of paint and litter of brushes, rags, and plastic pots. There was a small artists' colony around Walterboro, and this unusual woman was obviously one of the members. "Forgive us for the interruption. We did come to the front door, but the music—" It was then she realized that the frenetic "Bolero" had ended at some point in the cacophony. "We came around back when there was no answer."

"Actually, we're looking for someone," Julia added. "Someone we thought lived here."

"Oh," the woman said, making an exaggerated oval with her full pink lips. "You didn't come to see my work." She effected a kind of pout, like a disappointed child, but quickly brightened. "No matter. Do you want to sit down?" She cast her eyes around the room and gave a soft musical laugh. "Oh no. Better not in here. Y'all come on in the parlor."

She set the brush down, wiped her hands on her smock, and led the way into a large, well-appointed room with leather couches and polished tables of an earlier vintage. A gleaming Kawai piano covered by a fringed cloth and a bouquet of silk flowers dominated one corner. The room was too traditional in taste for the bohemian-like artist. "I'm Yolanda Carson, by the way," she said. "And you are?"

"Meredith Bellefontaine," Meredith said. "And Julia Foley. We have been looking into the background of a man whose plantation is being considered as a heritage site by Savannah's historical society."

She would have gone on, but Yolanda interrupted. "This is Rufus and Nana's home," she said, making a sweep of her billowy sleeve. "They're travelling abroad this year and gave me the run of the place." She chuckled. "I haven't told them about John Henri yet." The pink-flowered cheek dimpled when she laughed, making it look alive. "If you're looking for my grandparents, they won't be back for, oh, several months at least."

"No," Meredith said, curious that Yolanda would call her grandpa "Rufus." "We are looking for a Mr. Geoffrey Besset. We understood that he was living here—"

"Oh!" This time the pink lips turned down in sadness. "I'm so sorry," she said. "But you did know, didn't you? I mean that Mr. Besset passed away, God rest his soul." Her eyes drifted beyond the window where a small house was set back in a cove of trees. She shook her head, making the garish turban slip even lower over her left ear. "I'm the one who found him—out there." She stopped, angled her head to one side.

"We heard of his passing," Meredith said. "We're very sorry. Was he a friend of yours?"

"No," she said, "but he once worked with Rufus—my granddad. They practiced law in Charleston. It had to be ages ago. I hadn't seen him in years—well, not since I was a child. Then three months ago I lost my lease on my apartment in town, and Rufus said I could stay here while they're traveling. Isn't that absolutely marvelous of them?" She pointed to an elderly couple smiling from a silver-edged picture frame. "They're darlings—both Rufus and Nana."

Meredith tried to reel in her amazement. Geoffrey Besset, reputed to dislike black men, had practiced law with an African American partner. "Did he live here a long time?" she asked.

"Not long. Rufus rented him the cottage out back a few months ago. Mr. Besset told me I shouldn't bother him, and he wouldn't bother me, that he kept to himself. That sure was no understatement." She shook her head vehemently from side to side. "He cooked his own meals, hardly went anywhere, and didn't want to talk." She grinned. "Not much of an art lover either. I tried to cheer him up, but he just wanted to be alone." She frowned. "Something powerful struggled inside that man and wouldn't let go."

"You said you were the one to find him after—" Meredith let the question fall away.

Yolanda crossed her arms over her flamboyant smock and sighed. "Yes. I brought him some of my special Afang soup. I make it with crayfish—very tasty. It's a special Nigerian recipe made with palm oil and okazi leaf." Her expressive eyes glowed. "In the last few weeks he was failing. He was getting so thin." She hesitated, and the glow faded from her eyes. "I came in with the pot of soup, and there he was lying on the bed. It was all made up, smooth and neat as you please."

She was still for a few seconds, and Julia broke the brief hiatus. "What did you do after you found him?"

"I called the local funeral home. He had made all the arrangements in advance and told me that when the time came I should call them. I asked couldn't I call someone from his family, but he just put a note in my hand with the funeral parlor's number on it. It was the saddest thing ever."

Meredith felt the lump in her throat thicken. A quietness settled in the grand living room as they sat looking out the window toward the small cottage finished in the style and coloring of the main house.

"It's not right to die with nobody caring," Yolanda said in a hushed voice. "Not even Toby was around when the time came."

"Toby?" Meredith asked.

"My grandparents' gardener. Just a kid when he started working for Rufus. Kind of troubled. Dirt poor. But Toby was the only one Mr. Geoffrey ever talked to. Took a real liking to him."

"Is he here?" Julia asked, leaning forward.

"No. He went off to university in Atlanta shortly after I got here. My guess is that Mr. Besset paid for him to go." Yolanda closed one eye in a slow wink. "Paid his rent on the cottage every month in cash."

Meredith tried to absorb the information falling from Yolanda's lips. Tried to square it with the general assessment of Geoffrey Besset's reputed character. "Did he ever talk to you? I mean maybe toward the end?"

Yolanda shook her head in slow motion, pressing her lips together.

"Do you think we might have a look in the cottage?" Julia asked, exchanging a quick glance with Meredith.

"You're not looking to rent, are you?" Yolanda's head shot up with interest.

"No," Meredith said, "but it might help us in our research."

"Well, I don't think Rufus would mind, but there's nothing to see. After all his personal effects were removed, I had Nu Visions Remodeling come in and paint and get everything ready for the next tenant. Rufus doesn't like to leave the cottage without renters."

Meredith swallowed, trying to tamp down her disappointment. But she couldn't withhold the urgent question. "What happened to them? Mr. Besset's personal effects, I mean."

"There wasn't much to take away. He didn't have much at all. A few books and things. The furniture came with the cottage. My oh my! The man lived like a hermit. Clean and neat, though." Yolanda was on a roll, and Meredith was amazed at the woman's spontaneous life zest. Her hoop earrings shook as she continued talking. "Can you imagine not having music and art and friends around you? I'm used to living alone—never married or had kids, but I got to have joy in my days and sweet thoughts when I lay my head on the pillow at night. I declare the blessed Lord creates them new every morning and sets them out like manna on the ground!"

Meredith tried again. "Ms. Carson. Yolanda—"

Yolanda stopped and took a breath.

"What happened to them? Mr. Besset's things."

She gazed at Meredith and tilted her head. "Why, it was that nice brother of his. Came and took care of everything. Backed up a

U-Haul and got it all loaded up before I had time to finish my *Dance of Spring* painting. That's the one I showed you with the heavenly magenta swirls."

Meredith felt her heart drop. "His brother?" she repeated, stupefied.

"Why, yes. A charming man—cosmopolitan sort—with wavy hair and great muscles. Wonderful name—Langston. Like one of my favorite poets. No one could write like Mr. Langston Hughes." She launched into lyrics from "The Weary Blues."

"'Down on Lenox Avenue the other night
By the pale dull pallor of an old gas light
He did a lazy sway....
He did a lazy sway....
To the tune o' those Weary Blues.'"

She stopped, perhaps upon seeing her visitors' faces, which likely reflected "weary blues" of their own. She stood, reached over to a table near her chair, and handed something to Meredith. "He left this card." She looked down at it and shook her head once more. "Mr. Langston Butler. Sad that he never got to say goodbye to his brother. And even sadder that Mr. Besset didn't want him called when he got so low. Can you imagine? He never even said he had a brother."

Chapter Fourteen

"CAN YOU BELIEVE IT? THE gall of that man!" Julia thumped the arms of Meredith's kitchen chair. "Just charging in and taking over when he hadn't given his so-called father or Geoffrey a by-your-leave for forty years!"

They had returned from Walterboro after an afternoon of shopping for antiques to enjoy a light supper of packaged cheese tortellini and sunflower salad at Meredith's house. While they prepared the meal, they went over the details of the day's discoveries.

"What I can't figure out," said Meredith, "is where the man is getting his information. He knows more about this whole Besset thing than he let on to us."

Julia rummaged in the crisper drawer for salad ingredients. "Somehow he convinced Yolanda Carson that he's Geoffrey's brother and had the right to his belongings." She sighed. "And maybe he is within his rights. With no will extant and no executor named, he could be next of kin."

Meredith popped the tortellini into the boiling water. "He probably is the next of kin. We know his mother was married to Charles for a little less than a month. Maybe Charles didn't want any more children after losing Harriet and decided to divorce her when she got pregnant."

While Julia got busy preparing the salad, fuming over Langston Butler as she chopped, Meredith placed a call to Quin Crowley, who greeted her with warm surprise.

"I'm sorry to bother you—" she began nervously. No doubt her anger and frustration at learning of Butler's move spilled over in her voice.

"It's no bother at all," he quickly responded. "It's good to hear from you."

She shook off the memory of the camaraderie they'd shared over coffee to launch her rebuke. "I suppose your client told you that he has taken possession of Geoffrey Besset's effects."

Quin was silent. She pressed on, feeling indignation rise.

"As his legal counsel, I suppose you assured him that he was within his rights, but I think it only fair that you advise Julia and me of his future plans so we don't waste further time and money investigating on behalf of the historical society." She ran out of breath and struggled to maintain her composure.

"I don't think I can do that," came Quin's quiet response.

"Can't or won't?" she challenged.

After a few seconds he said in his calm, infuriating way, "Won't, because I don't know. Can't, because I'm no longer his lawyer."

The shock of the statement threatened to close off her vocal cords. "You're not?" she asked weakly.

"I've been fired." There was a touch of amusement in his voice. "He'll be looking for a more accommodating attorney to push through his claim. No doubt he'll find one."

Meredith fumbled through an apology for her outburst, too stunned to express herself clearly. There would be no need for further collaboration. No need even to see each other again. She hung up, feeling unexpected regret.

Julia had finished preparing the salad, a smile having replaced her earlier angst. That was something about Julia. She could rant and rave over something like Butler hauling away Geoffrey Besset's personal effects, then shake off her anger, like water over a duck's back. Maybe Meredith could shake off Quin Crowley just as effectively.

Halfway through their meal, Meredith reflected on their adventure in Walterboro. "Yolanda was quite the eccentric."

"You think?" Julia responded with a massive eye roll.

"Imagine tending a white peacock—and creating those bizarre paintings with music blasting through the neighborhood!"

"She was pretty bizarre herself," Julia said. "Never saw a tattoo that covered half a face! But I liked her. I liked her unapologetic sense of self and flair for life."

"There was a softness in her too," Meredith said. "She tried to help Mr. Besset even though he didn't appreciate it."

"Too bad Rufus and Nana weren't there instead of Yolanda. Talking with the grandparents might have been very illuminating," Julia set aside her glass of sweet tea.

"We could still contact them. I'm sure they could shed some light on our illusive plantation owner, but I don't know that there's any point in it. Probate will take a long time, but Langston Butler will likely be confirmed as next of kin. I'm not sure the historical society will have any further use for us." Meredith sighed, feeling a sense of defeat. Quin was out of the picture too.

Julia carried her dishes to the sink and came back to stand at the table, arms folded over her chest. "But the mystery still remains. What happened to Harriet?"

"Maybe it won't ever be solved," Meredith said. *Whatever made me think that Julia and I could unravel a sixty-five-year-old mystery when no one has managed to in all these years?* The old fear and insecurity threatened to override her earlier sense that they had been somehow chosen for that very task.

Julia stood poised, chin forward, her gaze fixed. After a long moment, she asked, "Were you as surprised as I was when you saw the grandparents' photo and realized that Geoffrey had gone into partnership with an African American?"

"Blown over, to tell the truth," Meredith said. "I got the impression from everyone that he didn't have much use for anyone who wasn't white."

"What Yolanda said about the gardener—that Geoffrey had taken an interest in him and might even have paid his way into university—sure gives one pause," Julia said. "Which one do you think is the real Geoffrey Besset?"

"Maybe they're both real," Meredith mused. "Could be something happened to change his perceptions over the years."

"A leopard changing its spots?"

Meredith believed in redemption—had experienced it in her own life. One of her father's favorite quotes by Kierkegaard popped into her mind. *God creates out of nothing. Wonderful, you say. Yes, to be sure, but He does what is still more wonderful: He makes saints out of sinners.* She picked up their empty glasses and nudged past Julia to the sink. "Or being changed by some power beyond himself," she said quietly.

"I'd sure give a lot to know," Julia said, "but we had better get a move on." She grabbed her sweater from the back of the chair, at the same time picking up Meredith's car keys from the table. "We have another case to worry about," she said, handing the keys to Meredith. "We promised Charlene we'd come over at seven."

"Yes, *we* did," Meredith said, emphasizing *we* with mock irony, for Julia had made the promise on her own. "Seriously, I'm glad you went ahead and made the appointment. I'd like to help Charlene. She was so distressed the day she came to the office."

"I don't understand how her mother could simply break off ties with her only daughter," Julia said. "And her granddaughter too. And not even let them know where she was going."

"It is hard to understand," Meredith agreed.

Twenty minutes later, the partners climbed the steps to Charlene Jackson's midtown condo. It was a refurbished complex likely built twenty years earlier. Clean and roomy but nothing fancy. Charlene's business was taking hold, but no doubt finances were tight and would be for a while.

Charlene answered quickly, opening the door wide. "Please come in! Thank you for coming." She smoothed the folds of her dress as she stepped back to usher them in. "I just got home—I was afraid I'd miss you. Things always seem to come up at the last minute at the diner and—" She paused with seeming embarrassment. "Let me make you some coffee."

"Please don't bother. Julia and I just had supper." Meredith patted her stomach and smiled reassuringly.

"Yes. A late supper at that," Julia concurred, looking up into the handsome woman's face. Julia, who usually had to look down in greeting, was shorter than Charlene by a good two inches.

Charlene directed them to a brightly decorated living room with tall, narrow windows that faced the street. The drapes were designed in bold stripes of the same burgundy, green, and gold as the flowered couch and love seat. A low mahogany table contained some papers and photographs that Charlene must have assembled for a tutorial, meager though it appeared, on her mother's life.

Meredith set her purse on the floor at her feet and laid the photo Charlene had left with her earlier on top of the other documents. She cleared her throat and got down to the business at hand. "We're having a bit of difficulty in our initial search, Charlene. Do you have any other family names we can research?"

"My great-grandmother," Charlene said wistfully. "She raised my mother after her parents died. She died five years before I was born, but my mother often spoke of her." She pulled a yellowing sepia photograph from the small pile on the table. The image inside the five-inch oval revealed a light-skinned African American woman with somber features. Charlene set it down next to the photo of her mother. "Louvenia Emmaline Clement. She died in 1961 when she was eighty-two, so I guess that means she was born in"— she paused—"1879."

Meredith saw some resemblance, but neither photo was clear. "Do you have a birth certificate or other official document for your mother?"

Charlene shook her head. "I found a few things she left behind in her house, but she wasn't a saver. She lived very simply." She riffled through the items and handed Meredith a newspaper clipping. "It's from 1998 when Spencer Elementary made her teacher of the year," she said with animation. "It was a difficult, underperforming school, but she helped so many children to excel." Charlene passed a small, ragged clipping to Julia. "And this one is from her retirement in 2010."

Meredith and Julia read silently, exchanging clippings until both were read. It took only a few seconds. *The Daily Telegraph* for April 25, 1998, commended Louvenia King for her faithful service to children and declared her "teacher of the year."

The second clipping, only slightly longer, was little more than an official statement of Louvenia Brown King's retirement—not even accompanied by a photograph.

Meredith could feel Julia's eyes roll without looking at her. She tried not to show her own frustration that there was so little to aid them in locating Charlene's mother. "How about a driver's license?" she asked, though they'd already tried to locate her through the DMV.

Charlene's eyes misted as she shook her head. "My mama never drove. We walked to school every day, summer and winter. We took the bus if we went anywhere—which was never far—or we caught rides with friends in our neighborhood."

Charlene had always referred to her parent by the formal name "Mother." Something in the way she now said "Mama" touched Meredith. She tapped another photograph of a much younger Louvenia Brown with a strapping young man of seventeen or eighteen. "Who is this young man?" she asked quietly.

"My uncle Benny's boy," Charlene said. "I never got to meet him. He—" She paused so long that Meredith had to prompt her to go on. "I don't know if he's even alive. He—well, he got into some trouble when he was young—like to break my mother's heart. 'You got to pray hard for your cousin,' she would say. 'Pray that the good Lord won't let go of him.' But we never heard from him. Word was he got to drinking a lot."

"How about your uncle?" Julia asked.

"My uncle Benny was an activist for civil rights. A really strong advocate in the fifties and sixties." Charlene tugged at an earlobe, today unadorned by her usual gold hoops. Her voice lowered to a whisper. "In 1962 he was brutally beaten by some men when he was working to register black voters, and died from his injuries. My mother said he was one of the smartest and best people she ever knew." She looked off into the distance for a long moment. "I wish I knew more about my mother when she was young. She just never talked about her childhood."

"Do you have any idea why she would have my husband's business card?" Meredith asked.

Charlene shook her head. "I didn't know about it until I found the card at her house."

"You said your mother was secretive about her past, that maybe she was afraid of something." Julia peered closely into Charlene's dark eyes. "Do you have any idea what that could be?"

She shook her head again. "We moved a lot when I was growing up, but always in our Live Oak community. Things would go along just fine, and then we'd up and move again. Mama would say that there was a better chance somewhere else, more opportunity for people like us."

"You said she left a note under your door telling you not to contact her. When was that?" Meredith asked.

"It was two years ago." She wrung her hands nervously. "It made me angry because she still wouldn't say where she was or when she was coming back. I—I threw the note away." She covered her face and then straightened, struggling to regain control.

"Have you heard anything more? Have there been any calls? Anything?"

"Nothing," she began slowly, staring again through an adjacent window. "Strange, though, I had the funniest feeling the day of my Clarissa's wedding. That was about a year ago—right here in Savannah's old Second African Baptist Church. It's where some say that Martin Luther King Jr. practiced his 'I Have a Dream' speech. Anyway, Clarissa and Philip were dancing at the reception, and it seemed like—" She let the sentence drop for several seconds while Meredith and Julia waited in silence. "I know it sounds crazy, but it seemed like she was there in the room," she finally continued. "I remember looking among the crowd of dancers and watchers, the feeling so strong inside me. She and Clarissa were very close." She shrugged. "But maybe I imagined it because I wished so much she could be there to see her only granddaughter married to such a fine young man."

Meredith absorbed the story, tucked it away for further thought. Seeing her mother might well have been Charlene's imagination, yet she had received a note under mysterious circumstances. Could it be that her mother was surreptitiously keeping an eye on her family? "Perhaps," Meredith said. "But if you should have any further intimations along that line—or anything else that might help us locate her, let us know. In the meantime, we'll keep these items and see what we can do."

Charlene studied her hands briefly and looked up. "And now, Clarissa is going to have a baby," she said softly. "I'm going to be a grandma. And Mama will have a great-grandchild. I want her to know. I want her to come home—" She broke off with a heavy sigh.

"I know," Meredith said gently.

"I keep thinking," Charlene said, drawing her eyebrows together. "I keep thinking that folks at the library have to know something about that woman who was Mama's friend. But they couldn't—or wouldn't tell me anything even though I called them several times."

"We haven't checked with the library yet," Julia said gently, "but we will soon. Someone may remember."

"Do you think there's any hope?" Charlene asked, tears trembling in her eyes and threatening to spill over.

"There's always hope," Meredith said, reaching across to take Charlene's hands. "You believe in God, don't you?"

"I do," Charlene said. She pressed her lips together briefly and looked down at her hands. "But sometimes my faith slips and I—"

Julia reached over and joined her hand with Charlene's and Meredith's. "When we reopened the agency," she said confidently, "we agreed that God would be central to our work, and prayer would be one of our strategies. So let's keep our faith strong and pray for an answer."

Meredith said a simple prayer, affirming her confidence in God's power. She gave Charlene's hand a squeeze before releasing it. "If you think of anything else that might help us, call right away," she said. "You have our cell numbers, right?"

Charlene nodded. "I can't tell you how much it means to me that you're willing to help me."

They stepped out of the apartment together and paused briefly at the top of the stairs. The air was still hot, but darkness had eased it, and a faint breeze stirred the air.

"What on earth?" Charlene rushed out to the rail on the small stone porch. "What's going on down there?"

Meredith stared down to the curb. She had pulled up directly behind Charlene's Ford Fusion, and both cars were flanked by a row of trees. There was a flash of light, and a figure leaped back from the curb and disappeared behind the row of cars. Meredith hurried down the stairs with Julia and Charlene following. But the street was quiet, and there was no sign of anyone in the area.

"There has been some vandalism around here," Charlene said. "But not for some time. Probably just some kids looking for an unlocked car."

With a start Meredith wondered if she had locked her car. It was her habit to do so, but in the press of things and hurrying to get to Charlene's condo on time, she might have forgotten. With sinking heart, she checked the front door and realized that she had indeed left her vehicle unlocked. She and Julia checked the interiors as well as tires and windows on both Meredith's and Charlene's cars but found nothing out of the ordinary. Nothing appeared to have been touched, nor was anything missing.

"No problems I can see," Julia said.

"Lord knows there's nothing in my car anybody would want," Charlene said. "But you never know what mischief some kids might be up to."

Meredith sighed with relief. For all their beauty and culture, Savannah's neighborhoods were not immune from trouble. They said goodbye to Charlene, then waited until she was inside before pulling away.

As she drove away from Charlene's street, Meredith found herself recalling the dark sedan that had lingered on her street just before she'd had lunch with Carter and the kids. She had put it out of her mind, but was it possible that someone was marking their movements? Did someone think the investigators knew something they didn't?

An incoming call registered on her instrument panel. She pressed a button and heard Charlene's voice. "Everything okay?" Meredith asked, anxiety rising.

"Everything's fine," Charlene said quickly. "And I want to thank you again for coming. I'm calling because I just remembered something about my mother's close friend that might be helpful. I still can't remember her name, but I do remember that she was Jamaican."

"Okay, we'll remember that," Meredith said, feeling her nerves relax and seeing from the corner of her eye that Julia had made a note in her cell phone. She caught Julia's eye for confirmation. "That will help, and we'll check things out at the library. Good night, Charlene."

"It's been a long day," Julia said, tucking her phone back into her purse. "Let's go home."

"My thoughts exactly." Meredith pressed firmly on the accelerator, drawing a deep breath. She felt unnerved and disoriented; the day had been too full, too long. Or maybe all that talk of mysterious pasts and sudden disappearances was making her paranoid.

Meredith was approaching Julia's neighborhood when her phone rang again. She pressed the button on the steering wheel. "Hello?"

"Meredith?" A pause. "Quin Crowley here. Is this a bad time?"

"Quin," she said, irritated to be suddenly befuddled. "No. It's fine." She risked a look at Julia and frowned at the raised eyebrows of her friend.

"You still interested in a revisit to Mr. Armstrong in Hinesville?" Quin asked. "If so, could you get away tomorrow? Perhaps we could stop for lunch first."

"That sounds like a good idea," she said. "Should I meet you somewhere?"

"No, I'll be around your neck of the woods tomorrow. I'll come pick you up at the office. Say eleven thirty?"

Meredith sent another fierce look at Julia. "That sounds fine. Thanks, Quin. I'll see you then."

"I look forward to it. Goodbye, Meredith."

Meredith said goodbye and clicked the END CALL button, probably a bit harder than she needed to. She turned to Julia. "What?"

"The lawyer you don't like?" Julia's eyes betrayed the tongue-in-cheek question, her lips twisting in a thoroughly Julia smile.

"I never said I didn't like him," she countered. "And he isn't working for Langston Butler anymore. He just wants to help clear up the matter of the Besset inheritance and thinks I might help." She shrugged, adding, "Besides, it's a business meeting. Cord Armstrong may remember something else from his days living next door to the Besset plantation."

She parked in Julia's driveway, and Julia opened her door and got out. Before shutting the door, she leaned in. "I hope your 'business meeting'"—irritatingly, she used air quotes—"goes well tomorrow," she said. "As your business partner, I'm obliged to hear every little detail." She laughed and shut the door. "Good night, Meredith."

Meredith couldn't help but laugh. She had to admit, this was one business meeting she was looking forward to.

Chapter Fifteen

LOUVENIA DIDN'T STEP FOOT OUT of Delyse's cottage for the next two days. She knew her paranoia wasn't logical. Learning that Geoffrey Besset was dead should have taken the burden off her back and the fear from her heart. And yet something wouldn't let her go. Maybe she'd gotten so used to living with her eyes looking back over her shoulder that she couldn't look forward anymore.

Geoffrey Besset was dead. There was no one looking for her, was there?

Louvenia ate her breakfast of wheat toast and strong coffee at Delyse's small kitchen table. For the third day in a row the sky was the color of slate, and bilious clouds vented their anger in teasing spurts. There was no sense in making the half-mile walk to see Delyse until the weather cleared. If she could get up the courage to step out the door.

She touched the faded book that seemed to follow her around the cottage, from her bed to her knitting chair to this table, all day long, never far from her thoughts. With a deep sigh, she opened the pages and continued reading.

May 30, 1956

We learned about a lady called Harriet Tubman in school. Miss Johnson says she lived a hundred years ago and helped slaves escape to freedom on something called the Underground Railroad. This lady helped more than 300 slaves go free, my teacher said.

I can't wait to tell Harriet that the lady had the same name as her. That's why I went running to the summerhouse right after school. It was one of Clementine's good days, so she didn't need me to help, and I promised I'd do all my homework before I went to bed.

I was plumb tuckered by the time I ran to the Besset plantation and snuck through the old abandoned gate. I sat down near the magnolia tree to wait and let the sweet perfume fall over me. Sometimes I wait a long time till Harriet comes, but I love it here in my special place. I love getting to ride the back trails with her and hope we might go today. She will ride Bella, of course—the most beautiful horse Mister Besset owns. I usually ride Polly, a gentle old roan with white whiskers. I tell her she is a good girl, even though I secretly wish I could ride Bella.

Polly is one of the mounts the help get to use if their duties make a trip by horseback necessary. The sign in the back section of the stable where they keep those horses reads, "For Blacks Only" just like the signs in town by water fountains and restaurants.

But today, it seems Harriet will never come. Maybe her mama isn't any better. Or maybe Miss Persimmon won't let her go. I wait, thinking about the lady Miss Johnson told us about. The "Moses" who worked so hard to help people get free. And I wonder if Harriet is free.

I hear the bushes rustle and know she's coming. Her skirt swishes as she breaks through the tangled vines; her long blond hair streams over her shoulders. She drags her left leg a little, and it gives her a funny lopsided look. Maybe the sack she's carrying has something heavy in it. Maybe she's brought sweets from the kitchen for us to eat while we read Little Women or The Wind in the Willows. I have the two cookies Clementine gave me after school to share with Harriet.

I jump up all excited to see her. There had been a week of heavy rain, and I had been kept close to home. "I thought you'd never get here," I say. I ask if she's all right on account of her eyes look funny. Kind of sad and worried.

She gasps and plops down on the scarred bench. I figure she ran too fast. She should be more careful with her bad leg. I wonder if Miss Redbraids or some of the other girls were mean to her. Or maybe it was Miss Persimmon who nags Harriet a lot and tells her to stay out of the way.

I try to cheer her up. "Guess what we learned today? There was this really brave lady a hundred years ago who ran a railroad. Well it wasn't a real railroad but a bunch of secret routes and safe houses that helped slaves escape to Free states like Canada or Nova Scotia. Her name was Harriet—just *like yours! Harriet Tubman, but some people call her Moses. You know, like Moses in the Bible."*

"I know about her," Harriet says, nodding. But she doesn't sound excited. Usually she's the one telling me something she learned in school from a book we don't have in ours. She looks down at the sack by her side. I think maybe she wants to show me, but I can't wait to finish my story.

"This brave lady used songs like a kind of code. She would sing to tell the slaves things they needed to know about the next escape plan. The song 'Wade in the Water' meant to travel by water to avoid being tracked. 'Steal Away' meant that a slave would soon be escaping. 'Sweet Chariot' told slaves to get ready to go North because the Underground Railroad was coming." I laugh and think how clever this Miss Moses was.

Harriet shakes her head like she is listening, but I can tell she's thinking about something else. "What's wrong? Your auntie been mean? Is your mama sicker?"

Big tears form in Harriet's blue eyes, but she presses her lips together like she can't let the words get through. She scrunches up on the bench with her arms wrapped around her stomach. I wait, wishing Granny Luv was here to pray for whatever was hurting Harriet.

After a few minutes, she opens her mouth, and her chin juts out. "Auntie Amelia says it's only a matter of time and Mama will be out of her pain. Only a matter of time before she goes to heaven."

I know Missus Besset's been spending more and more time in bed. It's the same with Clementine. Granny Luv just shakes her head and says the good Lord knows what's best. And I think how can being sick and dying be best?

Harriet's talking like somebody dreaming. "I helped your granny turn Mama and fix her bed today. She never even woke up. Mama's not very heavy, but it's hard to make a bed with somebody in it."

I think about Granny Luv lifting Missus Besset, about the way she comes home at night so tired she can barely walk. It scares me, and I get mad that she works so hard. Benny says one of these days she's gonna fall and not get up. And then I get mad at Benny.

Harriet pushes her lips out like she does when she's thinking hard. She turns to me, and her eyes go big and round as cogwheels. "Something fell out of Mama's mattress when we were changing the sheets. Your granny said I should put it back or give it to my father. I asked your granny to look at it. She told me it wasn't any of her business."

I can imagine Granny Luv shaking her head hard as she snaps sheets and pounds a pillow. She's a big believer in minding her own business—especially when it comes to white folks.

Harriet reaches into the bag and pulls out a thick paper. Her hands shake as she begins to unfold it. She unrolls the wad four times until it's one long sheet. She leans toward me. "Read it, Maggie. You gotta read it."

I stare at the handwritten print filling the paper. I see Mister Besset's name right off. Charles Pendell Besset. He prints in a funny backhand way, the letters small but clear. "Being of sound mind..." I make a face at Harriet and turn back to the words. "...hereby bequeath the whole of my estate..." I think "hereby" sounds like the Bible. I'm used to hearing that, but I'm not sure about "bequeath."

"I think it means to give away," Harriet says. Her face goes whiter than the paper. "And look there!" She traces her finger under her own name, Harriet Elizabeth Besset. "Is Daddy dying too and giving this plantation away?" she asks, her voice rising.

I shake my head, and I'm afraid for her, because she looks so scared. "I think it's what people call a will," I say. "It doesn't mean they're dying—at least not right away. They just want to be ready and to say who they want to give their stuff to."

Her eyes stay round and scared. "That's what I think too, but I don't want Mama and Daddy to die. And I don't want them to give me anything. I—"

"You should put it back," I tell her, pushing the paper toward her. "Does anybody know you took it?"

Harriet bites her lip and stares into my face. "Auntie Amelia saw it. She saw me and your granny in Mama's room." She scrunches up her nose and mimics Miss Persimmon. "'What is that, young lady? Give it to me!' And she grabbed it and started to read it, but then Daddy came in the room. Right away, she put it behind her back and dropped it on the floor. She told Granny Luv to go and then she went out with Daddy, whispering how Mama was sleeping and was there anything she could do for him. You know how she gets that funny smile with Daddy and follows him around."

"And you took the letter?" I ask, imagining Miss Persimmon all syrupy with Mister B right after being nasty to Granny Luv and Harriet.

"I shouldn't have taken it, but I—" Harriet breaks off and rocks a little on the bench. "Maggie, this has been a terrible, awful day. I want Mama to get better. I don't want things to change. I want—"

"You got to go put it back," I say.

But she doesn't take it. She just rears back like the paper might bite her. "No!" she says, getting up from the bench, "I don't want those awful dying words in Mama's bed." Her eyes widen, and she grabs my arm. "Will you keep it? Hide it somewhere?"

I start to shake my head, but Harriet looks like a deer spooked in the forest. "But your auntie—won't she be asking about it? What if—"

"I'll pretend I don't know what it was, that I don't know what happened to it." Her jaw juts out, and her eyes gleam with that dose of stubborn I think she takes every morning like medicine. "Mama's going to get well." She puts her hands on her hips like grown-up ladies do and stamps her strong foot. "I simply won't allow any dying words in her room."

I start to say that it would be a lie, and I'm thinking it's not a little one. I begin to fold the paper back like it was and imagine myself stuffing it away in my treasure box. But I'm thinking how we better ask forgiveness like Pastor Ray Bill Samuels says. Like Granny Luv says.

Harriet hugs me and heaves a big sigh. "You're my best friend in the whole world, Maggie Lu."

"But—"

"I just know Mama's going to be okay. We'll keep praying, like you say." She shuts her eyes real tight and grits her teeth. She doesn't say anything. I know she's waiting for me to do the praying.

My teeth chatter, but I try my best. "If You're listening, God, we're needing help here. You say You can do anything. We're asking You to make Harriet's mama better. And about this big paper—" I stop because I don't know what to say, and I wonder if God will turn His listening ear away on account of the lie we're gonna tell.

"Amen," Harriet says and jerks her head up.

That's when we both hear it—not a thunderbolt from heaven calling down fire on us, but a familiar whiny voice calling Harriet's name. "Har—ri—et!"

I picture Miss Persimmon in her little sleeveless dress and hair piled up on her head like a beehive. She'll be wearing orange lipstick and maybe a string of Missus Besset's pearls that she likes to borrow. Harriet says she sneaks jewelry from her stepsister's box lots of times. Wouldn't surprise me if she's hankering to have the whole plantation to herself. And Mister B besides.

"Come on now, it's time for your piano lesson," comes the cajoling voice that hides a heap of mad in it. "Har—ri—et!"

Miss Persimmon never goes far from the big house. She's still a long way off, but her shrill voice seems to carry for miles. I cringe against the magnolia branches, prepared to leap into the woods.

"Shh!" Harriet says, and her eyes glitter with purpose. She's her sassy self again. "I'll sneak back to the house through the woods and be sitting at the piano when she gets back. Don't worry. She won't find you."

And she's gone like a streak. Even her limp is gone. I crouch down low in the thick underbrush and wait. I risk another prayer that Harriet's auntie doesn't catch her. Miss Persimmon is still hollering, but I can tell she's turned back toward the house, probably stumbling in her strappy high heels.

I stay still a long time till I'm sure no one is coming. I stuff the paper away and bury my treasure box back under the magnolia tree. The day is spoiled. I decide to go see Benny. I head toward the stable. Maybe I'll tell him about the stolen paper. Maybe I won't. But I need to feel his big strong arms right now.

When I get closer, I hear loud voices. A few of the field workers watch from behind the fence that divides the corral and stable from the fields. On the other side, a man holds something in his fist and shakes it in the face of another man. "I asked you where you got this, boy."

I realize with a catch in my throat that the angry, shouting man is Little Bee—Mister Geoffrey. Hair slicked back from his forehead, black eyes flashing, he presses what looks like a pamphlet toward Bob Henry Biggs.

Biggs is a short, thick man who likes to sing while he works and often fishes candy from his pocket for me. He knows I love the sweet, peanut buttery taste of Mary

Janes. Now he holds his hands out like he's afraid of being hit and shakes his head. Sweat shines in his round face.

I hover in the shadow of the stable door. I stare at the pamphlet, and I can almost smell the stuff used in the ditto machine that makes words. I catch a glimpse of purple print and feel a sinking in my stomach.

"This belong to you, boy?" Little Bee demands as Bob Henry takes a step backward, still shaking his head. Mister Geoffrey wheels around to the group of men by the fence. "Maybe you'd like to tell us about it!" His voice is like hot steel.

"No, sir. Don't know nothin' about it," Bob Henry Biggs says.

Little Bee slaps the pamphlet into the palm of one hand. Smacks it again and looks at Biggs and the other men. "Trash!" he fumes. "Ungrateful rabble-rousers trying to get your fingers in the pockets of hardworking men who made this country what it is. If my father catches any of you with this stuff you'll be out of here faster than you can say hog grits and catfish."

Silence falls until suddenly Benny appears at the stable door. He looks like he has just come out for a stroll. His hands hang in his pockets, and there's an easy expression on his face. But I see what his eyes say. And I know he's in for it from Mister Geoffrey.

He's in for it because he knows right enough about those pamphlets. On account of he wrote them. Sometimes when he comes home from his "meetings," I can smell the chemicals *from the ditto machine. Smell the power of the words that burn in my brother's soul. Words I think for sure gonna flare up and lick us all up in a fiery heap.*

Little Bee saunters over to where Benny stands. He mimics Benny's posture, stuffs his hands in his pockets. He glares at Benny, whose handsome face doesn't show the least flicker. "Don't think my father won't hear about this, boy," he says low and soft with a snake's venom in his words. "I reckon we all know where this garbage comes from."

"We do you no harm, sir," my brother says quietly, but his eyes match Mister Geoffrey's steel for steel. "We only want what's right as a free people."

"You've had your freedom for almost a hundred years, and you still don't know what to do with it." He starts to say more, but Big Bee's truck is pulling into the stable yard. Little Bee straightens, his face like a balloon going flat. "Watch yourself," he snarls at Benny before turning away. "Remember what happened to Tommy Roy."

I crouch deeper into the shadows and feel my heart thump hard. Tommy Roy Grant got beat up bad because he dared to drink from a "Whites Only" water fountain on the wharf. He'd been attacked in the very woods where Harriet and I had seen Waylon Jute in his nightshirt.

Little Bee's threat rings in my ears. Things were bad between him and Benny before. Now, it's ten times worse. And if he knew that his little sister was hiding his daddy's private papers and that his daddy had willed his whole estate to Harriet, none of them would ever be safe again.

Right off, I think of Moses—the Moses who was Harriet Tubman. The Moses who helped three hundred slaves get free on the Underground Railroad. And I'm scared. Powerful scared. But I look at Benny and I'm proud. Prouder than a full-feathered peacock rising from the dusty barnyard.

Chapter Sixteen

MEREDITH PRETENDED THE DAY WAS no different than any other. Yet she took her time dressing, mumbling to herself as she tried first one outfit, then another, before deciding on a green dress that flared out gently and was splashed with large white flowers. Perhaps too bold and showy, but the sleeves were three-quarter length and the neckline modest but airy. *Who said a girl shouldn't look as youthful as possible?*

GK, sitting in the doorway, watched the drama with mild amusement on his whiskery face. His pose was meditative, his tail wrapped sedately around his blue-gray paws.

"Don't you know it's not polite to watch a lady in her boudoir?" she scolded him laughingly. And gave him an extra treat before leaving for the office.

It was just lunch, after all. A simple convenience since she had agreed it was time for a second visit to Cord Armstrong. His recollection of things pertaining to Geoffrey Besset had been sketchy at their initial visit. Yet his remarks about sharecroppers and Geoffrey's prized horses had shed some light on the dead man's character. Perhaps a second visit might reveal more. Memory was like that. Something would trigger it and bring to the fore a long-forgotten face or event. She would spend the morning at her desk before Quin arrived, and then they would set out for Hinesville.

Quin picked her up right on time, coming into the office to escort her to his Land Rover. They made small talk as he drove to a small diner a few miles outside of Hinesville. Upscale but not stuffy, boasting old-world revival décor with still life prints of fruit and flowers and not a few French language plaques encouraging patrons to live life joyfully. *Profite de la vie!*

The restaurant was pleasantly cool. A smattering of early diners gathered around small, square tables. Men in suits or white shirts from nearby businesses, women in casual attire enjoying a ladies' day out, a father with a young girl perhaps enjoying a daddy-daughter date.

"The service is good," Quin said after seating her. "The food is even better." He sat down across from her, briefly resettled the silverware, and smiled. "I'm glad you were free."

"Yes," Meredith conceded. "We're still working for the historical society, but we haven't uncovered much useful information. And we remain in the dark about what happened at the Besset plantation. So I don't know how long we'll remain employed." She shrugged and returned his smile.

He had left his coat in his Land Rover along with his tie and looked considerably more relaxed in his white shirt, sleeves rolled up to the elbows. She was aware of tanned arms beneath a light covering of silver hair. "I'm sorry about Butler," she said.

His turn to shrug. "He wasn't happy with my way of doing things, I guess. Didn't like me getting too deep into his past."

Quin broke off to give his order to the waiter, a young man sporting a black tie and faded jeans. Quin ordered a French dip with coleslaw and sparkling water. Meredith chose a chicken salad croissant and raspberry iced tea.

"Frankly, I'm not sorry he's gone on to greener pastures," Quin continued. "But Butler's crazy to think a court is going to just turn over a potential gold mine without a thorough check."

Meredith released a sigh. "He wasn't overjoyed to learn that we'd alerted the city council—and the Chamber of Commerce, mind you—about the deal he was involved in in New Orleans." Briefly, she outlined the details of the development built on property without a local water source. "The company duped those buyers who had no idea what the cost of piped-in water would amount to."

A look of admiration flashed in Quin's eyes. "Good detective work," he said. "I'm impressed."

"Just lucky. It was Carter—my son—who made the connection and passed it on. He's a banker, gets around a lot in money circles." She bit into her croissant, thinking she'd like to ask Quin about his extraordinary eyes that pulled a person in against their will. Hardly a business lunch question. She studied her glass of iced tea before downing a good third of it.

Keep things on a professional level, she told herself. *No point in giving him the wrong idea.* Which was what? came the swift counter thought. She rarely had difficulty making new friends, finding common ground for conversation. So why this hesitancy where an available man was concerned? Of course, people would assume, "He's a widower; she's a widow. It's only natural." She emptied her glass and had barely set it down before the young waiter was at her side, refilling it.

"Thank you." She smiled and sat back, only to realize that Quin was watching her intently.

"So, are you enjoying your new role in the detecting business? You and that former judge who has quite a number of my colleagues talking." He touched his napkin to his mouth. "Quaking, to be more accurate. They say she was a formidable opponent to those who challenged her."

Meredith laughed, thinking about how Julia would set her jaw and try not to look pleased at such a compliment. "We try to cross all our t's," she said. "There's only one letter difference between 'defective' and 'detective,' you know." She glanced away from his appreciative smile then sobered. "We're still learning the ropes, but we feel we're in the right place for this time in our lives."

"It always interests me how people determine they're in the right place, as you say." He blinked, studying her briefly. "I know you said you were taking over the agency your husband started, but have you always been interested in investigations? How did you know it was the right place for you?"

Meredith folded her hands in her lap and reflected on the question. "I think there's a reason why each of us is here. I believe the God who created us knows just where we fit and helps us find that place." She drew a breath, wondering how this sounded to Quin, but she couldn't stop herself from finishing. "I think this is where He led me—Julia and me."

She looked up to meet his eyes. They seemed lit from within, an alluring mix of oceanic blue and copper brown with no strangeness about them.

He nodded. "I think I knew this about you from the first time we ran into each other." His cheeks reddened slightly.

"You mean *I* ran into *you*!" She laughed.

"Sorry. I didn't mean—" He shook his head. "What I mean is, I could tell you were tuned in to the important things. I too try to follow those higher purposes God places in us." He turned to press his plate closer to the edge of the table to assist the waiter who stood with an inquiring glance.

"May we offer dessert?" the young waiter asked in speech undoubtedly foreign to the kid who would likely pull out his skateboard after work.

"Nothing for me," Meredith said hastily to cover the lovely sense of discovering that she and Quin Crowley might be kindred spirits.

"We're good," Quin said. "The check, please."

"Separate checks, if you don't mind."

"Not today, Madam Sleuth," Quin said with a return to his first-impression assertiveness.

"In that case," Meredith said grandly, "it'll be my treat next time." She felt her cheeks flush, realizing she had hinted there might be a next time.

Their conversation was easy and lighthearted for the remainder of the short journey to Hinesville. They entered the now familiar foyer of the care home and asked to see Mr. Cord Armstrong.

"I believe he's in the solarium," the attendant said after turning the sign-in register toward them. They entered their names and arrival time and followed directions to the solarium off the east wing. Light reflected on the glassed-in sun parlor with its abundance of green plants, benches, and aviaries where tiny colorful birds flitted and sang.

Meredith and Quin wound their way to the rear, smiling and nodding to seniors in various stages of rest and unrest.

They found Cord Armstrong in much the same position as on their first visit. He stood with just a slight stoop to his shoulders staring through the glass. His profile was fixed and unreadable. She recognized the narrow face, reddened cheeks, and aristocratic nose. The same white mustache and bushy sideburns.

When he turned, he stood up to what might be his full height, his face brightening. He took a step toward them, his eyes fixed on Meredith. Then he stopped short and put out a hand to steady himself on a nearby table, his expression immediately altered.

"Oh," he said in little more than a whisper. "You're not Trudy."

His daughter? A good friend? It hurt to see the disappointment in his eyes.

"Meredith Bellefontaine." She put out her hand. "It's good to see you again, Mr. Armstrong."

"Arthur Crowley," Quin said, also extending a hand, which Armstrong didn't take, perhaps because the stretch was too much, or perhaps because he simply didn't want to.

Mr. Armstrong seemed to grow suddenly weary and dropped down on a chair by the table at his left hand. He took a long breath, then said, "I'm sorry. I thought you were—" He broke off, looked at them each in turn, and seemed to restore his dignity. "You're the people who were asking about that Besset fellow."

Good. He remembered. He hadn't suddenly lost his memory or pleaded to be left alone. Clearly, he had hoped to see someone else, but, ever the gentleman, he would entertain their intrusion.

"I've been investigating a very old mystery, Mr. Armstrong," Meredith began, relieved. "When we were here before, I asked you about a twelve-year-old girl who went missing. You mentioned that the police questioned everyone in the area and anyone who had dealings with the family."

"Yes, I remember," Mr. Armstrong said. He shook his head, as though to clear the cobwebs of the past. "Getting old is funny," he said, though his features reflected nothing remotely amusing.

Meredith leaned closer.

"It's strange, I mean. The past becomes all there is. All there is that's important anyway. What little happens now seems trivial and some-how not real." He touched a slightly trembling hand to his mouth. "I'm sorry. I didn't mean to say that you are not important. Forgive me, I—"

"We understand," Quin broke in, his expression thoughtful. "But things that happened in the past can change the present, and they can make a difference in the future."

"Most young people aren't interested in the past," Mr. Armstrong said, giving Quin a keen glance. "Unless it helps them advance their careers or make more money." He looked over at Meredith with the same intensity. "Maybe the two of you are different. Maybe not."

They must have seemed young to him, but Cord Armstrong was surprisingly insightful, Meredith realized. He could be a force to be reckoned with. She wondered if his family appreciated that. Appreciated him. "Our interest in the Besset plantation is for the benefit of society and to solve a sixty-five-year-old injustice that should be brought to light," she said quietly.

"What do you remember about growing up?" Quin asked. "Your father was a rancher, wasn't he? You mentioned he raised horses like the Bessets did."

"I remember that growing up on a farm was a lot of work. Of course, my father had hired hands, many of them African Americans, but he saw to it that my brother and I did our share of taking care of the stock and helping in the fields." He paused. "We were not as wealthy as some, but our stock brought a good return. My father was a fair man and paid his hands a decent wage. Wasn't a bad life, but I didn't want to go into farming." He lifted his chin slightly. "I had my sights set on engineering—building things that wouldn't crumble in a drought or be flattened by a freak windstorm."

"Your place was just to the west of the old Besset Plantation, wasn't it?" Meredith asked, trying to lead his thoughts back to his former neighbors. "You left as a young man, but did your parents ever speak of them? Perhaps visit?"

He thought for several moments, leaning forward with his gnarly hands on his knees. "Like I said, there wasn't much time for socializing. My folks were old-fashioned, very strong on the law and minding their own business. Don't think they saw eye to eye with Charles Besset, and they didn't want us mixing with Geoffrey."

"Yes, you said he was rather wild and unruly," Meredith said.

He nodded. "He got into a lot of fights. But I suppose we were all a bit wild and unruly as kids."

A young woman approached, bearing a tray. Her white pantsuit and cherry-red smock were a compelling contrast to her dark skin and hair. "Sorry to interrupt, Mr. Armstrong," she said in a soft voice. "It's time for your two o'clock meds."

"Yes. Thank you," he said, straightening, and obediently downed the contents of the little paper cup.

"Would your guests care for something? I could bring some fresh coffee." The CNA smiled with what appeared to be genuine concern and laid her hand gently on the elderly man's shoulder.

"Myra's right. The coffee's good here," Mr. Armstrong said, looking up at his guests to determine their pleasure.

"Thank you so much, but please don't bother," Meredith said.

Quin shook his head as well. "We have to be on our way soon."

As the nursing assistant walked through the solarium, Mr. Armstrong watched her. He seemed subdued or sleepy and said nothing until she had long disappeared into the outer hall. He angled his head toward one of the nearby aviaries as though arrested by the twittering activity inside its bars. Was their discussion over, the interruption turning him away from memories of his long-ago life on a Southern plantation?

Disappointed, Meredith said nothing. She glanced at Quin, who shrugged. Well, at least they had done something worthwhile by visiting a man time seemed to have forgotten. A man Trudy—whoever she was—had perhaps forgotten too.

"It was wrong, you know," Cord Armstrong said suddenly, probing the silence. He waited a good ten seconds before continuing. "The Bessets never could get over what happened. Charles neglected his son in favor of his horses, and they both blamed a whole race for the actions of two men."

Meredith felt her pulse speed up. "What was it they couldn't get over, Mr. Armstrong?"

"I was only a child when it happened," he said as though pushing through a hazy curtain. "But I remember my parents talking about what they saw that day. About what happened to poor Sarah Jean."

"Sarah Jean Besset? Charles's first wife?" Meredith asked.

Mr. Armstrong twisted his hands slowly in his lap. "There was trouble back in those days—bad trouble. Hatred on both sides. Things would go along peacefully for a while. Then—" He broke off and continued to stare at the twittering birds.

Meredith leaned forward, pressing her fingers hard into each other.

"Sarah Jean was attacked one night just yards from her house," he went on. "She was carrying a baby in her arms, and her little boy was running by her side." Mr. Armstrong's eyes widened with remembrance. "Two men were chasing them, saying terrible things and threatening to—" He shook his head. "To hurt Sarah Jean. She tried to outrun the attackers, her little boy clinging to her skirts and running too. They got away, but the baby fell from her arms. It was Geoffrey's little sister."

"Harriet," Meredith breathed.

"Yes," Mr. Armstrong said. "Her leg never healed right."

"How awful," Meredith whispered.

Mr. Armstrong wagged his head again, slowly from side to side. "Charles changed after that. Kept to himself. Never had much to say to anyone. But it was Geoffrey who suffered most. Charles ignored him, even belittled him, as though he was to blame somehow for what happened. But he was just four years old! And he needed his daddy."

"Did they find the men who attacked Sarah Jean?"

"They did," Mr. Armstrong said, still staring into the bird cage. He turned to look at Quin and Meredith, an ancient horror reflected in the rheumy depths of his eyes. "They were hanged before they ever got to trial."

Chapter Seventeen

THE NEXT MORNING MEREDITH FOUND Carmen at her desk in the agency, the telephone receiver cradled between her shoulder and chin. She looked up, widened her eyes, and gestured to Meredith.

"Ah, here she is now," Carmen said into the phone. "*Un minuto.*" She covered the receiver with her hand and tossed her head of abundant black curls. "It's Miss Enterline for you," she said in a hushed voice.

Meredith headed into her office, where she picked up the phone. "Good morning, Beatrice." She pictured the historical society director behind a familiar desk in the office she once occupied. Seldom so grandly, though, she imagined. Beatrice would be perfectly turned out in a classic business suit, ringed fingers poised on the receiver. "Sorry to keep you waiting."

"No matter, dear. Just checking in."

Meredith sighed. Beatrice was two decades younger than she was, yet she delighted in referring to her as "dear" or "darling." Well, it was simply her way. Over the top, as always.

"Anything new with the investigation?"

Meredith cleared her throat. There was so little to report that would please Beatrice. Nothing that would give her hope for the historical society's procurement of the coveted Besset property. "We've had a look at the home where Geoffrey was staying at the time of his death," she offered. "Unfortunately, Langston Butler found it before we did." Meredith released a long breath. "If there were any legal documents there, he may have found them."

"Why, that sneaky polecat!" Beatrice erupted. "Does he have a legal right?" she asked quickly, her voice rising.

"That hasn't been confirmed, though he certainly makes the claim. But according to Julia, who as you know has connections in legal circles, there's nothing on the court docket—no petition to probate at this point. Also, no sign of a will."

Beatrice spoke as though thinking out loud. "If he can prove he's the rightful heir, he may be open to selling the plantation, but I bet the price will be pretty steep since he knows we're interested."

Meredith hurried on, wanting to say something positive. "We frankly don't know what to make of Geoffrey Besset. Butler says the estate should never have gone to him. Says Charles cheated his mother, lured her into becoming his wife, then annulled the marriage, leaving her destitute. Now that she's dead, he says the estate should be his as Geoffrey's legal half brother." She paused. "We're hearing some contrary information about Geoffrey."

"You don't say," Beatrice exclaimed.

"The big surprise is that Geoffrey's law partner was African American. Besset was living in seclusion in a small house on his partner's estate."

"The same house that Butler managed to search before you and Julia could, I presume," Beatrice said with considerable irony.

"Sadly, yes." Meredith released a sigh. "He must have sounded quite convincing to Yolanda," she continued, swiveling her chair to look out the window and feeling the sting of defeat. They hadn't really learned anything to further the historical society's cause or to solve the mystery of young Harriet.

Julia entered the agency with a wave in Meredith's direction. Meredith glanced her way and turned her attention back to Beatrice. "If there's any good news here, Butler wouldn't still be snooping around if he had a solid case."

"He's looking for something," Beatrice said thoughtfully. "A will, maybe." She was quiet for a moment, then seemed once again to think out loud. "You don't suppose that's why—"

"I'm sorry we haven't been able to—"

"We just assumed it was kids snooping around."

Beatrice was talking on some wavelength Meredith couldn't reach. She leaned forward in her chair, perplexed. What was Beatrice talking about? "Has something happened?"

"Someone got into the house. Pried up the lumber around the lock on the front door. Must have happened during the night. The police are investigating."

Someone broke into the Besset mansion? Bored kids stringing toilet paper from the trees or curious vandals with paint cans—those were the usual suspects. But a break-in? Meredith recalled the huge man who had warded off more than one curious visitor, including her and Julia. How had someone gotten by the surrounding fence and right up to the mansion without his notice? "Where was Lucky?"

"Apparently, he was nowhere around. It's not like him. He's been vigilant up until now. He can see cars approaching from that shack of his. And it isn't more than a quarter mile past the woods to the estate. Well, the police will get to the bottom of it. In the meantime, they're installing official police tape around the house, which may or may not prevent curiosity seekers or vandals." Beatrice sounded weary.

"Lucky," Meredith said thoughtfully. A nickname. Beatrice had told them almost nothing about the man. Nor, Meredith realized with a pang of regret, had she inquired. "Do you know what his real name is?"

"I can't remember. Shouldn't be too hard to find out, though." Beatrice sighed. "Well, gotta run. Got a tour fixin' to start in half an hour. My public awaits."

Meredith hung up, leaving her hand on the receiver for a moment. She looked up, aware of Julia in the doorway, her expression registering acute curiosity. "That was Beatrice," she said, trying to absorb the surprising news. "Someone broke into the Besset mansion."

"Who was it? Do they know?" Julia came all the way into Meredith's office and dropped down in a chair by the desk.

Meredith shook her head. "The police were doing a random check and found someone had jimmied the front door."

"But there's nothing inside to take, is there?" Julia drew her brows together. "We always understood that the place was cleared out long ago."

A view through clouded glass windows gave that impression, but who really knew what was inside? The police checked the premises from time to time, but they wouldn't invade a private residence. Certainly not without a warrant. "Well, someone was hoping to find something of value in the old place." Meredith crossed her arms over her chest.

"And they got by Lucky the Terrible?" Julia gave a little shiver.

"That's the odd part. He wasn't around." Meredith held her friend's gaze. Lucky had been more than diligent keeping intruders off the grounds. He'd been fiercely protective. What had happened? Where was he? Well, he couldn't be on guard every second, she rationalized. Maybe he was off fishing or something. She stood and drew a sharp breath. "I think we should go have a look."

"Now?"

Meredith picked up her purse. "Now. Tell Carmen we'll be out for a while, please."

"Got it. *Hasta luego!*" came a voice from the outer office, drawing twin eye rolls from Meredith and Julia.

The road, now familiar, grew narrower as they drove, overgrown shrubs and trees forming a sort of canopy over it. Meredith squinted into the distance, saw the outline of the mansion but drove on past the forested area toward the house Beatrice had told them about. A little house with a clear view up the hill to the mansion and a narrow creek running along its western perimeter.

"That's the section where sharecroppers once lived," Meredith said. "There's only one house still standing. It's on the other side of the creek. That's got to be Lucky's place."

"It sure is quiet. Doesn't even seem the air is moving." Julia fanned herself and cranked the window all the way down.

"Well, that's Savannah in late May for you," Meredith agreed. "It's already hotter than a blister bug in a pepper patch."

"My daddy used to say that. He said the good Lord made blister bugs to shoot out a chemical that poisoned any predator that came around." Julia laughed. "Probably not two-legged ones, though."

"Ah, this place," Meredith breathed as she drove on. She found herself speaking almost in a whisper, feeling the odd sense of presence she had noticed before on the Besset property. "I found out something about Harriet."

"About why she disappeared?"

"Sadly, no," Meredith said, releasing a long breath. "But yesterday Cord Armstrong said that Harriet had a crippled leg. It happened when she was a baby. Her mother was attacked by two men." Meredith nodded toward the forested vista through the open window. "Somewhere out there." She shivered, remembering Cord Armstrong's haunted eyes as he related the story.

"What happened?" Julia asked, wide-eyed.

"Sara got away, but she dropped the baby. Harriet's leg was damaged and never healed right, according to Mr. Armstrong. Geoffrey was with her too. He was only four years old."

"That's awful," Julia breathed. "Did they catch the guys who did it?"

"Two black men. Lynched before they got to trial." Meredith heard Julia's horrified gasp. "Charles wasn't the same after that. Mr. Armstrong said it was almost as if he blamed Geoffrey, his own son, for the tragedy. He turned all his attention on his prized horses and all but ignored his little boy. He and Geoffrey both turned bitter, especially toward people of color, blamed the whole race for the sins of two."

"Those were terrible times," Julia whispered.

They drove on in silence until the road suddenly ended. "I see the house," Meredith said. "But I guess we walk from here."

At the end of the narrow thruway was a log cabin, obviously quite old. It appeared to have been jacked up and the foundation relaid with stones of various sizes. The chinking, probably made of clay and sand or lime, was unevenly slabbed between the logs. Set among fir trees on hardscrabble ground, the cabin stood only slightly crooked and boasted windows with rugged frames.

Meredith and Julia exchanged glances as they approached the slatted door, which might have been fashioned of old barn wood. The ground around the house had been cleanly swept, and a good-sized garden had been dug behind the cabin. Next to the door, a scarred table held a small pot of red flowers.

Meredith knocked, touched by the occupant's obvious attempt at homeyness. There were no signs or numbers and no mailbox, but clearly, someone lived here. It had to be Lucky. They waited. Only the sound of small birds flitting in and out of pine branches and twittering filled the late morning air.

Julia knocked again then looked at Meredith with wide gray eyes. "He'll come home eventually, won't he? Should we wait?"

Meredith scanned the area around the house. She was about to peer through a window when something like a moan emanated from inside. "Did you hear that?"

Julia put her ear to the door and touched a padlock twined through an old-fashioned hasp. It fell open. "Someone's inside," she whispered. "It sounds like someone's sick or hurt." She lifted the lock, and the door creaked open.

Meredith blinked to adjust to the dark interior, which was surprisingly cool and uncluttered. They were in a kitchen, which perhaps was the only room in the cabin. She quickly took in a table, a chair, an ancient refrigerator, and a butane stove. A fabric curtain attached to cup hooks hung from the ceiling at the far end. She glanced at Julia and approached the curtain. She drew it aside tentatively.

A low groan came from the bed where a large black man lay fully dressed. A blanket was tangled around him, as though he had been tossing and turning through a long night. He turned toward them, eyes huge in his face, which was surrounded by thick gray hair.

Meredith rushed to the bed. She saw beads of sweat on the man's face. His eyes shone too brightly in the dim room. "Lucky? What's happened? Are you sick?" She whipped out her phone. "We can call a doctor."

"No, I'm—all right," he rasped, trying to rise but falling back against a striped tick pillow. "Just been feeling poorly the last couple of days," he stammered. "No need for—" But he seemed to run out of the strength to say more.

Meredith put her hand to his brow. It was clammy but cool. She looked around the small enclave that had been curtained off for a bedroom, found it well-ordered and clean. A shelf held an oil lamp, a thick china mug, and a Bible. A few clothes hung from pegs on the wall. "Can I get you some water?" *Is there running water?* Then she remembered seeing a pump a few yards from the cabin.

"In there," Lucky said, pointing. Meredith looked toward the curtain that divided his sleeping quarters from the kitchen. He made another attempt to rise, then fell back and closed his heavy-lidded eyes.

"Just lie still," Meredith said, trying to straighten the twisted blanket.

She handed Julia the mug, heard her move into the kitchen and open the refrigerator. She was back in a flash with the mug half-filled with water. "Can you drink this if we help you sit up?"

"I'm sorry," the old man sputtered, obviously embarrassed. But he allowed her and Meredith to prop him against the pillow. "Don't get sick much," he said, panting with effort. "I'll be all right. Sorry for the trouble."

"Drink," Meredith said, hushing his apologies and feeling quite winded herself from lifting the huge torso. "I think your fever's broken now. How long have you been sick?"

He swallowed the water eagerly and leaned back against the pillow. "Just a day or two. Been clearin' brush." He put a big hand over his enormous chest and closed his eyes. "Sometimes I forget I'm not a young man anymore." Suddenly, he opened his eyes wide. His brow furrowed deeply. "Is everything okay at Mr. Geoffrey's place?"

Meredith looked at Julia. "Well, someone broke in last night. We knew something was wrong. That's why we came to find you."

The water seemed to revive him. His eyes roamed back and forth between the two women at his bedside. He made fists with his hands and thumped them against the mattress. He wagged his head from side to side on the pillow.

"It's not your fault," Meredith said quietly. "You would have stopped them if you weren't sick." But a bell had begun to ring in her mind. The historical society had hired him because his old shack was nearby, because he needed something to do with his time. Because—

Then she saw it on a ledge in the corner of the room. The bottle they had seen in his pocket the first time they'd encountered him near the old summerhouse. It was empty, clean, the sun glinting through the amber glass. Beatrice had inferred that Lucky was a recovering alcoholic who needed a place to stay, some work to keep him focused. "Did you—know Geoffrey Besset?" she asked, her gaze still trained on the empty bottle.

Lucky nodded wearily. "The man helped save my life," he said just above a whisper. He released a breath and rolled his eyes before closing them briefly. When he opened them again, he stared at the bottle on the ledge. "Never thought I'd be anywhere but the gutter. City to city, good for nothin'. Hit bottom in North Charleston. Shoulda' died there."

Lucky closed his eyes and didn't speak for a moment. Meredith waited, intrigued. Charleston was a magnificent city, but people were warned to avoid North Charleston, where the crime rate soared. The chance of becoming a victim of violent or property crime there was one in fifteen.

"He got me dried out," Lucky said thickly. "Near three years now." He rolled his eyes toward the Bible on the table. "Says in that Book God forgives people who go wrong. It's taken me some time to see that means all of us." Lucky was looking off into space, perhaps to the small window where the sun settled on the whiskey bottle. "I keep it to remember," he said, as though in a trance. "To remember and never to go back."

He reached for the mug in Meredith's hand and took a long drink of water. "Mr. Geoffrey said he owns this house, and he let me stay here." He drew a deep breath, then struggled through a cough. "He asked me to watch over his place." He shook his head and looked at Meredith with sorrowful eyes. "I wonder what's going to happen now that Mr. Geoffrey's gone?"

Stunned by what she was hearing, Meredith didn't know how to respond. "We—really don't know," she began haltingly. "The historical society is hoping to see the property rebuilt, but—"

"I love this place—this old cabin and Mr. Geoffrey's land," Lucky broke in. His eyes seemed relit from within. "I take good care of it. At least until last night." The light left his eyes.

"You were sick. And besides, no real harm was done. The police saw to that." Of course, Meredith didn't know what had happened, what the intruder might have taken—if there was anything to take in the broken-down place. But Lucky would have stopped it if he could. "Mr. Geoffrey would understand."

"I've been on my own since I was ten. Can't hardly remember a home. But this place—" He wagged his head slowly. "Somethin' about this place just seems like home. Like I belong here."

"What's the last place you remember?" Meredith asked. "Was it here in Savannah?"

"A little place in Alabama—Jones—where my mother's people were. Don't remember my mama, and my daddy was killed when I was a boy. Never was one to back down when his people were hurting. Uncle Thaddeus had a little ole farm. I was sent there but left as quick as I could—" He stopped and closed his eyes tight, like he was trying to shut out the images coming to mind.

Meredith's heart ached over lost life, lost opportunity, lost love. She looked down at the man on the bed. "Lucky." The irony of the man's nickname washed over her.

Lucky was shaking his head again. "I've been a bitter man. Had a hard time forgiving a lot of what I've seen." He laid one hand on his chest, but an inner light seemed to shine in his face. "But there's something rising in me now. Something I can't explain. 'Cause I've been forgiven."

Thank God! The tears tugging at the corners of Meredith's eyes slipped down her cheeks. Lucky had been touched by grace—God's unmerited favor. Nothing was more important than that. Not pride or a centuries-old piece of property, not land disputes, not economic advancement. Maybe "Lucky" wasn't such a bad name. She laid her hand over his.

"I think you're more than Lucky," she said gently. "But that must be a nickname, isn't it? What's your real name, Lucky?"

He closed his eyes, pressed his lips together briefly before answering. "My name is Luke. Luke Benjamin—after my daddy." He closed his eyes and opened them slowly. "Luke Benjamin Clement."

Chapter Eighteen

LOUVENIA PULLED BACK THE CURTAIN in Delyse's living room—the curtain that had remained closed for so many months. She knew she had to go home. Not so much to face the past but to find some answers. Questions and regrets had plagued her in the past few days. Questions and regrets that grew bigger and stronger than her fear of some unknown danger. But first she needed to finish reading to Delyse.

She slipped into the nursing center, carrying her past with its final pages in her shoulder bag. Would Delyse know her today? Would she ask her to read? What was left unread were the heaviest, darkest, scariest words of all.

She didn't bother signing in. She was like a fixture in this place, and the aides were happy that she helped with her friend's care. She made her way to Delyse's room and stopped at the threshold when she saw that Delyse wasn't alone. A man was standing beside her bed.

Louvenia thought it must be her grandson who, though he paid for her private care, never had time to visit. But this man was white, with dark hair. Silver flecks gleamed in the sunshine pouring through the window. She saw his tall back, his expensive suit, and good shoes. *Maybe it's a doctor,* she thought, *but one I don't remember seeing before.* How would she know? The doctors came and went, made the obligatory check of vital signs, and consulted the computerized chart at the nurses' station. Every one of them looked too young to be practicing, though this one looked to be in his fifties.

She went quietly back to the front desk, not wanting to be seen. She smiled at the receptionist and slipped into the recessed coffee room to wait until she was sure he was gone.

When he finally left, Louvenia returned to Delyse's room. Her friend's hands were folded over the blanket, but her eyes, more gray than brown, were focused on the ceiling. Her hair was wrapped in a red turban, and someone had affixed hoop earrings to the edges of the bright wrap rather than to her delicate lobes.

"Good morning," Louvenia greeted her. "I bet that doctor says you're too young to be in this place."

Delyse gave her a stern look. "You're late, and we got to sort through all these duplicates today. I know there's twelve copies of Homer's *Odyssey*, and we haven't checked one out in six months."

"The library's closed today," Louvenia said, realizing her friend was not here in bed but sorting through books like she used to. "But don't worry," she added. "I'll get right on it tomorrow." She smoothed Delyse's dry forehead and clasped her hand. "Can I get you a drink? Coffee? Ginger ale?"

Delyse said nothing for a full thirty seconds, and Louvenia was beginning to think she may have fallen asleep, but then she opened her eyes and fixed them on the tapestry bag Louvenia had placed on the chair by her bed. Her voice was deep but insistent—a statement, not a question. "You gonna read to me now."

Louvenia's fingers shook as she lifted out the notebook. All day the day before, she'd heard Granny Luv in her mind as she pondered her next steps: "When you can't stand no more, kneel." Her heart bowed as her eyes fell to the final yellowed pages—the darkest, most painful of her memories.

July 13, 1956

Summer is growing old, weary. The fields are brown from the wicked sun beating down on them. Workers wear themselves out with the weeding and watering and hoeing as they pull the beans and peas and potatoes from the ground. Soon they will harvest the corn, and the fields will get to looking like sticks poking up like flags of surrender. I peer through the trees in the old summerhouse and see how things are changing. I'm changing too, growing old like the season. And I feel all quivery. Like something is going to happen. Everything's got to change, and I will change too. And I wonder if I will like what I turn into.

It's Friday. Harriet and I have planned to go riding. Granny Luv is already at work in the big house. She left me my chores to do. But Clementine said it's too beautiful a morning to dust and polish. She winks at me over Luke's chubby head and tells me to go on, to find a four-leaf clover for her. The sickness seems to have lost its hold on her, but I worry it's only hiding, ready to jump out and attack again.

I'm sketching Bella's mane with my ochre-colored pencil when I hear Harriet's footsteps. She slips under the gate and through the dense Skip Laurel bushes with a bundle under her arm. Probably her clothes for riding. A bunch of wrinkles sit on her forehead like ripples in a creek when the wind passes over it. And I'm suddenly wary.

"Hey," I say and put my pencil down on the scarred log. "You all right?"

She sits down beside me, stretching her bad leg out straight, and sighs. "Auntie Melia's been on the warpath ever since yesterday. Says it's long past time the house had a thorough scrubbing. Mama's room first, then mine. She inspected every inch and made me pull out every drawer."

"You think she was looking for that paper?" I ask.

"Of course, but I didn't let on I know anything. And she's too scared to ask Papa, to let him know what she saw. She made your granny empty her purse too."

I cringe, hating Granny Luv being shamed that way.

Harriet's eyes go wide suddenly. "You still got it, don't you? You didn't tell?"

"No!" I say. "It's safe." And my eyes go to the ground under the magnolia tree.

Harriet heaves another sigh, and then she notices my drawing. "That's really good," she says, and I swell with pride that she thinks so. She suddenly sits up straighter. "Let's go find Bella. I can't wait to ride today." She snugs her bundle under her arm, and we head for the stable.

It's quiet in the horse barn. Nobody around but Benny, who's filling the feed troughs. I notice he looks tired and remember that he didn't come home until late last night. Another meeting of "the brothers"? Or is he worried about Bob Henry Biggs, who ain't been around since Mister Geoffrey caught him with the pamphlet? I shiver and swallow a lump in my throat bigger than a pawpaw.

"Beautiful day for a ride," Benny says with a wink. He glances around, and I see the twitch in his temples. Big Bee and Little Bee have gone off somewhere, and I'm right happy about that. Benny drops a bucket on the floor and leans against one of the stalls. "Now, you take the double-loop trail but keep steady on the path, and don't go too far. Those rocky glens past the river can be dangerous."

Benny goes off to find Polly among the horses reserved for black riders only. I like to watch his strong shoulders roll when he walks. "I'll have 'em tacked and hitched behind the barn for you," he says, glancing back.

"Okay," I say, and follow Harriet up into the loft where she always puts on her shirt and jodhpurs. It takes her a while to get her fancy dress off and switch her shiny black shoes for boots. I hear something as I wait, and when I look down, a figure flashes around the corner of the stalls. I shrug and hope no one spoils our plans for a ride.

When she's ready we climb down and head for the horses. Bella stands patiently in the late summer sun, pointed ears erect, her mane golden silk. Polly turns her shaggy head and switches her wispy gray tail to greet me, and I feel bad for thinking she's old and clumsy—not beautiful like Bella.

I stroke Bella's soft mane, and Harriet cocks her head, watching me. "Looks just like your picture." She has a gleam in her blue eyes like she's just thought of something. "You like Bella a lot, don't you?"

I nod. "Prettiest horse I ever saw."

Surprising me, Harriet grabs the pommel on Polly's saddle and swings herself up. "Let's switch today," she says. "I'll ride Polly, and you ride Bella."

I stare at her. "We can't... Your papa... Mister Geoffrey..." I stammer.

"They're not here," Harriet says, frowning. "Bella's my horse, and I want my best friend to ride her." She sticks out her chin in that stubborn way she has. "You're going to ride Bella. Because I say so."

I cringe and look around, but we're alone. I feel my heart racing because I can hardly believe my good luck. "You sure?"

"Go on," Harriet urges. "I'll race you." And before I can mount, she's off and racing toward the double-loop trail.

I love the way the sun sits on my shoulders and how the wind hits my face. Bella flies, tossing her mane, and I imagine myself a grand princess or, better yet, Annie Oakley, who could ride standing up and shoot targets at the same time.

I easily catch up to Harriet, and we ride side by side where the trail is broad and even. We talk about all the things we see—Indian paintbrush that glows in fields green as emeralds. The lazy blue creek snakes along the trail heading toward the river that we will come to soon. Up and down we go along the winding trail, and I feel my stomach flip over with excitement.

Bella's gait is smooth as butter, but I notice that Polly is kicking out her back feet and switching her tail like she's nervous or uncomfortable. Harriet talks soothingly, but she's having a struggle with the reins. Harriet's a good rider, even with her bad leg. She says her daddy taught her from the time she was five years old.

"Is she always skittish like this?" Harriet asks, pulling back on Polly's reins as the horse wriggles and squirms.

"No," I say. "Maybe she's picked up a stone or something." We draw up under some shade trees. Polly doesn't balk when I check her hooves and nickers softly, remembering my touch. "Her feet look fine," I say. I'm afraid Harriet's gonna ask to switch back to Bella, but I'm crossing my fingers and toes hoping she won't. I feel so strong on Bella's back. Like I could do anything, be anyone!

Harriet just shrugs, and we mount up again. She lands hard on Polly's back as she swings her bad leg over the pommel. Polly whinnies in protest but takes off with a jerk when Harriet nudges her flank.

"Hey, wait!" I yell. Because Polly breaks into a gallop, kicking up her feet, knocking Harriet back in the saddle. The trail has narrowed, and there are rocky valleys on each side now. "Slow down!" I yell. But it's useless. Polly's bucking and jerking like a jack-in-the-box that's just been sprung.

I push Bella to go faster, yelling at Harriet. But Polly's like a wildcat. Just when I round the curve, I see Harriet fly one way and the saddle fly the other. She hits the ground but bounces over the edge into a rocky valley below the trail. I rein Bella hard, climb out of the saddle, and scoot gingerly down the hill.

Harriet isn't moving. Her legs are splayed out on the ground. Her head is couched on a boulder, her eyes closed, *like she's fallen asleep on a pillow. Her yellow hair flares out from her still, bloodless face.* "Harriet!" *I scream and drop down beside her.*

Again and again I cry her name and tell her to wake up. But she doesn't move—not the tiniest bit. I shout for help, but there is only wilderness, the brilliant sky, and Polly galloping away. I scramble up the hill and run to Bella where she's munching on grass by the side of the trail.

Harriet! Oh, Harriet, my heart roars. What have I done? Just because I wanted to ride your beautiful horse and give you Polly in exchange! I dig my feet into Bella's sides, haunted by Harriet's marble-like face, her poor hurt leg angled against a rock. I make Bella fly like a crazed bat back to the plantation. Back to get help! Oh, Harriet! Dear, gentle Harriet!

There are men around the corral when I get there. I'm gasping and sobbing. I hear myself screaming, see eyes stare like I'm some crazy person. Benny is there and Big Bee— Mister Besset—who appears to be offering some of his prized stallions for breeding to men who slap their hats against their thighs in the afternoon heat.

Mister Besset's eyes flash and burn into mine. "What is this? What are you doing on that horse?"

I get down as he yanks the bridle, and I blurt out my story. Benny rushes to me, arms out, eyes dark, bulging circles. The men clustered around Mister Besset stop my brother from getting to me. I forget exactly what happened next, except that I was lifted onto a saddle, ordered to show them the place where the terrible thing happened.

When we get there, I feel my breath stop in my chest. Harriet is gone. We find the scuffed spot on the trail, the rocky slide, and the boulder where Harriet's head landed. I stare at the blood on the rock. One of the men points to Polly's saddle on the ground several yards away.

But there is no sign of Harriet.

A storm of words. Questions. Accusations. It seems to go on for hours before the order comes. One of the men will take me back to the plantation and call the sheriff. Others will spread out, comb the prairie to look for Harriet.

Did she wake up and wander away? Did someone find her and take her to a hospital? Or did something even more terrible happen? I think of Waylon Jute's anger the day we saw him in the woods. I think of Miss Persimmon wanting to be the mistress of the house and knowing Harriet is the one Mister Besset has chosen to inherit his fortune.

Something in me knows they won't find Harriet. I'm haunted by her still body, the way her chest didn't move at all. Somehow I know she was dead when I scrambled back up the hill to ride Bella for help. But where is she?

Much later I'm at home in my bed. Granny Luv is wiping my face and soothing me with her hushed words that sound like praying. I can't stop shaking, can't stop seeing Mister B's eyes like red-hot coals boring into me. Blaming me. And me blaming myself. I want to see Harriet pressing her lips in concentration over Jo's antics in Little Women. I want to hear her *laugh when Luke slurps noisily on his bottle and tugs at my hair. I want her to take my hand and tell me again that I'm her best friend in the whole wide world.*

When Mister Geoffrey gets back from Charleston, where his daddy had sent him, he falls to his knees at the news. And then he screams and cries like a wild animal. He rages at Benny, at me, and it takes four men to hold him back with strong arms. The police seem to be everywhere, asking questions, looking for clues, some hint to help them find the missing daughter of Charles Besset.

Benny returns after hours spent at the police station. He and Clementine sit in the living room in the dark, their faces grim and set. We know that none of us will return to the Besset plantation—ever. Mister Besset has made it clear.

In the days that follow, the accusing looks are everywhere. Then rotten vegetables are thrown into our little yard. Loud voices pierce the walls of our house. Someone tosses a rock through the window close to Luke's crib.

Even after they stopped searching, the threats continued. So did Granny Luv's praying. She prayed for Sarah Jean. "Who's gonna look after her now?" She prayed for us and for the angry men who wanted to frighten us away.

In the end, we knew there was no other way. In the dead of a September night, we packed up a few small bundles and left the plantation.

Benny and Clementine and Luke would go to Clementine's parents in Alabama. Granny Luv and I would escape to her cousin Noma, to a place she knew where we would be safe.

But I knew I'd never be safe from my fear. Not just the fear of Harriet's daddy but of Mister Geoffrey, who threatened to pay me back for what happened to his little sister. "Wherever you go, I'll find you!"

Louvenia looked up from the notebook. She'd come to the last page, smudged where her useless tears had fallen all those years ago.

Seeing Delyse with wide eyes fixed on her shocked her back to the current reality. *I'm an old woman, who still doesn't know what happened that dreadful July day so many years ago.*

Delyse's thick hair restrained by the red turban made Louvenia think of blood on a boulder. Her eyes were clear, brighter than Louvenia had ever seen them, and they locked on her with magnetic fierceness. "You been runnin' since that day?" she asked.

"I suppose I have," Louvenia whispered. The memories couldn't hurt her anymore, and she'd kept her family safe from the vengeance of the past. Safe from the man who couldn't forget. His pain was buried now. And Louvenia's pain? She looked down at Delyse in the bed and knew that she would lose her soon—as she had lost Harriet.

"I am sorry," Delyse said softly. Louvenia knew that Delyse was fully present—in the moment. No disease veiled her mind. She touched her old friend's hand, wanting to tell her that she'd been a good friend.

But Delyse spoke before she could get the words out. "That man who was here—" She left a gap so long Louvenia wondered if the curtain of her mind had dropped down again.

"You mean that doctor who was here a little while ago?" Louvenia stroked her hand gently.

Her eyes fluttered open and focused with unusual clarity. "I didn't tell him. He thinks I'm out of my mind."

Louvenia stared at her, not comprehending, but suddenly alert in every fiber.

Delyse's voice was strong. "That man was no doctor. He was looking for you, Maggie Lu. But I didn't tell him. I didn't tell him!"

Chapter Nineteen

"I HAD AN AUNT—MY daddy's sister." The words resounded in Meredith's consciousness. Lucky was Luke Benjamin Clement! It had to be the same man Charlene had told them about—the cousin who'd "taken to drinking" and been lost to her and her missing mother.

Meredith stared across the desk at Julia, excitement building. "Lucky's father was killed when he was a boy. Charlene said her uncle, who was Lucky's father, was killed for registering black voters. It all fits."

"It's incredible—too strange to be true," Julia said, leaning forward and clasping her hands. Their searches had concurred that Benjamin Clement had married Clementine Jefferson, and the couple had one son, Luke Benjamin.

"We have to tell Charlene right away," Meredith said, looking across at Julia. Could she have imagined she had a cousin living right here in Savannah and that he had risen from the grip of alcohol addiction?

"Sadly, Lucky can't tell us how to find her mother." Julia crossed her arms over her chest and wagged her head slowly from side to side. "It's remarkable to find this connection to Charlene's case while working on the Besset mystery for the historical society."

"Mm," Meredith said with a sigh. She'd been thinking along the same lines. They'd learned nothing to explain what happened in 1956 to Harriet Besset, whose possessions they thought were in the safe at their agency. And someone—very possibly Langston Butler—was actively working to take over the antebellum mansion.

Julia looked at her watch. "We still have some time before lunch. How about we hit the library and see if we can find out anything?"

Meredith groaned. "We can try. Why would they talk to us if they wouldn't talk to Charlene?"

Julia stood up. "Because we're professionals and we know what we're doing, that's why." She grinned. "That's my story, and I'm stickin' to it."

Meredith laughed. "Lead the way, Miss Marple."

"Not technically a professional, but I'll take it," said Julia.

They bantered their way out to Julia's car. While Julia drove, Meredith called Charlene and caught her up on the news that they had discovered her cousin. Charlene was thrilled, of course, but nothing was going to truly satisfy her until her mother was found. A few minutes after Meredith hung up, Julia parked on the street a few yards down from the beautiful old library.

Julia exited the car and approached the library, but stopped as she reached the building's historical marker. "This has got to be a trip down memory lane for you, Meredith," she said. "How long has this marker been here?"

Meredith caught up to her. "The Georgia Historical Society put it up about five years ago," she said. "Our society hosted the reception. We were so glad this site finally got the recognition it deserves in Georgia history. It is, after all, the oldest public library in Georgia."

They went up the steps, pulled open the dark green double doors, and entered the hushed atmosphere. Meredith took a deep breath. She wished she had several hours to settle in, relax, browse, discover. But duty called. And so did Julia.

"There's someone we can ask," she said, pointing to a woman who looked to be about their age rolling a shelving cart. Julia walked briskly toward her. "Excuse me," she said, "we were wondering if you could answer a couple of questions for us."

The woman, whose name tag said her name was Rebecca Thompson, looked up and smiled. "I'm happy to help you if I can," she said.

Meredith took out a business card and handed it to her. "My name is Meredith Bellefontaine, and this is Julia Foley. We're look-ing for a woman who used to volunteer here about three years ago—Louvenia King. Do you remember her?"

Rebecca smiled even broader. "I sure do. She was a gem. All our patrons just loved her."

Julia opened her bag and pulled out a small notepad and a pen. "We're wondering if you could tell us where or how we could get in touch with her." She tapped her notepad with the pen. "A phone number, an address, anything that could help?"

Rebecca was shaking her head before Julia stopped speaking. "I'm sorry. We aren't allowed to give out that information, even if we had it. Our policy forbids it."

Even though this was what Meredith had expected, she was still keenly disappointed that they'd hit another dead end. "We appreciate your time," she said to Rebecca. "Please keep our card and call us if anything turns up that you're able to share that might help us."

Rebecca nodded. "I can do that," she said. "Please come back anytime." She held up the card. "In your line of work, you probably do a lot of research. No better place than a library." She grinned. "And no better library than ours."

Meredith laughed. "We'll keep that in mind, I promise you." She waved. "Thanks again."

As Rebecca moved off with her cart, Julia put her notepad and pen back in her shoulder bag. "Oh well. We knew it was a long shot."

"That we did," said Meredith. "Let's go."

"Wait," said Julia. "I'm gonna find the restroom. I'll be right back."

Meredith perused the New Fiction rack while she waited. In a few minutes, an excited Julia appeared at her side.

"Meredith," Julia puffed, obviously having rushed to get to her, "come look at what I found. You won't believe it."

Meredith let Julia pull her down a hallway that led to some conference rooms and the restrooms. Julia stopped halfway down the hall and turned Meredith so that she was looking at a series of photographs that lined one wall. "What do you see?" she asked.

Meredith quickly found the plaque underneath the row that united all the pictures. HALL OF FAME VOLUNTEERS it said in shiny brass. The fine print informed her that a volunteer made it into the Hall of Fame when they'd reached their tenth year of service. Her eyes swept the pictures, finally landing on a familiar face. The brass plate under the picture said LOUVENIA KING.

Meredith frowned. "Okay. I see a picture of Louvenia. She was a volunteer here. What does that tell us we didn't know before?"

Julia clapped her hands together. "Keep looking, keep looking."

Meredith slowed down, started at one end, and studied each photograph. A woman, maybe in her fifties, with a beautiful smile. Another woman, with wire-rimmed glasses and big blue eyes. A man, maybe in his forties, with a very loud tie. Two more women, an elderly woman with a brightly colored turban, the other, younger, with impeccable makeup. Then Louvenia, then three more women, all with big smiles.

"Okay, I've looked," said Meredith. She turned to Julia and shrugged. "What am I missing?"

Julia bounced on her toes. "Remember what Charlene said? Her mother left to take care of a sick friend. A friend she met at the library. A *Jamaican* friend. What if she met her at the library because they volunteered together?"

Meredith jerked her eyes back to the pictures on the wall. A woman in a turban… There she was. And underneath the picture there was a small brass plate with a name.

Chapter Twenty

MEREDITH AND JULIA DISCUSSED THEIR find back in Julia's office over sandwiches they picked up from a local deli. Julia tapped her pen on a notepad by her telephone. "So we have a name."

"We do," said Meredith. She was running Delyse's name through a search engine to find her address. "Bingo. It's a little ways from here. You up for a ride?"

Julia gathered the wrappings from their sandwiches and threw them in the trash can. "I think I'll stay here and let you handle it. I've got some paperwork to finish up for my certification for the agency."

Meredith spent the thirty-minute drive to Delyse's house thinking about the twists and turns of the two cases they were working on, and how they dovetailed into each other. She prayed that Delyse Watson would be the key to finding Louvenia King and that they could get a clue somewhere soon about Harriet's disappearance.

She strained to see house numbers as she drove slowly down the street. About halfway down the third block she found the address. She parked the car at the curb, got a business card out of her bag before shouldering it, and made her way up the sidewalk. It was a small house, not more than two bedrooms, surely. She walked up the few steps to a tiny porch and rang the doorbell. Not hearing it echo inside, she tentatively knocked on the door.

There was no answer, so she rang again, then knocked again. Suddenly she heard a voice at her elbow, and she jumped. "Are you looking for Miss Delyse?"

Meredith whirled around to see a little girl, she would guess about eight years old, who was looking at her quizzically. "I am," she said to her. "Do you know if she's home?"

"She's not home," said the child, pulling at one of her beaded braids. "Me and my mom, we take a walk sometimes to go see her at the nursing home, just down that way." She pointed over her shoulder. "She doesn't always know me, but she's always really nice. We're gonna go again tomorrow, my mom says."

"I think that's wonderful, that you can go see your friend," Meredith said with a smile. "I'll go see her right now, and I can tell her you'll come tomorrow. Should I do that?"

"Oh yes," said the girl, her eyes lighting up. "Tell her Lily will come see her soon."

"I'll do that," promised Meredith as she waved goodbye and went back to her car.

As soon as she was settled in the driver's seat, Meredith pulled out her phone and typed in "nursing homes near me." Only one was within a mile of where she sat, and she figured that must be it.

It was tempting to rush over there, find Delyse, and find the answers they'd been looking for, but she had to consider her client. She knew without asking that Charlene would want to be the one to ask Delyse questions about her mom.

She called the Downhome Diner and asked for Charlene. In just a minute, she heard Charlene's voice. "Hello? This is Charlene."

"Hi, Charlene, it's Meredith. I have some good news for you—it looks like we've found your mother's Jamaican friend. Do you think you could get away for a couple of hours so you could come see her with me?"

Charlene's voice was trembling as she said, "I'll make the time. Where do I need to go?"

Meredith gave her the address of the nursing home and told her she'd meet her there. After they said goodbye and Meredith hung up, it occurred to her—what if Lily was wrong? What if Delyse Watson wasn't the right Jamaican friend? What if she was not the one Louvenia left to take care of?

In the middle of her doubts and questions her phone rang. Her pulse jumped at the name on the screen. "Quin?" she asked hesitantly.

"Just checking in," came the mellow voice that reminded her of water flowing over smooth rock. "Anything new on the Besset plantation?"

When she didn't immediately respond, he laughed softly. "And how are you? Which is what I really want to know."

"Fine," she said, slightly breathless. "I'm on my way to meet a client. Not our client. I mean—" She floundered, realizing they didn't have a mutual client. "But I did want to talk to you—"

"You did?" he asked, cutting off the rest of her sentence.

She felt a warm flush rising. "About the break-in at the plantation. Did you hear about it?"

The tone in his voice turned from playful to serious. "No, I didn't. At the mansion?"

"Someone must have used a crowbar or something like it to break the panel on the door." She went on to explain briefly that Lucky had been ill and hadn't noticed an intruder.

"Are you all right?"

"Of course," she said. "Julia and I heard about it and went looking for Lucky, who, by the way, turns out to have known Geoffrey Besset." For an instant she considered telling him about how Lucky's real name was Luke, and about Louvenia and Charlene, and even Harriet, but just as quickly dismissed the idea. Her clients trusted her to keep their cases confidential, no matter how intriguing a certain lawyer happened to be. "Geoffrey helped him stop drinking and gave him that cabin down the road from the plantation."

"Wow," Quin said at length and was quiet, perhaps absorbing the information. "Geoffrey Besset was full of surprises." He paused briefly before continuing. "I thought you'd be interested to know. Word on the street is that there's an outstanding warrant on Butler in Louisiana. For fraud."

"What does that mean for his case?" asked Meredith.

"I think it means he won't have undivided attention on the Besset Plantation right now," Quin said.

Meredith checked her rearview mirror. A dark sedan pulled away from the curb about a block down. The driver gunned the engine and buzzed by her. She had a momentary flutter of nerves as she recalled a similar vehicle idling on her street. "Get a grip, Meredith," she whispered. There had to be thousands of cars in Savannah that looked like that.

"What was that?" asked Quin.

Meredith rolled her eyes at herself. "Nothing," she said. "Just reminding myself I'm not in some second-rate film noir of the forties."

Quin chuckled. "Should I take that personally?"

Meredith laughed along with him. "No, you most definitely shouldn't," she said. "But I appreciate your calling and letting me know about Langston Butler."

"Anytime," said Quin. "I'll be in touch, Meredith."

Meredith felt another flutter, but she was pretty sure this one had nothing to do with dark sedans. "I look forward to hearing from you," she said.

After they hung up, Meredith drove the short distance to Rutger's Nursing Home. She passed the time waiting for Charlene by first calling Julia and catching her up on what was happening, and then spent some time reading Facebook posts.

Charlene pulled up and parked beside her. "Do you think this Delyse Watson will know where my mother is?" she asked as they walked up to the glass double doors. As they stepped into a small vestibule, she added, "I know my mother spoke of her, but I've never met her."

A receptionist signed them in and showed them to a room at the end of the hall. The partially open door revealed a woman who made only a small mound in the bed. Her head, wrapped in a green striped turban, was propped on a white pillow. Her eyes were closed, but her lips gaped slightly open in a smile, as though she enjoyed a pleasant dream.

Meredith indicated that Charlene should go in while she stood just inside the door. She watched Charlene move close to the bed, bend to search the small, wizened face. "Ms. Watson?"

The woman's eyes fluttered open. Her cheeks were sallow, high in a nearly perfect oval face. Meredith thought she must have once been a very attractive woman.

"'Bout time you get here, Louvenia."

Charlene's eyebrows knit together in confusion. Her eyes flashed to Meredith at the door and back to Delyse Watson.

Meredith was just as confused. But more importantly, she was startled by the name "Louvenia" on the old woman's lips.

"Hello," Charlene stuttered. "I—I came to ask you about my mother. About Louvenia Brown King. You volunteered with her at the library, right?"

Delyse's eyes shuttered once more above that same half smile. Had she mistaken Charlene for her mother? They did look a lot alike. Meredith could feel Charlene's anxiety, her barely restrained enthusiasm.

Charlene bent lower. "Can you tell me where she is?"

Delyse's eyes fluttered briefly and closed again. "Sidney behaving himself?" she asked, satisfied expression fixed.

Charlene looked back at Meredith, who had taken a chair to the left of the door. Meredith shrugged, hope sagging that Delyse Watson would be lucid enough to help Charlene.

"He never learned to keep off my divan," Delyse said. "Cats are connoisseurs of comfort, don't you know?"

"Please, I'm looking for my mother," Charlene pressed, clearly agitated. "I know you were friends. I've just got to find her. If you know anything—"

Meredith could tell Charlene was close to tears. She wondered if she should suggest to her that they come back another time. But just as Meredith was about to rise from the chair, she heard footsteps. A tall woman stopped and stood still in the doorway.

She was wearing a light tan dress, belted at the waist, and carried a large fabric bag over one slightly stooped shoulder. Hair not yet completely gray nestled at the base of her neck. She seemed suspended in time, her feet in sensible lace-up shoes planted on the threshold. She trained her eyes on the scene at the bedside and seemed not to notice Meredith. She was a picture of Charlene. Older, an inch or two shorter, but astoundingly like her, regal as an Egyptian princess.

Meredith watched what happened next as though in a slow-motion film reel. Charlene raised her head, saw the woman at the door, and reached toward her with both arms. The woman stepped inside, compelling eyes fixed, and dropped the large bag to the floor.

"I was coming to you today, baby," came the resonant voice. "But here you are, coming to me!" The older woman embraced the younger, rocking her back and forth as though she *were* a baby needing the consolation of its mother.

Questions, half phrases, garbled, passionate. "Are you all right?" "I've missed you so much!" "I'm so sorry." These words of regret were repeated over and over by both women while Delyse watched from her bed, a broad smile spreading over her features.

Meredith thought to step out of the room to allow the reunion the privacy it deserved, but suddenly names on Louvenia's lips sent shock waves rolling through her brain. "Mr. Geoffrey's gone, and I have to trust Harriet to God. Wherever she is, I've got to believe she's at peace. Just like this old woman now!" She patted her own chest. "I know if I don't let the past die, it won't let me live!" Meredith saw her raise her eyes heavenward over Charlene's shoulder in a look of rapture.

Charlene stepped back, confusion clouding her face. Then she seemed to shake herself, as though whatever her mother was babbling about was inconsequential. "Oh, Mama. I can't wait for you to see Clarissa—and meet her husband. They're going to have a baby!"

"Yes, child," her mother said, nodding sagely and taking both Charlene's hands in her own. "I know and I'm so proud. I saw them at the wedding. You know I couldn't stay away."

Charlene shook her head, eyes wide. "I didn't know, but I felt you there. How did you—"

"A mother has her ways. I only wish—" But she broke off, declining to express her regretful wish. "I had to keep you safe, keep you away from him because he couldn't forgive. Couldn't forget."

Charlene cocked her head, once again looking bewildered. Then she seemed to suddenly remember that Meredith was in the room. "Oh!" she exclaimed as she turned around. "This is my friend, Meredith. She's been helping me search for you." She steered her mother back toward the door. "Meredith Bellefontaine."

Mr. Geoffrey? Harriet? Meredith's mind whirled feverishly. She held out a shaky hand. "I'm—so glad to meet you."

Louvenia's face registered shock, but she quickly regained her composure. She looked into Meredith's eyes and took her hand. "I believe I might have met your husband—or at least another searching Bellefontaine—some time ago." She lowered her head. "I've been hiding these years and sorry for it. And for the trouble I put you all to." She turned once more to Charlene. "Especially you and my sweet Clarissa."

Meredith drew in her breath, mind spinning spidery connections in all directions. "How do you know Geoffrey?" She swallowed. "And Harriet?"

"Harriet and I both grew up on Mr. Besset's plantation. My people worked for him, and sometimes I helped my granny there. We were good friends, Harriet and I—until that day." She turned her face away, the deep, pain-filled eyes dark with memory. "But come along. I'll try to explain it to you. We'll go back to the cottage. It's just a short way. I've been hiding there for three years. And I've been walking here most every day to visit Delyse." She squared her shoulders and walked to the bed, where Delyse watched now with what appeared lucid awareness.

A smile spread across her features as Louvenia bent over her. "You goin' home now, ain't yuh?" Delyse asked. "'Bout time. Yuh been wearing me down." But the look in her eyes was tender, knowing.

"Don't think I won't be back right soon." The tall, gracious woman shook a finger close to Delyse Watson's face. She touched her lips to the turbaned forehead. "And you don't worry about Sidney and the cottage. I'll notify that son of yours."

Meredith gathered herself together enough to give Lily's message to Delyse, who nodded and fell asleep smiling.

They rode together in Meredith's car. Louvenia seemed anxious now to tell everything about her past. She spoke rapidly, as though fearing there wouldn't be enough time for the unburdening. She told them about Geoffrey Besset's threat to find her wherever she was, about years of apparent quiet when she was protected by her community, then the reappearance of the vengeful man. When the tenacious detective—Meredith's husband—came around three years ago, intent on finding her—at what she was sure was Geoffrey's behest—she had to distance herself from her family to keep them safe.

Meredith drove, listening with rapt wonder that the case of Charlene's missing mother had all along been linked to the mystery of Harriet Besset. How could Geoffrey be what Louvenia said he was and appear so completely different? What about Luke? What about Rufus, Geoffrey's associate and friend in whose home he'd spent his last days? And what could one make of Toby, the gardener Geoffrey had helped get into college?

Louvenia was holding tightly to Charlene's hand. "Best tell you right now, honey," she said. "I've been Louvenia Brown King since I married your daddy, but my real name is Magnolia Louvenia Clement King. I was always called Maggie Lu by Granny Luv and Benny and Harriet, and I'd like to be called that now." She took a deep breath. "And I loved Harriet like a sister until the day she disappeared."

"Do you know what happened to her?" Meredith couldn't stop herself from asking the direct question.

"That's the worst of my regrets," came the despairing response. "It's all my fault." Maggie Lu seemed to visibly shrink in the seat.

Silence fell as the question burned in Meredith's mind. What had this woman—Louvenia Brown King or Magnolia Louvenia Clement King—done?

"Turn left here," Maggie Lu said, thrusting her hand out to point the way. Meredith decided not to mention that she'd already been to Delyse's house.

For the second time that day she pulled up to the curb in front of the small house. This time, a large yellow cat peered through one window with glowing green eyes. Delyse Watson's home. Here Louvenia—Maggie Lu—had sheltered, hovering in fear of Geoffrey Besset. Or of her own struggling conscience.

"Oh!" A gasp fell from the older woman's lips.

"You have a visitor," Meredith said with surprise, for a man in dark trousers and jacket rounded the corner from the back of the house. He stopped and raised his head—a handsome dark-haired head with a well-tanned face Meredith recognized instantly. Langston Butler!

Chapter Twenty-One

THE TRAPPED SURPRISE ON BUTLER'S face quickly morphed into a self-assured, cocky expression that Meredith thought must suit him. How had he found this place, and what on earth did he think he was doing? She saw him glance furtively at his car parked a few yards away, half visible beyond a bushy mimosa tree. He seemed to gauge the possibility of getting to it without confrontation and realized it was hopeless.

"Were you expecting anyone, Mama?" Charlene asked, opening the rear door of Meredith's car.

Maggie Lu's face blanched as she gripped the door handle. "No! I thought it was all over. I thought—"

Butler was coming toward them with a jaunty step, his smile broad and ingratiating.

Meredith fixed him with a fierce glare. "I suppose you have a good reason for trying to break into this house."

"Ah, Ms. Bellefontaine," he said, his smile fading. "You've got it wrong, I assure you. I didn't break in, though I don't see that it's any of your business." He narrowed his eyes at Maggie Lu, who had gotten out of the car and now stood facing him. "I came to see this lady here," he said. "But when no one answered the door, I merely stepped around back to look for her."

Meredith was at a loss to understand what was going on. How had Butler found Charlene's mother? What did he want with her? She struggled to decide what to do next.

But Maggie Lu took a step closer, squaring her shoulders and jutting her chin out. She was nearly as tall as the man she confronted. "Just what do you want?" she asked, steel in her voice. "And what were you doing pestering my sick friend?"

Meredith saw Butler's face go pale.

"I saw you there yesterday," she accused. "Thought you were one of those doctors come to see about Delyse, but it was you! You best explain yourself. You've got no business coming around here." Her fiery eyes blazed.

Butler held his fists rigid at his sides and the veins in his temples pulsated like miniature jackhammers. "All right. You can drop the act. I know that my father's estate went to that worthless son of his—Mr. Geoffrey Besset." He spat the name as though it tasted bad. "And I know that he wanted to turn it all over to a—a—" He closed his mouth, struggling for control before finishing. "To a hired servant, who once worked for my grandfather. Well, if you think you can cheat me—his own blood kin—out of what's rightfully mine, you'd better think again! You'll be hearing from my lawyer!"

Without another word he turned and strode rapid-fire to his car hidden among the Mimosa branches.

Meredith started after him, but he slammed into his car and roared away.

The three of them stood gazing after the fleeing man until Charlene grasped her mother's arm. "What is he talking about?" Her eyes were wide and frightened.

Maggie Lu held a hand over her mouth. She was shaking her head, clearly at a loss. "He's a crazy man," she said. "Crazy. I don't know what he's talking about." She took a few steps toward the cottage. "I never cheated him out of anything, but if he's tampered with Delyse's things I'll have him drawn and quartered!" She dug in her purse and, after finding the key, unlocked the door and pressed in, Charlene and Meredith behind her.

While the intrepid Maggie Lu searched the small house with the cat traipsing along behind, Meredith sank down on a flowered upholstered chair in amazement. Did Langston Butler discover something? Perhaps when he maneuvered his way into the house in Walterboro where Geoffrey had died? Had he found his will? Clearly, he believed the woman she now knew as Maggie Lu was involved.

"Guess he didn't get in after all," Charlene said, finding Meredith in the front room. "Mama says nothing's out of place."

Meredith swallowed. Her first instinct was to call the police—but if there hadn't really been a break-in, what could the police do? She had to get back to Savannah and work out this new wrinkle in the two cases. The cases that were not two but one.

"Mama wants you to read this," Charlene said, handing her a worn, yellowed notebook. "She says it will answer a lot of questions. I'm taking Mama back with me now, but we'll come by your office later." Charlene's eyes glowed with happiness. "Thank you for everything," she said, clasping Meredith in a sudden hard embrace.

***

Later that afternoon, Meredith and Julia sat in Meredith's office huddled over Magnolia Clement's journal open between them.

Coffee and pastries, which Carmen had prepared, were largely ignored as they absorbed the fascinating story of two young girls growing up in an era marked by racial unrest and injustice.

"The metal box belongs to Maggie Lu, not Harriet," Julia breathed after reading the girls' long-ago adventures. "All those items we found in it—the book and the blue ribbon, the sketch of a horse, the scrap of poetry. It's just amazing."

"When she comes to the office with Charlene, we'll give it to its rightful owner," Meredith said. "What a reunion that will be between her and Luke. God preserved them both through those tempestuous years. It's really a miracle, isn't it?" She felt a shiver engulf her whole body. "But how did the box come into Ron's possession?"

"It had to be Geoffrey, didn't it?" Julia asked. "We know he experienced a huge change in his life. Maybe he found the box after Maggie Lu and the rest of the family were chased off the plantation and scattered. Maybe he was sorry for all the trouble he caused them and for blaming Maggie Lu and her family for his sister's disappearance."

"From what we've learned about his later life, that does seem plausible." Meredith traced circles with her finger on the desk. "And according to Langston Butler, Geoffrey wanted Maggie Lu to inherit his estate."

"How are we ever going to prove that?" Julia asked with exasperation. "We have only Butler's word, and if he's pressed to divulge what he knows, he could simply deny finding anything."

"And continue to press his claim as next of kin," Meredith said, nodding. "He could say that the conversation outside Delyse's house never happened, that he knows nothing of a will—unless Maggie Lu can produce something in black and white."

Julia took a sip of coffee and made a face. "The law is clear on the matter. When a person dies intestate, the next of kin stands to inherit."

Meredith leaned back against the couch she and Julia shared as they reviewed the astonishing journal. "Butler believes Geoffrey's will is out there somewhere," she said, releasing a long breath. "I think he was looking for it when he convinced that eccentric artist to let him remove Geoffrey's personal things. Maybe he found it—or burned it or—"

"Or he hasn't found it yet, and he thinks Maggie Lu has it," Julia said. "If you hadn't arrived when you did, he probably would have ransacked Delyse Watson's house...or worse."

"He's come close to criminal behavior in his efforts. Maybe even crossed the line." Meredith paused, recalling the black sedan at Charlene's and at her own house the day Carter and his family came to visit. And just that day when she was outside Delyse's house. In each case, it could have been the same car and the same driver— Langston Butler. Had he been following her since the day she and Julia had gone to see him?

Meredith closed the fragile journal and laid her hand on top of it gently. "But we still don't know what happened to Harriet after Maggie Lu left her to get help," she said.

Carmen knocked on Meredith's half-open office door and stepped in hesitantly. "Charlene is here with her mother. Anything I can get for you?" she asked.

"Would you please bring that metal box from the safe?" Meredith asked. "Oh, and thanks for the coffee."

"*De nada*," she answered, giving her black hair a toss over her shoulder. "I'll bring some coffee and pastries for your clients. Maybe they will be hungry."

"*Bueno*," Julia said, grinning.

Maggie Lu stepped in wearing a dark green dress with small white polka dots. Her hair had been brushed and refashioned at the nape of her elegant neck that was much like her daughter's.

Charlene too had changed her clothes and was wearing a white linen dress. She held her mother's arm companionably—though a bit too closely, as though to make sure she didn't disappear again. "Mama likes the Downhome Diner," Charlene said proudly. "Without her I would never have had the courage to—"

A gasp from Maggie Lu halted Charlene's praise of her mother's generosity. "Oh!" She faltered, causing Charlene to grasp her arm more firmly. Carmen had come in the room holding the box, and Maggie Lu was now staring at it, one hand on her chest. Carmen put it down in the center of the coffee table. "Where did you—? I never thought I'd ever see—"

"Please sit down," Meredith said, indicating the chair directly in front of the box. "We thought this might belong to Harriet Besset, but now we know it must be yours."

Maggie Lu's fingers trembled as she touched the box and began caressing the dents in its hammered surface. She turned the key set in the lock and with a shaking hand lifted the lid.

Everyone sat in silence, giving Maggie Lu her private moments with her long-ago treasures. They watched as she pressed aside dry pinecones and seeds and lifted out the faded blue ribbon that

Meredith assumed was the same one Harriet had placed around Maggie Lu's wiry curls the day they had met at Harriet's birthday party. She cupped her fingers around the plastic balls that formed the clown rattle. Tears tracked down her wrinkled cheeks, and no one moved as Carmen quietly placed cups of coffee and another plate of pastries on the table.

"My own Luke," she whispered. "Law, how I loved that baby, and God has brought him home."

"Yes, Mama," Charlene said softly. "We will see him tomorrow."

Maggie Lu traced her fingers slowly, almost reverently, over the faded copy of *Little Women*. "It was Harriet's favorite," she whispered. "Mine too." Her tears flowed unabated.

What happened to Harriet? Meredith wanted to shout the question that hung in the air. The last chapter of Maggie Lu's journal had ended without an answer. Maggie Lu had been swept away from the rocky valley where she had left Harriet. But who had moved the body? The greedy Aunt Amelia who coveted her brother-in-law's possessions? Waylon Jute, the boy they'd read about in Maggie Lu's journal? Geoffrey himself? But he had seemed to cherish and protect his little sister and vowed to avenge her. Was Maggie Lu herself guilty? *"Oh, my poor Harriet! I am so sorry,"* she had written in her journal. But hadn't she run away, fearing to be discovered? Had she merely pretended to be hounded by Geoffrey all these years?

Maggie Lu put the scrap of paper with her little-girl poem close to her face. The words formed on her lips, but no sound came out. *Is that You God...high in the sky... Or do You hide from me still...* She set it down on the table with the other items she had withdrawn from the box. Finally, she picked up the sketch of the golden horse called Bella, stared, then dropped it as though it were too hot to hold. She shook her head over and over.

Meredith recalled the story of the girls' decision to switch horses for the ride and then the tragic accident.

"It wasn't your fault, Mama," Charlene assured her, leaning in close to Maggie Lu's bowed head.

A long silence ensued until Maggie Lu raised a tearful face to Meredith and cleared her throat. "Do you have a letter opener?" she asked quietly. "Or a knife?"

Julia went to the desk to retrieve the opener. Meredith said nothing but watched as Maggie Lu pressed the blade along the four inner sides of the box. She pried with considerable strength, despite the trembling of her hands. And when suddenly the bottom sprang up like a jack-in-the-box, Meredith felt her breath stop in her throat.

A false bottom. Maggie Lu's treasure box had a hidden compartment! Meredith recalled the story of Harriet's finding the will her father had left in his wife's mattress. The document Harriet had asked Maggie Lu to hide. She must have hidden it in the box.

Maggie Lu picked up the inch-high packet with her shaking fingers, but instead of opening it, she handed it to Meredith.

"Is this what Harriet wanted you to hide?" she asked, carefully unfolding the pages that comprised the packet. It had been so sad to read about Sarah Jean Besset, how Harriet had bravely tried to fend off death by removing her father's little-understood document from her mother's room. Obviously Sarah Jean had succumbed to her illness—records confirmed it. And then Charles had remarried—foolishly perhaps, since he annulled the union so quickly. His legacy had then gone to his son, Geoffrey. Meredith looked down at the pages in her hand. They were too crisp and white to be old, certainly not sixty-five years old.

Maggie Lu closed her eyes and, head bowed, seemed to brace herself for whatever was to come. "Please," she whispered, beseeching Meredith. "Read it."

"'Dear Magnolia Clement.'"

Shock sprang to Maggie Lu's face. "That isn't—" She pressed toward Meredith and peered down on the page. "That isn't the document I put there!"

Meredith drew a breath, and read on.

"'If you are reading this, it must be that the items inside this box have been returned to you. What I cannot give you are the years of regret and trouble I have caused you and your family. I blamed you for the losses that fell to me and tried to punish you for something that was my fault. Only mine. For you see, I was responsible for what happened to my sister—your friend.'"

Meredith heard a gasp in the stunned silence of the room as she continued to read the astonishing letter, a letter Geoffrey had obviously planted in the false bottom of Maggie Lu's box of treasures.

"'In my blindness and bitterness, I hated your friendship with my sister. I blamed every one of your race, using as excuse the tragedy that befell her and my mother at the hands of cruel men. Not knowing that my sister would trade horses with you for that fateful ride all those years ago, I placed burrs beneath old Polly's saddle pad. I wanted to scare you, to punish you, but it was Harriet who got thrown into the ravine and died.

"'Yes, I found her. I buried her outside the summerhouse where you used to meet my little sister. The old magnolia tree wept over her as my heart bled. As yours bleeds. The shame of my actions broke me. I could make a success of nothing. I hated my life—until grace dawned in my heart and drove me to my knees.

"'My efforts to find you have been unsuccessful—perhaps until this moment. No doubt, the kind detective who pledged to find you has kept his promise, and you now hold the memories of your life with gentle Harriet. No apology is sufficient for the gravity of my past wrongs, but I give it to you with a humble and penitent heart. You will see by the attached that I leave to you the plantation which you and your family served so nobly amid the destruction of my disdain and resentment.

"'I have nothing more to give except a prayer that God will keep you safe and restore to you the "years the locusts have eaten." In sincere regard, Geoffrey Besset.'"

Wordlessly, wonderingly, Meredith placed the letter into Maggie Lu's hands that lay open in her lap. Maggie Lu's voice shook as she said, "Mr. Geoffrey must have found my box when he buried Harriet."

"Oh, Mama!" Charlene whispered, her tears matching those that fell down Maggie Lu's cheeks. "I'm so sorry. All these years we never knew… We couldn't have guessed…" She embraced her mother in the hushed office that had become a sanctuary.

Meredith felt a rising sense of awe. Maggie Lu believed her former enemy continued to pursue her to do her harm, while he was seeking atonement for his sin. How could she have known of Geoffrey's change of heart, of the transformation that had taken place that lifted him from revenge to redemption? Each had been rising, and they converged through a divine embrace that nothing could diminish.

Chapter Twenty-Two

Two days later Meredith sat at supper with Julia at the Down-home Diner. Most of the business crowd had left the district, so there were just a few scattered diners. The windows were open, and she could smell the sweet fragrance of flowers.

"I can't believe our first case is solved," Julia said. She shook her head and a silky swatch of silver hair grazed her eyebrow. "And we survived." She was quiet for a while, and then she said, "But can you believe the stamina of Charlene's mama at age seventy-five?"

"Mm," Meredith acknowledged, feeling somewhat drowsy with the scent of wisteria. "I can only hope for half her energy when I reach her age." Charlene had taken her mother to spend a few days with Clarissa and her husband. Maggie Lu was making up for lost time, eager to embrace her granddaughter.

"Maggie Lu is amazing," Meredith said, drawing a deep, satisfying breath. "Especially when you know what she's been through over the years—taking her grandmother's name and earning her degree—teaching all those years while raising a family."

"She's overcome so much pain and loss," Julia added, "all the while keeping her secret—and Geoffrey's. You know, I think she suspected all along that Geoffrey had found Harriet. But could she have imagined him burying that poor child? I'm not sure what will be done, now that the truth is out. But I think about the awful guilt and terror Geoffrey must have experienced. He was really just a boy when he dug the grave. It's no wonder that the man became a virtual hermit."

"Until God broke through," Meredith said, feeling a deep sense of wonder. All those years gone by, He honored the prayers of Maggie Lu's grandmother—the "prayin'est woman in the county"—and tenderly watched over the little family.

"He's done quite brilliantly for two fledgling private investigators as well," Julia said, flashing her gray eyes upward. "Could we have imagined when we took on Charlene's case that finding her mother would mean solving Besset Plantation's sixty-five-year-old mystery?"

"Amazing," Meredith said, aware that the word *amazing* had sprung from her lips frequently in recent days. It was satisfying too that she had been able to fulfill a promise her husband had made to Magnolia. Somehow, it sealed the little crack left open in her trust that she could succeed in the course she'd undertaken at God's direction.

"All those naysayers who questioned our sanity," Julia said. "They'll have to eat their words now that we've solved a mystery that's baffled Savannah for decades."

Meredith couldn't help but think of Carter, her no-nonsense banker son. "Guess Bellefontaine Investigations may have made something of a name for itself." She paused, thinking that the name wasn't truly representative now. "Speaking of names, maybe it's time we found something more suitable."

"I suppose, but I don't mind conceding Foley to Bellefontaine."

Meredith tented her fingers and regarded her friend and business partner. "What would you say to something descriptive of the area as well as its feminine leadership? Something to give our enterprise a fresh new appeal?" Her idea grew large in her mind, even as her gratitude swelled. "What do you say to 'Magnolia Investigations'?"

Julia looked up in surprise, then a smile spread over her face. "I love it—and what a fitting tribute. Especially since the lady herself has made her wish known that the plantation should go to the city of Savannah and the historical society. I bet Beatrice is still pinching herself." She pointed over Meredith's shoulder. "Look who's here."

Quin Crowley, silver hair immaculate, stepped inside the diner, compelling eyes searching the room. His light jacket flared to reveal an open-collar shirt of Mediterranean blue. Catching their eyes, he sailed toward them.

Meredith smiled and waved. He was like a colorful ship on a buoyant sea. "He said he might stop by when his meeting finished," she told Julia nonchalantly, hoping her pleasure remained hidden.

"Ladies!" he greeted them, doffing an imaginary hat. "I'm glad you're still here."

"Still nursing the diner's special blend," Julia said brightly. "But we saved some for you." She reached across the aisle to grab an empty cup and saucer. Handing it to him, she said, "I hope you two will excuse me. I promised Beau I'd be home in time to go to a movie."

"No problem," said Meredith. "See you tomorrow morning."

"Bright and early," said Julia with a smile. "Bye, Quin. Nice to see you again."

Quin waved. "Sometime we'll have to exchange war stories," he said.

Meredith took a drink of her coffee as Julia walked out of the diner. "I'm glad you're here," she said, warmed by his smile. "You can be the first to congratulate us."

"I believe I'd be a mile down the list in that department," he said. "Everyone's talking about you."

Meredith felt herself blush. "I don't mean that. I mean, congratulate us on the new name for the agency. We've decided it will be 'Magnolia Investigations.'"

"I like it," Quin said, drawing his chair in. "Magnolia Clement is a remarkable woman."

He was handling legal matters for Maggie Lu, at Meredith's recommendation. They'd already had two meetings, which included negotiations with the city council.

"She's agreed to turn the property over to the city as long as Luke Clement is retained to watch over things." He lifted his cup to his mouth. "She wants to donate it, but I'm trying to convince her to accept a reasonable sum. Just to make things tidy legally and give her a small nest egg."

"That sounds fair," Meredith said. It felt right for him to be sitting there—an experienced colleague but more—a friend she hoped wouldn't be moving anywhere anytime soon.

"I haven't heard anything from Langston," Quin said. "But I'm guessing it doesn't make a whole lot of difference now if he's a true son of Charles Besset or not. The will is airtight."

"Thank you for guiding her in this process, Quin."

"It's my pleasure. I'm glad I came to this city. Never intended to, but somehow—" He broke off and gazed through the open window.

"Meredith, remember what you were saying about how God knows just where we fit and helps us find that place?"

"Yes," she said softly.

"I guess maybe He knew I should be here. To rise to the challenge, so to speak." He gave her a self-deprecating smile.

"'Everything that rises must converge,'" Meredith said, feeling the power and peace of those words. "Everything rises toward its full realization in God."

He closed his hands around his cup and held her with an affectionate gaze. "Have I ever told you," he began, "how glad I am I ran into you? Whoops! It was the other way around, wasn't it?"

Dear Reader:

What an honor and delight to write the first book in the Savannah Secrets series created by those masters of inspiration at *Guideposts*. Every step along the historic Georgia streets, with plantations shaded by stately elms dripping with Spanish moss, has been a delight. As you walked with me through these pages, I hope you caught the scent of magnolias and the dazzle of azaleas, and embraced God's enduring promise as He interacted with His creation.

Writing *The Hidden Gate* with its cast of characters, historic and contemporary, has led me to greater understanding and love drawing ever upward, uniting each to the other. "Everything that rises must converge."

—Marlene Chase

About the Author

MARLENE CHASE IS A LIEUTENANT colonel in the Salvation Army, having served people in various communities in the Midwest for forty-three years. She retired as editor in chief and literary secretary for the Army's National Publications headquartered in Alexandria, Virginia. She continues to serve the ministry endeavors of the organization and to write from her home in Rockford, Illinois. She is the author of twenty books and numerous articles, poems, and stories. She has two daughters, four grandchildren, and one great-granddaughter. She holds a Bachelor of Arts degree from Mid-America Nazarene University in Kansas and is an ordained minister in the Salvation Army.

Get to Know...

FLANNERY O'CONNOR

THOUGH A MIDWESTERNER BY BIRTH, I have always been intrigued by the South with its flamboyant history and larger-than-life characters. Among its literati is Flannery O'Connor, who grew up on Savannah's Lafayette Square during the Depression. Known mostly for her short stories, such as "A Good Man Is Hard to Find" and "Wise Blood," she is much anthologized and perennially appears on student reading lists. She was born in 1925 and attended Catholic schools, later Georgia State College for Women (now Georgia College & State University), where she graduated with a social sciences degree. She studied journalism at the prestigious Iowa Writers' Workshop at the University of Iowa, meeting important writers and critics like Robert Penn Warren, John Crowe Ransom, and Andrew Lytle.

O'Connor possessed a deeply sardonic sense of humor and often featured the disparity between her characters' limited perceptions and the awesome fate awaiting them. When challenged about her often "grotesque" characters, she replied, "Grace changes us, and the change is painful." A quote borrowed from Teilhard Chardin informed her short story "Everything That Rises Must Converge" and provided the theme for *The Hidden Gate*. She did much more than teach a chicken to walk backward; she imparts to all who embrace her the way to walk uprightly—through the grace that changes.

Today you can visit Flannery O'Connor's childhood home at 207 E. Charlton Street in Savannah. The nineteenth-century Greek revival townhouse is owned by a nonprofit corporation maintained partly as a memorial to O'Connor and partly as a literary center for Savannah.

—Marlene Chase

SOMETHING DELICIOUS FROM A
Downhome Southern Kitchen

BRUNSWICK STEW—GEORGIA STYLE

Brunswick stew (named for Brunswick, Georgia) was originally made primarily with squirrel and a few vegetables. (Sounds gamey!) But try this fast and easy modern recipe with chicken or pork. Our characters enjoyed something like this at the Downhome Diner after a tour of Savannah.

Ingredients:

2 lbs. chicken or pork (cooked and diced)

½ teaspoon black pepper

1 teaspoon hot sauce

2 tablespoons Worcestershire sauce

3–4 tablespoons bacon drippings

½ cup favorite barbecue sauce

1½ cups ketchup

2–3 cups diced cooked potatoes

3 (15–16 ounce) cans cream-style corn

Optional: 1–2 tablespoons dried minced onion

Directions:

Place all ingredients in stockpot or Dutch oven. Place pan over high heat and bring to a boil. Reduce heat to low and cover pan; simmer until hot and bubbly. Adjust seasonings according to taste with more salt, pepper, or hot sauce as needed. Serve with freshly baked cornbread and a tossed salad. Makes 6–8 servings. Yum!

Read on for a sneak peek of another exciting book in the Savannah Secrets series!

A Fallen Petal

BY RUTH LOGAN HERNE

"I CAN'T BELIEVE THE CEILING actually collapsed in my office," Julia Foley remarked as she typed furiously on the electronic notebook she'd set up on the deck of Meredith Bellefontaine's historic Savannah home in early June. *Typed* may have been too generous a word for her actions.

Stabbed was more like it, and each finger-poke made a tiny *click!* that punctuated Julia's frustration. She puffed out a breath against a wayward lock of pale silver hair and choked back a sigh. It came through, though, so she didn't choke it back all that well. "I appreciate that Arnold Mains is an old friend of yours, Mere, but that man does not understand how to move fast, and that's coming from a Southern woman. We are traditionally more understanding of such things, but not at this moment."

"Bug infestation," Meredith lamented. "It seems the exterminator wasn't doing proper inspections or treatments for the past two years. He simply cashed my checks and gave a stamp of approval, so that brought the ceiling down."

"On my refurbished desk." Julia loved that desk. She'd brought it with her from Atlanta when she and her husband, Beau, decided the quieter setting of Savannah would suit them better. Despite its flaws, the old desk was perfect. An aged kneehole with a chestnut-toned finish and not one bit of gloss, exactly how she liked things. Solid. Well-made. Not showy. Now the poor thing was pockmarked with shots of wallboard all over the antique finish. But in the end, it was just a piece of furniture.

She shrugged. "It's fixable. And furniture is just furniture, after all. Still, the whole thing was a surprise and a disappointment because I was so excited to have my own office. My own desk again. In its own place, away from my house."

Meredith laughed. "I hear you, and it will happen soon. Just not as soon as we thought. Ron used to tell me I trust the wrong people, but then, he didn't trust too many, good or bad, so I suppose it evened out."

Meredith had lost her husband Ron over eighteen months before. He'd died suddenly, leaving a gash in her heart and a thriving business that had ground to a standstill without him. A standstill, that is, until she and Julia decided to reopen and rename Ron Bellefontaine's private detective agency.

"Still, I should have double-checked the exterminator's reports. I didn't realize the company had changed hands right before Ron died."

"They should have sent a letter explaining that. That's the norm. This is on them, not you." Julia had spent years rendering decisions on guilt and innocence as a state-appointed juvenile court judge. She saw things in clear tones. Black and white worked for her, but occasionally she made way for life's grayer moments.

"They might have," Meredith replied. "I wasn't myself for a while, and there's probably a lot of stuff that got by me."

"Oh, honey, that's the way of it. And Ron was a law-and-order guy from the get-go, wasn't he?" Julia took a long draw on her Diet Dr Pepper, then pressed the glass to her forehead. The coolness of the condensation felt good, but she was careful not to let it drip onto her keyboard.

"He was, and he hated red tape, which is why he left the police force and opened his own agency. Ron liked getting to the bottom of things, while I like trusting people—*most* people," she added firmly. "If we're running a business I have to make sure the i's are dotted and t's are crossed. Businesswomen can't afford costly mistakes."

"I just made sure it's costing us nothing but time," Julia crowed, then read aloud from her email. "'Dear Ms. Foley: While admitting no wrongdoing, Southeast Pest Control will cover the cost of all damage incurred at the aforementioned property and will refund the customer's retainers for the past two years. Per your request, payment for repairs will be made to Arnold Mains Construction.'"

"They caved?" Meredith's eyebrows shot up. An expression of relief eased the worry that had carved a *W* between her eyes since the weekend ceiling collapse. "So quickly? Do you think the title 'former Presiding Judge, Chatham County Juvenile Court' swayed them to make a swift decision?"

"Clout helps," said Julia cheerfully. "They probably figured I'm buddies with everyone in the county court system. Of course, that's nowhere near the truth, but if the implication pushed them to take responsibility, I'm fine with that. And they're lucky we don't sue them for time lost and potential loss of income, but that would be hard to prove, since we just opened the business."

"Since we're only working from the house temporarily," added Meredith. "Let's just consider this a bump in the road for two entrepreneurs. No big deal."

"And we're in a gorgeous setting," Julia conceded, looking down at her keyboard. *Tap, tap, tap!* "Right here in the heart of Savannah's historic district with that pretty view of Troup Square. Who knows how many people will come seeking our help now that we've fixed things up so nicely with the Besset Plantation and sweet Maggie Lu?"

It felt wonderful to have their first case under their belt and a successful outcome. Meredith blotted her face with a folded square of paper towel. "May I ask again why we are conducting business on the deck when there is an expansive and delightfully air-conditioned living space just beyond that door?" She indicated the door of the house with a thrust of her chin. "June here in Georgia is not what some folks would consider porch friendly," she reminded her old friend. "Summer comes early. And stays a long while."

"We need to acclimate ourselves," Julia explained. "You and I are not the steel magnolias we used to be, and if we want to get Magnolia Investigations up and running, we've got to be prepared to 'glisten'"—she made air quotes with her fingers—"with the best of them. Lady detectives do not swoon, nor do they quietly retire to their fainting couches."

"And this is why we'll make a great team," Meredith declared. "You have all that big city go-get-'em personality going on, and I like to delve into the nitty-gritty in the shadows. That's why this will work, Julia."

"That and the fact that you were a bigger part of some of Ron's cases than anyone knew," Julia replied. She finished typing a reply to the exterminator and hit SEND. "Ron certainly showed a lot of wisdom and foresight when he made sure you got your certification years ago—"

"I suppose it was more to avoid a finger-pointing lawsuit than the thought that I was any kind of real help," Meredith cut in dryly.

Knowing Ron's Southern upbringing, Julia thought Meredith was probably right. Raised with fairly old-fashioned, traditional views regarding the roles of men, women, and genteel propriety, he loved his wife but turned a skeptical eye toward the importance of history. That was then, and Ron was more intrigued with the present. Julia nodded at Meredith. "I think he knew you'd help him any way you could, but that you would be demure and stay behind the scenes. I know that's how you helped him with that case out near Fort Pulaski. Still, you and I both realize the days for demure are long gone."

"Drug smuggling under the guise of historic boat rides," declared Meredith. "That was simple from the get-go. Those captains didn't know Georgia history at all. That was a lucky find on my part."

"Not lucky. Smart," Julia corrected her. "Your work with the historical society gives you a deeper perspective on things, and if there's one thing I found out by being a judge, it's that many of today's misfortunes lie in the ruins of yesterday's crises. Some folks can muster up. Some can't. You have that cause-and-effect well in hand, Meredith, and that's not a gift. That's years of hard work and study bearing fruit."

Meredith smiled at her. "Well, thank you, my friend."

"Now Ron was amazing with numbers," Julia noted as she finished clearing her inbox. "He came from money, he understood corporate financial structures, and he could smell an embezzling scheme like a hound dog on a raccoon. He lacked an appreciation of history and its effect on the present, but that's where you excelled. Still, his absence does leave us with a weak spot," she added.

"Auditing and finance."

"Yes. Neither one of us has the nose or education for that kind of thing," Julia noted, "but if we get into a pinch, we've always got Wyatt." Wyatt was Julia's nephew, the son of her absentee sister. He'd become a CPA and accidentally fallen into the role of forensic auditing when he discovered a hidden deficit in a major corporation's finances. His discovery led the embezzlers to jail time and brought his firm multiple new clients and a sizable bonus for himself. "He's our backup quarterback, and speaking of football, are you keeping your season tickets for the Bulldogs?"

"You know, I think that was one of the biggest adjustments of widowhood," Meredith told her, but not with angst. Humor laced her tone more often now. "Getting used to fall weekends with no one yelling at the TV or rushing out the door on Saturday morning while lamenting game-day traffic. Have mercy, how that man loved his Bulldogs." She raised her glass but then didn't sip it. Just held it. "I thought the boys would want to go, but they only managed one game last season. I'm not sure if that was lack of time or lack of interest, and I didn't have enough energy to second-market the seats. I'll see how this year goes. If Carter and Chase don't care to go, I'll drop the tickets. Some fan will be thrilled to get them."

Ron and Beau had gone to at least one game together each year. It had become a tradition. "I'm not pushing," Julia told her as she set the electronic notebook aside. "Beau's friend Riley was asking. He noticed your seats were empty a lot last year. He's in the deck above you and would like to move down."

"Ron loved taking the boys when they were young. And he went through years of trading up to get better seats until he finally got the ones he wanted. It's funny how letting go of something I never used makes me feel like I'm closing the book on a whole chapter of life. Maybe that's why I was hoping the boys would use them," she added. "To keep some life in those ridiculously expensive seats." She rolled her eyes. "Of course, Carter and Chase are total opposites, so maybe they'd prefer alternate weeks. How can siblings be so completely different?"

Julia knew exactly how siblings could be that different. Her younger sister was the direct opposite of her, and yet they shared two wonderful parents. "That's a question I've been asking for decades." Her dry tone highlighted her confusion. "And no pressure," Julia assured her. "You'll be able to sell them instantly, I'm sure. Just thought I'd mention there's a buyer waiting in the wings. Kind of like we'll be waiting on Arnold and his crew."

"There's no rushing the Mains."

"I see that," Julia muttered as she tucked the notebook aside.

"Fortunately, entertaining clients in one's home is a perfectly acceptable practice. So we'll be relegated to the living room until the official office space is revamped."

"Of course you're right," Julia replied. "Blame my reluctance on my former career. Judges, prosecutors, and cops stay under the radar for a reason. We make people mad. Sometimes really mad. The Whitaker Street office gives us a measure of invisibility. In a business like this, a slight separation is never a bad idea." She tipped her black-rimmed glasses down and faced Meredith. "We're not exactly young, and it hasn't even been a year since your heart episode, my friend. I'm simply thinking an ounce of prevention isn't a bad idea. But you're right, it's only a few weeks' time, and I'm being a pest."

"The heart scare was my wake-up call, for certain," Meredith agreed. "It's what drove me to step aside from running the historical society after all those years. Did I want to help others, or preside over them? Old money talks here."

"Money talks anywhere, but old money whistles a sharp tune in the South," noted Julia. "Which might be another reason to keep the business away from your residence. Middle-aged women with money are easy targets."

"But we have our delightful Carmen with access to the internet and a fully-stocked kitchen, and our gal does love to bake. This current situation could be in our favor."

Carmen Lopez was their Gal Friday for the office—once they had an office again—and that young Hispanic woman wasn't afraid to run a tight ship, speak her mind, or bake amazingly fun treats, three qualities her bosses liked and respected.

"You're right, of course." Julia sighed purposely this time. "I'm being silly by letting one minor setback bother me. We call it the 'courtroom curse.'" She aimed a wry look at Meredith. "When you're wearing a judicial robe, everyone listens. People jump. They snap to attention when you walk into a room. It's a head rush, and the reason we called it a curse is because you start expecting life to bend your way outside the courtroom. And life doesn't work that way. You're right—folks are just as likely to come knocking on a front door on East Charlton as they are to search out downtown. One thing I can say about our sweet city, it takes history quite seriously and makes it absolutely approachable."

"Except for the inevitable family scandals and closet skeletons," Meredith noted. "Every old Southern family has some, and most are quite adept at hiding them."

"Until the past comes creeping up on the present." Julia paused and looked down from the raised deck overlooking the historic park-like square. "Speaking of the past, isn't that Harlowe Green coming our way?"

"Oh my word, it is."

Julia followed close on Meredith's heels as Meredith hurried down the steps to meet the elderly gentleman. Harlowe had the somewhat dubious honor of being the oldest person in Savannah, and at one hundred and four years old, he was an amazing figure as he clomped around town with his walker. He'd hired a young man to drive him places, and a housekeeper, who played the keyboard at Julia's church, tended his Historic District home. However, Harlowe prided himself on doing as much as he could himself. Meredith's deck steps, however, would have bested the aged fellow.

Meredith reached him on one side, as Julia took the other. "Harlowe, good morning." Meredith took the aged gentleman's right arm gently. "Were you coming to call on me?"

He gazed at her.

Then Julia.

Then Meredith again. And then he did something that grabbed Julia's heart.

He started crying.

A Note from the Editors

WE HOPE YOU ENJOY THE Savannah Secrets series, created by the Books and Inspirational Media Division of Guideposts, a nonprofit organization that touches millions of lives every day through products and services that inspire, encourage, help you grow in your faith, and celebrate God's love in every aspect of your daily life.

Thank you for making a difference with your purchase of this book, which helps fund our many outreach programs to military personnel, prisons, hospitals, nursing homes, and educational institutions. To learn more, visit GuidepostsFoundation.org.

We also maintain many useful and uplifting online resources. Visit Guideposts.org to read true stories of hope and inspiration, access OurPrayer network, sign up for free newsletters, download free e-books, join our Facebook community, and follow our stimulating blogs.

To learn about other Guideposts publications, including the bestselling devotional *Daily Guideposts*, go to ShopGuideposts.org, call (800) 932-2145, or write to Guideposts, PO Box 5815, Harlan, Iowa 51593.

Sign up for the Guideposts Fiction Newsletter
and stay up-to-date on the books you love!

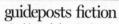

guideposts fiction
Inspiring reads chosen just for you!

What's New

Ordinary Women of the Bible

This one-of-a-kind series that brings you page-turning stories enriched with biblical and historical facts, which allow you to see how God called on everyday women to work His will. These groundbreaking stories are a thrilling way to experience God's love and power. These stories will open your heart as you immerse yourself in their world and see how they lived and worked...the difficulties they struggled with almost daily... their customs and traditions...and the hopes and dreams they held dear. You'll see how their faith, devotion, and love for God carried them through unimaginable situations. Learn More

Reader Favorite

Secrets of Wayfarers Inn

Secrets of Wayfarers Inn is everything you love in a great mystery; intriguing plots, secrets from the past, and faith-filled characters with the added excitement of unexpected surprises from one of the most unique periods in American history. The historic town of Marietta, Ohio, once an important stop on the Underground Railroad, is the setting for these thrilling mysteries. You'll love piecing together clues from the past that help unravel present-day mysteries. And you'll absolutely adore the energetic trio of friends who have vowed to never let their lives be boring. Learn More

From Our Editors

Mysteries of Lancaster County

Welcome to Bird-in-Hand, Pennsylvania, a quaint village in the heart of Lancaster County's Amish Country. It's here, amid rolling green hills and well-tended farms, where the Classen sisters, Elizabeth, Martha, and Mary, reunite after inheriting their family home. Together, they operate Secondhand Blessings, a charming gift-and-thrift store, housed in the old homestead's barn. Little do the sisters suspect as they stock their shelves with Amish handcrafted gift items, antiques, and yummy baked goods that they're also filling their rustic store with a host of mysteries and surprises. Learn More

A perfect blend of faith, family and fun!

You'll get sneak peeks of new releases, recommendations from other Guideposts readers, and special offers just for you . . .

and it's FREE!

Just go to Guideposts.org/Newsletters today to sign up.

Guideposts.

Visit Guideposts.org/Shop or call (800) 932-2145

Find more inspiring stories in these best-loved Guideposts fiction series!

Mysteries of Lancaster County

Follow the Classen sisters as they unravel clues and uncover hidden secrets in Mysteries of Lancaster County. As you get to know these women and their friends, you'll see how God brings each of them together for a fresh start in life.

Secrets of Wayfarers Inn

Retired schoolteachers find themselves owners of an old warehouse-turned-inn that is filled with hidden passages, buried secrets, and stunning surprises that will set them on a course to puzzling mysteries from the Underground Railroad.

Tearoom Mysteries Series

Mix one stately Victorian home, a charming lakeside town in Maine, and two adventurous cousins with a passion for tea and hospitality. Add a large scoop of intriguing mystery, and sprinkle generously with faith, family, and friends, and you have the recipe for *Tearoom Mysteries*.

Ordinary Women of the Bible

Richly imagined stories—based on facts from the Bible—have all the plot twists and suspense of a great mystery, while bringing you fascinating insights on what it was like to be a woman living in the ancient world.

To learn more about these books, visit Guideposts.org/Shop